RECKLESS PRINCESS

KNIGHT'S RIDGE EMPIRE #8

TRACY LORRAINE

TRACY LORRAINE

Editing by Pinpoint Editing

Proofreading by Sisters Get Lit.erary

Photography by Wander Aguiar

1

JODIE

My entire body trembles as I race down the hallway of Toby's building wearing nothing but his incorrectly buttoned shirt. My makeup is a mess down my face, the tears continuing to fall as my legs move faster than I can control in my haste.

I trip over my own feet before I get to the corner which will lead me toward the lift, toward my escape. My body collides with the wall. My shoulder that's already smarting from the bathroom door frame screams in pain once more.

I use the agony to give me strength, focusing on that instead of the excruciating pain in my chest, the way my already crumbling world has just been stolen from beneath me.

A sob rips up my throat as memories from the past few minutes slam into me once more, the grief, the disbelief almost as strong as it was when this whole nightmare was playing out in front of me.

I make it to the corner, my eyes set on the thick, soft carpet at my feet when I run headfirst into someone.

"Whoa," a soft female voice says before small hands land on my upper arms, stopping me from falling on my arse. "Are you okay?" she asks, bending down so she can get a look at my face.

Her brows pinch in concern as I lock onto her blue eyes and flawless makeup.

"I-I'm s-sorry," I stutter, barely able to get the words out with my need to flee.

I twist away from her, ready to continue for the exit, but she doesn't release me.

"I-I really n-need to go," I plead, looking back at her. "H-he might c-come and—" I look back over my shoulder toward Toby's front door, and a torrent of emotions slam into me, most of which I don't have the capacity to identify right now.

"Okay," she says firmly. "Let's go."

To my utter shock, she wraps her arm around my shoulder and moves me forward.

"Let's grab you some clothes first though."

"N-no. I just need to leave. Please."

I glance back once more, terrified I'm going to see him standing there with that wrecked look on his face that I just left behind, and another sob bubbles up.

"My flat is right here, we can—"

"No," I say, firmer than I was expecting.

"Okay, we'll just go."

Bypassing the door to her flat, she leads me straight toward the lift.

I should probably shrug her off. I'm usually not all that much of a fan of being hugged by strangers, but right now, I need the warmth, the support. Anything that might help convince me that I'm not about to shatter into a million pieces.

She releases me to press the button and I have to slam my lips closed to stop me complaining about the loss.

"Here," she says when she turns back to me, seeing me trembling with my arms wrapped around myself. She unzips her hoodie and hands it over, leaving her standing in a pair of gym leggings and sports bra. She looks so put together, so... everything that I'm not right now.

"Thank you," I whisper, unable to resist reaching out and taking it from her.

No more words are said between us as we descend through the building. She just stands beside me, allowing me to soak up her warmth and support.

I have no idea who she is, but quite frankly, I don't care.

"This is me," she says, slowing down in front of a matte black Porsche which lights up before us.

I might not know who she is, but with a car like that, she's clearly one of them.

She opens the door for me and I drop into the passenger seat, the new car scent hitting me immediately. It's strong enough that it makes my stomach roll. I swallow down the extra moisture in my mouth, wishing I could do something about the putrid taste lingering from throwing up only minutes ago.

Curling up, I watch as she elegantly lowers herself into the driver's seat and brings the engine to life. Reaching out, she turns the temperature up and switches the heated seat on.

"It'll be warm in a few minutes."

It's not until she says that that I realise I'm shivering, wrapping her hoodie around me as if it's the thing that will literally keep me together.

"Thank you," I whisper, tightening my hold on my legs that I've pulled up to my chest.

We emerge from the underground garage and into the torrential rain that has started since we disappeared inside.

It just about sums up everything about my night as the huge droplets crash against the windscreen so fast the wipers can barely cope.

"Where are we going?"

"Oh... um..."

I can't get my brain to process where we are

enough to even consider giving her directions home.

Tapping the screen between us, she finds the search screen on her GPS.

"Postcode?"

Thankfully, I'm able to rattle it off without even thinking, and a few seconds later, the map shows my street and I have nothing to distract myself from what happened up in that flat only minutes ago once more. Grief and disbelief wrap around me, their icy claws digging into my skin, making my body tremble harder.

"What did he do?" she asks after long silent minutes. "I mean, you don't have to tell me. But I will go and kick his ass for you."

Looking over at her, I blink a few times as I register her accent.

"You're American," I blurt.

"That obvious, huh?" she deadpans.

"I'm sorry. I'm… uh… not really with it."

"I know Alex can be a pr—"

"Alex?" I question, a frown creasing my brow as I consider the fact that his manipulation has gone so deep he hasn't even given me his real name.

"Yeah… was it not Alex you were running from?" she asks hesitantly, her eyes darting between the road and my tear-stained face.

I've no idea what she reads in my silence, but suddenly she gasps. "Holy shit. Are you Jodie?"

I startle at the fact that she knows my name.

"Uh... yeah."

Her lips purse as her grip on the wheel tightens with anger.

"What did he do?" she grits out, her tone completely different from when she was asking me about whoever Alex is.

I shake my head. "I just want to go home and forget that the past few weeks, especially tonight, have happened."

Her attention burns the side of my face, but I refuse to look up at her as I wipe my cheeks with the back of my hand and blow out a shaky breath.

"I'm sorry he was a dick. When I get back, I'll make sure he hurts for whatever he's done," she assures me, her voice full of hurt and venom.

"I don't need you to fight for me."

"Who said anything about needing to."

Finally, I risk another glance over at her. Gone is her concerned expression from when she first saw me, and in its place is a hard, furious mask, one that is actually quite terrifying.

"You don't even know me," I say quietly, astounded that she assumes the worst of someone she does clearly know.

"That may be true, but I know Toby. I know all those boys better than they think I do. And I'd put money on him doing something really fucking stupid to have sent you running like this."

I scoff, unable to say anything about what he's done.

How? How can I possibly explain to anyone everything he just showed me without me sounding like a total crazy person?

If I hadn't seen him through the screen with my own eyes, then I'd think I was insane.

But he was there. The man I thought had died a few weeks ago. The man I thought was my stepdad who selflessly brought me up as his own.

A whimper breaks free as my mind takes me back to that bathroom floor as Dad begged me to get out, to run away from Toby as fast as I could.

"You need to ask him," I mutter, not interested in getting in the middle of whatever this is.

"Oh, I will. Don't you worry about that," she spits.

Silence falls around us once more and I quickly realise that the bullshit conversation with that stranger was better than allowing the voice to spark up again in my head, the questions, the doubts, the confusion.

Despite the car warming around me, my body still trembles. Shock, I guess.

"Here's fine," I say when she pulls up on my street. In seconds, she comes to a stop a little down from my house and kills the engine. "I've got it."

"I might live in that building with them, but I'm not a complete douchebag. Come on." She's out of the car before I can stop her and has my door open as I'm uncurling my legs from the seat.

The second I'm on my feet, she wraps her arm around my waist and I have no choice but to let her guide me to my front door.

I want to pretend it's not necessary, but seeing as she's holding up the majority of my weight, I think we both know that it is.

"Keys," she demands, reaching out.

Mindlessly, I shove my hand into my bag and dig around until I find them. Passing her the set, I stand uselessly as she fights to find the right one to open the door.

We quickly discover it's not necessary though, because the door opens and Mum's concerned face fills my vision.

"Jojo, what's happened?"

I shake my head, not ready to talk about any of it as she gestures for the girl clinging on to me to bring me inside before dragging me into her own arms and holding me tight.

"It's okay, baby. I've got you."

The whimper that falls from my lips is pathetic and weak. And I hate it.

"Don't be silly," I hear Mum say, her chest rumbling against my cheek with her words. "Come in."

"N-no, I really should—"

"I insist," Mum says in that tone of hers I

remember all too well as a kid that stopped me from arguing about whatever she was saying.

I'm pulled deeper into the house and directed into the living room before I'm lowered to the sofa.

Mum's warm hands land on my cheeks and I quickly find myself staring into her warm, dark eyes.

"What's happened, Jojo?"

I stare at her blankly as my thoughts, my fears, my confusion all war in my head.

My tears continue to fall and my bottom lip trembles as new thoughts hit me.

Did she know?

Has she known the truth all this time, or is she as naïve as me?

I shake my head. "I can't, not yet." Finding some strength from somewhere, I get to my feet once more. "I'm sorry, I just need—"

I march toward the door but stop when I'm standing in front of my rescuer, who's blocking my escape. Her eyes shoot around the room, taking in all the photos of my entire life that surround us. Photos of a man who might not have even existed.

"T-thank you, but I need—"

She thankfully steps aside and allows me the escape I desperately crave.

Voices from the living room carry up to me as I stumble up the stairs and damn near fall head first into the bathroom.

Dragging Toby's shirt from my body, I step into the shower and turn it on, desperate to wash him and this night from my body.

I'm blasted with ice-cold water for a minute or two that makes my teeth chatter and my skin erupt in goosebumps.

The second it begins to warm up, my knees buckle and I drop like a rock to the floor. Pulling my knees up to my chest, I wrap my arms around them and rest my head on the top. I drag in heaving, shaky breaths as my body begins to warm, although I never stop trembling. I think it'll take more than some warm water to rid me of the shock of this evening.

I have no idea how long I've been sitting there with the water raining down on me, but eventually, there's a soft knock at the door.

I ignore it, hoping that she'll leave me alone.

Sadly, though, that's not what happens. The door opens despite my silence and I squeeze my eyes shut, praying I could just vanish into nothing so that Mum can't see me bleeding out all over the bathroom.

But when a voice fills the small space around me, it's not Mum's.

"Oh my God, Jojo. What happened?" Bri demands.

I don't look up, I don't acknowledge her, but I

can't deny that her presence doesn't make everything a little easier to take.

There's a thud beside me which forces me to look up, and when I do, I find Bri in the shower, fully dressed—minus her boots—and dropping to her knees before me.

I shake my head once again, unable to even find the words. But she doesn't need them.

She just gathers me up in her arms, not giving a single fuck about the water raining down from above, and holds me while emotion climbs up my throat once more. I shatter all over again, my mind playing out the events of the evening so vividly it's as if they're happening all over again.

2

TOBY

I barely react to the loud crash that comes from my living room. It could be any of the many things that I've destroyed in the past hour as I tried to outrun my demons, my pain, falling off the walls and crashing to the floor.

Everything hurts. No. It more than fucking hurts.

I'm in agony. Every inch of me is suffering from the fallout of tonight, but nowhere more than my heart.

I might have delivered Jonas everything I've craved for almost all of my life, watching his face twist in pain as he watched Jodie, his daughter, learn the truth about the kind of monster he really was.

But nothing could have prepared me for how I would react to the look on her face.

I might have ripped Jonas's heart out with my own hands, but fuck if I didn't feel like I was doing exactly the same to myself.

It's not until the sound of light footsteps hits my ears that I finally drag my head from my knees and look up.

My heart pounds and my skin tingles with awareness.

Did she come back?

It's a pointless hope, because despite the fact that I'm aware I have eyes on me, my reaction is nowhere near as strong as it would be if she returned.

When my eyes finally collide with the person standing in the doorway to my bedroom, my breath gets caught in my throat.

I've seen Stella angry before. But fuck. I've never had it directed at me quite like it is now.

"Get. Up," she seethes, her voice low and terrifying.

Jeez, it's no wonder she had us all wrapped around her little finger almost from the moment she arrived. She's Cirillo through and through. And despite not being aware at the beginning, deep down, I knew. There was no other reason this beautiful, dark goddess was sent our way without her being one of us.

"I said... Get. The. Fuck. Up."

Unable but to do as she demands, I force my

body to move. Every single one of my muscles has locked up tight, and it physically hurts to do so.

Something Stella notices and seems to only look happier about.

"Does it hurt, big bro?"

"Stel, what are you—"

"I said, does it fucking hurt?" Her voice echoes around my silent bedroom.

"Yes," I concede.

"It's about to get fucking worse." Before I know what's happening, she's right in front of me. "This is for lying to me."

"Oof," I grunt when her fist collides with my stomach, forcing me to bend over to catch my breath.

"Stand up, you fucking pussy," she spits, her voice nothing but venom.

Sucking in a deep breath, I push my hands on my knees and stand to my full height, my eyes finding hers.

Gone is the usual light blue, replaced by a much darker, more violent shade.

"And this is for Jodie." She barely even gets her name out before her fist connects with my cheek, forcing my head to wheel to the side as pain explodes across it.

"Fuck," I hiss, lifting my hand to my cheek.

"You're a fucking asshole, Toby. I'm so fucking ashamed of you right now."

My eyes find hers for a beat, but unable to cope with the disappointment staring back at me, I shove past her in my need to escape.

"I don't fucking think so."

Grabbing my arm, she uses all her strength to drag me back around and land another punch.

And this time, she doesn't stop, fighting with me until I have no choice but to attempt to stop by blocking her painful blows.

"What's wrong, Bro? Jodie is fair play to hurt how you see fit, but you're going to go easy on me?" she taunts, her knuckles coated in blood and her chest heaving as she stares me right in the eyes. "You wanna play God, toy with people's lives for your own pleasure, then let's fucking play."

The roar that rips from my throat doesn't even sound like it belongs to me as I retaliate and allow myself to dive headfirst back into the darkness that has consumed me since I began telling Jodie the truth about our lives.

Our fists fly, grunts and groans erupting from us as we brawl. I treat her almost as if she's one of the guys because I'm more than aware she'll kick my arse even harder if she suspects I'm going easy on her. She's more than able to hold her own against each of us, something that I fucking love about her. My sister is a bad-arse and I couldn't be prouder to share blood with her.

She manages to dodge almost all my advances,

leaving me without a doubt in more pain than she is. Not that I don't deserve it.

I do. I deserve all her wrath and then some for what I've done tonight.

I was hell-bent on my revenge. It's clouded my every decision, my every judgement for almost as long as I can remember. But tonight… tonight was the first time I really appreciated just how toxic it's really been. How the words Mum said to me not so long ago about it killing me, my hatred for that man dripping poison into my blood, were nothing but the truth.

But watching Jodie shatter on my bathroom floor as I revealed everything… That was one hell of an eye-opening experience. I felt the pain I was causing her right down to my soul. I knew it was wrong, but hearing the pain in his voice was something I've craved for so long that I was powerless but to continue. To finally rip his cold, twisted heart out and stomp on it for ever thinking it was okay to treat Mum and me the way he has over the years.

"Come on, Toby. Use me. Get it all out," Stella demands as she bounces on the balls of her feet in front of me, her fists up, ready for my next strike. "The sooner you give up, the sooner your time is going to be up and I'm going to make you talk."

"Argh," I roar, slamming my shoulder into her belly, knocking her off her feet in one quick move.

We land on my thick carpet with a thud and I quickly start blocking her blows to my already sore ribs as she uses every ounce of her strength.

Eventually though, with her pinned beneath me, I manage to get the upper hand and lock her wrists to the floor above her head.

"Better luck next time, Princess," I taunt as she bares her teeth at me.

"Come on, baby. You can take him," a deep, rumbling voice comes from behind me, startling me enough to loosen my grip.

Stella flips us despite her pathetic weight compared to mine, and I quickly find myself at her mercy with a smug-as-fuck Seb grinning down at me from over her shoulder.

Stella's eyes track my injuries, my split eyebrow and lip, swelling eye, and what I'm sure is already dark bruising on my ribs.

My sister is fucking lethal.

"What exactly is going on here?" Seb asks, clearly the only one in the room who doesn't know what I've done.

"Go and find us some strong alcohol and Toby can confess," Stella says, finally getting off me after one more long warning look. "I hate you right now, just so you know."

"As you should," I mutter, sitting up and realising just how much it really does hurt now the adrenaline is starting to wear off. "I hate myself more though," I mutter quietly.

Stella takes off after Seb, leaving me alone to lick my wounds once more. But I know they're not going to let me hide for very long.

Hauling myself to my feet, I stumble through to the bathroom with my hand pressed against my ribs.

"Jesus," I mutter when I come to a stop in front of the mirror and take in the state of my face.

It had barely healed from our fight in the Wolves' Den last week. My lip has split back open in the exact same place, blood making its way down my chin.

Lifting my arm, I wipe it away with the back of my hand and hang my head, allowing myself a few seconds of self-pity before I have to go out there and face their wrath.

Stella knows. Fuck knows how, but she does. And the disappointment in her angry stare chilled me down to the bone.

The reality of what I'd done was already hitting me hard enough. I really don't need her telling me just how badly I fucked up tonight. Not that I think for a second I'm going to get out of it.

"Here," Seb says, throwing a bag of ice and a tea towel at me the second I emerge from the safety of my bedroom. "I know how brutal her punches can be."

"Thanks," I mutter, pressing it to my swollen eye.

"I guess you're going to need this too." He walks out of the kitchen with two bottles of vodka in his hand, two glasses in the other. He gives me one of the bottles before lowering the glasses to my coffee table and pouring generous measures for him and Stella.

"What, no glass?"

"From what I've witnessed so far, I'm assuming you're going to need the bottle," he quips. And to be fair, I can't exactly argue.

Falling down on the opposite sofa from the two of them, I twist the cap off the bottle and bring it to my lips, chugging down way more than I usually would.

Once my throat can't take any more and my belly is beginning to warm, I slam it down on the coffee table and stare my sister dead in the eyes.

"How'd you find out?" I ask simply, needing to know what she already knows before I figure out a way around this minefield.

"So... funny story..." she starts, making my fists curl with impatience. "I came back from a workout with Emmie and ran straight into this broken mess of a girl fleeing the building."

"Fuck," I hiss under my breath. But of course, she doesn't miss it.

"I assumed Alex had pumped her and dumped

her until she revealed that she had no fucking clue who Alex was. So that meant she could only have been running from one other person."

I fucking knew bringing her back here was a risk, but it was the only place I could successfully set up all the cameras without it looking like a totally kinky setup. Not that I really think she would have minded all that much.

"I took her home," Stella states. And although her voice is bitter and full of venom, something inside me breathes a massive sigh of relief that she looked after Jodie for me. That someone was there to help hold her together and deliver her back safely. "And this is where shit gets really fucked up," she says, making Seb pay even closer attention.

"Her mom invited me in. I followed them into the living room, and you'll never fucking guess whose photos damn near cover every surface of that room."

Seb's brows pull together in confusion as he looks between the two of us as if the answer is going to be written all over our faces.

"Go on," he prompts, desperately needing the answer.

"Jonas."

"What?" he asks, half shocked, half amused. "Why would they have photos of that cunt in their..."

"Yeah, Toby. Why exactly would that be?" Stella asks, her eyes narrowing on me.

Lifting my hand, I push my hair back from my brow, slumping lower on the sofa.

"She's Joker's sister. Jonas's daughter."

Silence rings out around the flat as they both absorb that information.

"Wait..." Seb says, sitting forward and holding his hand up to stop fuck knows who from talking. "You've been fucking Jonas's daughter?"

"Oh," Stella pipes up before I even get a chance to say anything. "It's so much worse than that. Isn't it, Toby?"

Dropping my head back on the sofa, I squeeze my eyes closed as an unbearable silence falls between us.

"Go on, put my imagination to rest. Because I've got to tell you, it's working on overdrive right now," she continues after a few agonising minutes where all I do is pray that they'll leave me to suffer in peace.

"I used her to hurt him, okay?"

"No, not really," Stella scoffs. "Did you see the state of her, Toby? It was like you'd literally shoved your hand inside her chest and ripped her heart out."

Her words cut me right down to the core, the pain in my chest only increasing as I think about

Jodie curled around the toilet in my bathroom once more.

"What did you do, Tobes?" Seb growls, clearly about as impressed by all of this as his missus.

"I did some of what that cunt has done to Mum and me over the years. I stripped everything away and then gave him the pleasure of watching his daughter fall from grace right before his eyes." I don't look up as I say this to judge their reactions. I don't need to. Their disbelief, shock, and disgust burn right into my skin.

"And how do you feel now?" Stella asks. "Vindicated? Free?" she offers.

Dragging my head from the cushion, I look into her angry eyes.

I just stare at her. Apparently, that's enough, because her expression completely changes.

"Toby," she sighs, the first bit of softness I've heard tonight flowing through her tone. "You've fallen for her, haven't you?"

My lips part to respond, to argue. Because I can't. I can't fall for the fucking spawn of Satan's daughter. I fucking can't.

But then images of our time together flash through my mind. Her wild smile that first night when we walked into Hades. How grateful she was the night I took her to the waffle shop, stopping her from spending another lonely night in with a tub of ice cream for company. The way she held me so tight the afternoon I rescued her from the coffee shop after she was fired.

"No," I state, refusing to accept that there is anything more than the revenge I craved so badly.

Seb scoffs at my answer, and I lift a brow.

"I may never have met this woman, but it's pretty damn clear sitting here that she's knocked you on your fucking arse, man."

"Fuck off. She was just a game. One that I've won."

"So what were you hoping for? You cause Jonas some heartbreak by hurting Jodie and it would suddenly make you even for all the shit he's pulled on you over the years?" Stella asks. The way she explains the plan I've been scheming up for years makes it sound insane.

"Something like that," I mutter, swiping the bottle of vodka from the coffee table and swallowing down shot after shot in the hope it'll eventually lessen the pain.

3

JODIE

I roll over, my stomach growling with its need for food and my mouth dry.

The scent of coffee permeates from downstairs where I'm sure Mum is sitting, wringing her hands together with worry. Just as she should be, when I finally find the strength to walk out of this room and start talking.

If it turns out that she knew about any of this—if I discover she hid the truth about my life, about who my father was from me all these years—then I don't know how I'm going to react.

I understand her need to protect me. But I'm nineteen. I'm an adult. I'm able to make informed choices about my life, drive a car, get married, every-fucking-thing. If she decided that I wasn't old enough, wise enough, or strong enough to handle the truth, then I'm not sure that this is even where I should be right now.

The betrayal and the lies are what sting the most. Or at least that's what I'm focusing on, because the pain in my chest is just too agonising to even attempt to address.

Just thinking about him makes a lump of emotion clog my throat and red-hot tears burn my eyes. I knew I was falling hard, and I knew it was wrong.

I wasn't in any kind of place to be falling in love while I was still drowning in grief. But that didn't stop me. And it sure didn't help that Toby seemed to be my perfect guy, the perfect boyfriend.

I knew it was too good to be true. I just wanted to believe that after all the shit that had been thrown my way, I was finally getting some good karma for once.

How fucking wrong was I?

There was nothing good about what we had. Hell, at this point, I'm not even sure there's anything good about the guy I let into my heart.

My fingers curl around the duvet covering me as pain lashes at my insides.

For the past four days, I've locked myself inside my dark room, only leaving for a quick trip to the bathroom. Bri has kept me stocked up with junk food, coffee, and alcohol. But aside from her visits,

I've allowed myself to finally be drawn under by the grief and devastation that is my life.

I don't feel good about it, but I haven't had the strength or brain power to do anything else.

Bri told Courtney that I was sick and was going to have to put back starting at the club, for which I think I'm grateful.

The thought of getting dressed up and shaking my arse for some sleazeball men right now makes my stomach turn. But the reality is that while I'm hiding in here, the world is still turning outside and we're still going to be evicted.

And even if Mum has hidden all this from me for all of my life, can I really see her out on the street all because she quite clearly fell in love with the wrong man?

No, I can't.

With a sigh, I try to muster up as much strength as I can and throw the sheets back.

Bri isn't going to be here today. She's at school and is busy tonight. I think she might be lying about that though to force me back to life, something I can hardly be annoyed about. She's spent days being my shoulder to cry on, allowing me to wallow, but it doesn't stop the frustration bubbling up beneath my skin that she's pulling some tough love bullshit on me to get me moving.

My body is stiff from days of zero exercise as I make my way to the bathroom. The sound of

Mum's voice downstairs hits my ears and I pause for a beat with my heart in my throat that someone else might be here. When I don't hear a response, I assume she must be on the phone and continue forward.

I'm gross. My hair is greasy, my skin is... ugh. I've been sitting around in my own filth for days. I really don't want to even think about it let alone see the evidence.

I brush my teeth as I have the past few times, without looking in the mirror in front of me. I dread what I might find staring back.

Standing under the stream of water, I try to force myself to let go of everything that happened in Toby's flat the other night. I try to forget that the man I've been mourning all these weeks isn't actually dead, because it's not like he's going to come back to us any time soon. And even if he did, he'd never be the same man to me.

Our connection might have shifted, our link stronger than ever, but it won't change anything.

Toby might be a liar, a master manipulator, and a sick and twisted fucking bastard, but there's one thing I believe him about, and that's how the man I've called my father all these years treated him and his mum. The pain that was in his eyes, etched into his every feature couldn't have been faked. It just couldn't. There's no doubt in my mind that both of them suffered at his hands.

Something twists at my insides, but I have no idea if it's relief or guilt.

My dad never laid a finger on me, and as far as I know he always treated Mum with the respect she deserved. He was only ever the perfect father, although I can't help wondering if he was just too good. Did he go over and above with us, knowing how he was treating his real wife, his other son?

But Toby isn't his son. Just like I thought I wasn't his daughter.

I drop my head into my hands as a loud groan rips from my lips.

As much as I might hate Toby right now and think his actions were deplorable, I can't stop a huge part of me understanding.

I wish I didn't. But I do.

I spent too long looking into the eyes of a scared little boy not to understand his need for revenge. His need to cause the man who hurt him and his mum the same pain.

But understanding is never going to make what he did right. And understanding and forgiving are very different things.

I put off going downstairs for as long as possible, despite the fact that Mum knows I'm alive because I found a cup of coffee waiting for me in my bedroom when I returned.

I've refused to talk to her the past few days, and

she's mostly respected my privacy to fall apart alone. I have no idea what Bri has said to her, but I know it's not the truth, because I swore her to secrecy with the details I gave her about that night. Not that I even came close to telling her everything. I mean, how can I even explain all of that? It was utter insanity. The kind of shit you expect to see in a fucked-up documentary. Stuff like that is not meant to happen in real life.

It's not until my hair is dried and straightened that I finally sum up the courage to head downstairs.

With my now cold mug clutched in my hands, I go in search of Mum. I can't put this conversation off any longer.

I need to know the truth. I deserve to know the truth.

The second I come to a stop in the kitchen doorway, she pauses what she's doing and looks up at me.

"Jodie," she breathes, as if she can't quite believe I'm standing here.

"Hey," I say quietly, stepping farther into the room, noticing that she's in the middle of baking my favourite cookies.

Whenever I was sad as a kid, she would always make them for me. Just the scent of them baking would cheer me up in an instant.

I'm not sure they'll have that effect today

though. My misery and pain are too deeply ingrained right now for sugar to fix much.

"Take a seat, I'll make you another," she says, nodding to the empty mug in my hands.

"Thanks." My voice is hard, void of the emotions that are causing a storm inside of me as I pass it over and do as she suggested.

"It's so good to see you up and about. I was so worried—"

"Did you know?" I blurt without meaning to.

I've spent almost as much time obsessing about her part in this as I have Toby's actions over the past four days that I can't hold it in anymore.

She pauses, the set of her shoulders hard as she grips onto the counter as if she needs it to hold her up.

"Did you know... about them? About his other family."

Mum doesn't say anything, but the way she hangs her head tells me everything I need to know.

"Baby," she starts, spinning around to face me.

"No, Mum. Don't *baby* me. I'm an adult. I deserve to know the truth. I've deserved it for a long time, actually."

"I'll tell you everything I know," she says sadly before turning back to the coffee machine.

I don't ever remember feeling uncomfortable in my mum's company before, but those few moments while she makes us both a fresh drink are unbearable. Uncertainty swirls around inside me like a brewing storm, reminding me that despite my hope, she's probably going to tell me something I'm not going to want to hear.

After what feels like an eternity, she finally walks toward me and lowers my coffee with a trembling hand.

"Talk to me, Jodie."

"Me?" I hiss in disbelief. "I'm not the one who needs to be talking. You'll tell me everything you know, remember?" I say, throwing her words back in her face.

"I know, I know. And I will. I just want to know what you already know."

"How about you assume I know nothing and tell me the truth like you should have done years ago," I suggest, the bitterness of my tone leaving no space for argument.

Her sad, tired eyes hold mine and just a little guilt tugs at my heart. What I'm asking of her is going to hurt. But that doesn't mean I'm going to let her off.

"You already know most of this but… I first met your dad when I was fifteen. He was…" She sighs, her eyes getting this glassy, far off look as she takes herself back. "Larger than life. The bad boy all my friends and I went weak at the knees for.

"We'd just been to the cinema and literally

walked into them loitering outside a corner shop, looking all angry and dangerous.

"The second our eyes connected, something changed. I always thought love at first sight was fantasy reserved for films and romance novels. But standing out there in that street, and at only fifteen, I knew. He was it.

"We started seeing each other from then on. Things got serious pretty fast. Your grandparents weren't impressed when I first took him home, as I'm sure you can imagine." A small smile graces her lips despite the loss darkening her eyes.

I think of my late grandparents. Prim, proper, and completely traditional in their ideals of the world. This isn't the first time over the years that their disapproval of Mum's partner has come up.

"I know this, Mum. What about the bit where you found out who he really was?" I prompt.

"Deep down, I always knew. There was a lot of gang trouble happening at that time around the city, so the day he turned up on my doorstep a broken mess, I was hardly surprised to discover his place in the world. I saw it that first night. The ultimate bad boy."

I shake my head, memories of Toby's face, the bruises on his body the night he rescued me from the coffee shop filling my mind.

"I think he expected the truth to scare me away. I was just sixteen when he finally told me, but there was nothing that could have separated me from him. I told him that I loved him, and that I would stand beside him through anything."

She lifts her hand, catching a tear that finally falls.

"He was such a good man, Jodie. My everything." My lips part to say something, but she beats me to it. "But I'm more than aware that he had many, many sides to him, and that we were very lucky to see the sweet guy that was mostly hidden beneath the surface."

"Lucky?" I spit. "He married someone else. Lived an entirely different life. He lied to me and Joe for years, Mum. How can you not see how fucked up this is?"

"Trust me, baby. I see it. But..." She lets out a heavy sigh. "I never could let him go."

Silence falls between us as I try to even comprehend what she's telling me. That she loved him so much that she allowed all of this to happen.

"I already had Joe by the time the truth came out about his other life, although I had been suspicious for a while. I begged him to let me be a part of his life but he always refused. Told me that I didn't have the right blood running through my veins for our relationship, our family, to be considered real in the eyes of the Family. But he had plans to change that. He assured me that one day, he would have enough power that he could do what he wanted, marry who he desired."

"And you believed him enough to just sit back and wait?"

"I know how it sounds, Jodie. Trust me, I do. But I had a young child, a man I loved, a home. I was happy. None of it was conventional, but it worked. The time we had apart only made the times we had together all that much more powerful. It made our connection stronger.

"The only time I ever had a massive issue with the whole thing was when you were born."

"Oh?" I ask, already knowing what's probably going to follow.

"Although he never said the words, I knew he wanted boys. I might not have been able to provide the full Greek DNA he needed to produce the little heirs as he really craved, but he could still make his own little army.

"Just like with Joe, we never found out your sex beforehand, but the second you were born, placed in my arms and it was announced you were a girl, nothing but pure happiness and love covered your father's face.

"I won't lie, I was worried, but he never treated you any less than Joe, never loved you any differently."

"But—" I prompt.

"But he felt a need to protect you in a way he never did with Joe.

"I was so angry when he came up with this story about you being someone else's and not putting his name down on your birth certificate. But he was worried you'd somehow end up in the middle of his other life, and he didn't want that for you."

"So you both just lied to my face. For years."

"I couldn't argue about keeping you safe, baby."

"And who would want me?" I say, the volume of my voice increasing with the sheer insanity of what I'm listening to. My gut twists as my mind takes me back to Toby's flat.

Toby. That's who was going to want me.

Not that Dad could have known that all this was going to play out, or maybe he did. He must have hurt enough people over the years who want to return the favour. I guess it all makes sense really, in the mind of a fucking psychopath.

"He had another family, Mum. How could you—"

"It was a loveless marriage of convenience, Jojo. It was something he needed to do as a part of his role within the Family. His heart was here, with us."

I shake my head, not needing any more evidence for where I get my naivety from.

"Did you ever think about them? About his wife? His son?"

"He's not Jonas's son, Jodie. She was playing away just as Jonas was."

She lifts her coffee and takes a sip. I don't follow suit for fear I'll bring it back up just as quickly as it goes down.

"That's not the point, Mum," I bark, pushing my chair out behind me. "Do you have any idea what it might have been like, being in that aspect of his life?"

"They just existed together for the sake of the Family," she says, deadly seriously.

"Jesus, Mum. Did you even know the man you gave your entire life to?"

"What?" she asks, her brows shooting up. "O-of course I did. I loved your dad more than anything. And he lo—"

"He was a monster, Mum," I spit, angry over her poor judgement.

"N-no, he was a good—"

"How much do you know about his other son, Mum?"

She shakes her head. "Nothing really. They lived separate lives."

"No they didn't. Their lives were very much intertwined, and he suffered, *they* suffered more than you can comprehend at the hands of my *father,*" I seethe.

She pales at my words.

"I'm sorry, Mum. But you made a massive fucking mistake with all of this. That man you've shared your life with is not the man you knew."

I storm toward the hallway, more than ready to escape this bullshit.

She's been brainwashed by him, of that I'm sure. She might not have suffered at the hands of Jonas like Toby and his mum has, but without doubt, he's worked his twisted fucking evil on her, ensuring she follows his plan and bends to his rules. I'd put money on it… if we had any.

"Jojo, what are you—"

"You really don't know who his son is, do you?"

She stares at me, her brow furrowed in confusion as grief and pain continue to darken her eyes.

I literally see the moment the penny drops. Her entire body jolts as realisation hits her.

"No," she breathes. "T-Toby?"

"Yeah, it seems you're not the only one who's been playing with the devil."

I take off, grabbing the bag I'd already packed before coming down here. The dread that has been sitting heavy in my stomach for the past few days told me how this conversation was going to go, and I just knew that I'd need to get away after it.

"Jodie, where are you going?" Mum shouts, rushing behind me as I pull my coat from the hook.

"I can't be here right now. I'm sorry, Mum. I just can't."

With my bag over my shoulder and my coat in my hand, I blow out of the house and into the cold, leaving the lies and the betrayal behind me.

If only it was that easy.

4

TOBY

I pull the door open only seconds after the buzzer rings through my flat and meet the eyes of the woman standing on the other side of the door.

All the air rushes out of my lungs as she steps inside and I all but fall into her arms.

"Oh, Toby," she says. Her voice is soft, but I hear the undercurrent of disappointment. "I knew that you'd find yourself on the losing end of all this eventually. What have you done, huh?"

Breathing in the familiar comforting scent of Mum's perfume, I find some strength from deep down and lead her deeper into my flat.

"Where's Galen?" I ask, not ready to dive into the heavy shit quite yet.

"With Stella. She said I should probably visit, and from the look of you, I see she was right."

Lifting my hand, I scrub at the days of scruff covering my jaw.

"If I knew you were coming, I'd have—"

"Sit with me," she says, lowering herself to the end of my sofa. "Talk to me."

Falling into the corner seat, I prop my feet up on the cushion and lower my head into my hands.

"I've dreamed for years about what I could do to him for the way he treated you. Us. I've been crafting a plan for as long as I can remember, and him doing what he did with Stella, it only played into it."

"You need to let it go," she says quietly. "I understand your need for revenge. Trust me, I've thought up enough ways of my own to hurt that man for everything he did to my kids. But what's the point? We're all here, we're together, safe. And he's… yeah," she mutters. I haven't given her any information on where he is right now, and I can only assume that Galen hasn't either. "I want us to put it in the past, where it belongs. We've got futures to look forward to, Toby. I don't want you tormenting yourself over things you can't change."

"I finally hurt him, Mum," I confess, pushing aside everything she just said. "I found his weakness and forced him to watch as I broke it right before his eyes."

Mum gasps in shock, but when I finally lift my eyes to meet hers, thankfully I don't see disappointment or hatred. Just understanding and concern.

She's grown up in this world, just like my boys and I have. She's seen plenty, heard even more. Experienced the worst of the monsters this life creates, so I doubt she'll be shocked by anything I've actually done. More surprised I'm actually capable of it, I'm sure. To her, I'll always be her little boy despite my training, despite my capabilities.

"Did you know about them?" I ask, testing to see how much Stella might have already spilled about what's going on.

Her eyes narrow on me suspiciously. "About who?"

"His other family."

"No," she says, shaking her head, hatred for the man she was forced to spend her life with darkening her eyes. "I didn't know they existed." She quickly adds, "I knew he wasn't faithful, but I never thought for a second he'd go to the effort of hiding an entire other life. A son."

Gratitude for my sister slams into me as she says that. Stella and Seb could have easily told Mum about all of this, but they didn't, even without me asking them to keep it to themselves.

"Joker wasn't his only kid," I confess.

"Oh?"

"J-Jodie," I choke out.

"Tobias," she warns, her eyes pleading with me not to say what she already knows is coming next.

"I was playing her to get to him."

Her teeth grind as she glares at me. "Toby, what did you do?"

Pain rips through me as I think of her shattering on my bathroom floor, of her pained cries and her tears. Her vomiting, unable to stand what I'd done before she called me a monster, compared me to him, and walked out.

Slouching down into the sofa, I pray that it'll just swallow me whole and make all of this go away.

"Everything she didn't deserve. But equally, I forced him to witness everything he needed to see."

Mum's lips part and then close again as she tried to read between the lines.

"I don't even know what to say to that, Toby."

"I thought it would make me feel better. I hoped it would rid me of some of the nightmares, knowing that I was able to make him hurt too."

"Did it help?"

I shake my head. "Now, when I close my eyes, I don't see him. I see her. I see her with a version of him staring down at her. Because to Jodie, I may as well be him. I am him."

"No," she says, sliding across the sofa and dragging my hand from my lap, holding it between hers. "You are nothing like him. I promise you, you're—"

"I broke her, Mum. I stood there and watched her world crumble around her. I made it happen. I pretended I was the one trying to make it all better, when really, I was the one pulling the strings."

"Tell me everything," she urges, thankfully not disgusted enough in me to walk out just like Jodie did.

"TOBIAS, to what do we owe this pleasure?" Damien asks as I close his office door behind me.

After Mum left, I took myself to the bathroom and finally scrubbed and shaved the past few days of oblivion from my body.

I hated the look on her face as I explained everything I'd done to trash Jodie's life just so I could let Jonas watch her fall from grace. She should have hated me for treating another person like that. Deep down, she probably does a little, but she never let it show. Instead, once I'd exhausted my list of crimes—missing out some of the filthier ones that no mother needs to hear about—she squeezed my hand and asked me the million-dollar question.

"How are we going to fix this?"

I shake my head as I walk to one of the chairs in

front of Damien's desk. Charon pushes from his seat on the other side of the room and walks over, standing behind the boss as they wait for me to speak. He doesn't look any different from when I believed he was my grandfather, but then, he knows and sees everything. He's probably known all this time that I'm no relation of his.

"I... uh..." I rub the back of my neck, knowing that I'm about to ask the exact opposite of what I did the last time I was standing in this office. "I need to talk about Joanne and Jodie."

Shock covers Damien's face for the briefest of moments before his usual mask is slammed back into place.

"And what would you like to discuss? You were more than certain of your decision regarding Jonas's money and your wishes for them the last time you were sitting in that chair," he says coolly, as if this is nothing more than a business transaction.

"I'm aware. Things have changed."

"Care to explain?"

"Not really. I've come to realise that I'm punishing the wrong people, and I'd appreciate it if you could ensure both of them get what they deserve. Not that anything he has to his name could ever be enough compensation for having him in their lives," I mutter, my eyes shooting to Charon.

Silence settles around us for a beat.

"I'll set things in motion. But there will be no changing your mind this time, Tobias. Once I sign off on it, it will happen no matter what."

"I won't be changing my mind again, I can assure you."

Damien nods once, resting his elbows on his desk and steepling his fingers as if he's over this conversation already.

I sit forward, more than ready to get out of his lair, but my eyes snag on Charon once again.

"You knew, didn't you? All this time, you knew."

His hard eyes hold mine, giving nothing away.

"You even helped cover all this up, didn't you?"

"You can leave now, soldier," Damien growls.

Standing, I round the chair, never losing eye contact with the man I believe to be on my side all this time.

"And to think, I always looked up to you," I hiss. "But you're no better than him."

"That's enough," Damien booms. "You do not talk to my consigliere like that."

"Pfft," I scoff, backing toward the door. "You should take this as a lesson, Boss, and be careful who you trust."

Damien's jaw pops with irritation, but he says no more.

"I need you working tonight. If you're capable."

"You don't need to doubt my ability, Boss. My loyalty to you isn't in question right now."

I blow out of the room without saying anything else. I'm pretty sure my parting statement pretty much said it all.

I don't look up until a familiar voice hits my ears, and when I do, I find the best sight before me.

"See, I fucking told you he was still alive," Seb taunts as my eyes fall on the others. On the guys I've kept locked outside my flat for the past few days.

"What the fuck, bro?" Nico barks, clearly pissed that I've shut him out while I drowned.

"Sorry, man. Sometimes things have just got to be done, you know?"

"Like fucking the hottest girl in the room every night of the week," he barks, his eyes sparkling with amusement as I step closer.

The second I'm in touching distance, he throws his arm out and wraps it around my shoulder, dragging me into his side.

"You're good though, yeah?"

I think about what I've just got Damien to agree to—more easily than I was expecting, I might add—and a small smile twitches at my lips.

"I will be, yeah."

"Thank fuck for that, because we're going to party," he announces.

I glance at the others and notice that they're not dressed for work.

"Don't tell me we're heading for Lovell again."

"Can't do that, man," Theo says. "No trouble tonight though. They've called a ceasefire of sorts. We're just going to hang with Archer and his boys, show our faces. Let those stupid fucks know we're still about."

I look down at my black hoodie and jeans, glad I left the sweats behind for the first time in days.

"Right, let's go then."

With Nico on one side, Theo on the other and Alex and Seb trailing behind, we make our way out of the hotel and to the car that's waiting for us out the front.

"What's this about?" I ask, looking around as the others pile into the back behind me.

"We're partying, remember?" Nico says as if it's obvious. "You didn't want to be capable of driving home, did you?"

"No, but I need to go back to school tomorrow," I say. Reality is calling.

"When has that ever stopped us?" Alex asks, lighting a joint. He takes a hit and then immediately passes it to me.

By the time we pull up at the Wolves' Den, I've got a nice buzz on, and that combined with knowing I did the right thing back in Damien's office means I feel lighter than I have in days, maybe even weeks. But it's not enough. And I know it won't be until I get a chance to see her, to talk to her, to attempt to apologise for everything I did. Assuming she lets me anywhere near her, of course.

"This place looks better than the last time we saw it," Seb says as we nod at the two Wolves guarding the door. They're clearly expecting us, because neither says a word as we let ourselves inside, finding the place tidied up from our previous visit.

The last thing I remember from this place was broken furniture, loud grunts and groans and the odd gunshot that echoed around the vast space as we ushered the girls out to safety.

Back in the day, it used to be a soft drinks factory, but it's been out of commission for years. Luis Wolf took it over when he was a teenager and gave his father little choice but to buy it and the land it sits on when the council demanded they stop squatting inside.

It's been the place the younger Wolves hang out ever since. It's pretty impressive really, all things considered. There's a huge communal party area, back rooms that are more intimate places to meet or hang out, and even a mezzanine with bedrooms above them. Not bad for a bunch of Lovell reprobates.

"Maybe this place isn't as bad as we always

thought," Alex mutters, obviously impressed with the cleanup job they've done. If we weren't here the week before last to witness the carnage, then it would have been hard to imagine.

"Ah, Cirillo royalty are back. Twice in two weeks... we must be moving up the ladder," Jace says, appearing on the balcony that leads to the bedrooms and dragging his hoodie over his head as he peers down at us.

Dax appears behind him, shirtless and doing up his fly, an obvious bullet wound in his shoulder as he glares down at the man who put it there.

"You still pissy, Daxton?" Theo taunts. "I do hope whoever you two have just spent time with back there wasn't married."

"Un-fucking-likey," Jace mutters, shooting a look back over his shoulder.

"You fuckers here for business or pleasure?"

"Little bit of both," Theo says with a grin while Dax snarls at him. Touchy fuck. He deserved that bullet hole for even thinking about laying a hand on Emmie all those weeks ago.

"Where's the boss?" Nico asks.

"In the sanctuary. Careful though, when we left he had a girl on her—" A door slams deeper in the warehouse before a female cry echoes around us.

"You're a fucking arsehole, Archer Wolfe."

His deep rumble fills the air, but it's too low to

decipher—not that I try too hard. A second later, a woman with dark tears staining her cheeks comes running our way. Her hair is a mess, her dress all twisted up, barely hiding the goods as she flies past us, a whimper on her lips.

"You playing too rough with your toys again, Archie?" Jace teases as he jogs down the stairs.

"Fuck you, man," Archer booms as he emerges from the shadows with a smirk playing on his lips. I get the feeling he got exactly what he wanted from that girl. Something that I'm sure wasn't reciprocated.

"Ah, just pissed off I left her with you instead of letting her play with the real men, then?"

Archer flips his boy off before stepping closer to us.

"Boys." He nods. "How's it going?"

"It's good. Boss sent us for a peacekeeping meeting or some shit," Nico says. "Although personally, I think I prefer the party."

"Come on," Archer says, beckoning us to follow him down to his sanctuary.

Theo and Nico are totally unfazed as they take a step forward, but I briefly look over at Seb, who shoots me a similar look. Being invited into the Wolves' Den in one thing, but their inner sanctum? That's something else entirely.

It seems like this peace treaty and support thing we've got going on with Archer and his boys really is serious. Something I never thought would happen. Well... while they were being headed up by Archer's big brother, anyway. We might not have known the depth of his desire to rip the Cirillo family apart with Ram, the prez of the Royal Reapers by his side, but since everything with Emmie was uncovered it's become clear that that was their number one objective. They wanted power, money, and all the respect that came with it.

It's a real shame they underestimated their opponents.

Our world is different now. With Archer heading up the Wolves and Cruz, Emmie's uncle, taking the gavel over in the Reapers compound, we can only hope that the future might just be a slightly tamer one where we can all just get on with business instead of fighting amongst ourselves. The only other motherfuckers we need to worry about are the Italians, and seeing as they've been making moves to claim our businesses recently, and helped to hide Ram when he disappeared, something tells me they're sitting back, watching all the drama and waiting for their turn to strike.

"The OGs have calmed their shit since that night," Archer informs us after inviting us into what is basically a self-contained studio flat at the back of the building.

Grabbing beers from his fridge, he throws each

of us one as we find seats on the sofas arranged around a coffee table.

"But I'm assuming you're not expecting it to stay that way, seeing as we're sitting here now," Theo guesses.

"They're licking their wounds, planning their next hit. Those brainwashed cunts are fully on board with Luis's dictatorship."

"So what are you saying?" Nico asks before taking a pull on his beer.

Archer stalks toward the final empty sofa and falls into the middle of it as Dax drops down beside him and Jace stands guard at the door with his foot casually pressed against the wall.

"They're not going to just roll over and toe the line."

"They're going to need to be taken out?" Alex finishes for him.

"We've got a couple of moles within their ranks. They're keeping us informed with what's going on."

"And what is going on?" Theo asks, ignoring the beer hanging between his knees, his eyes fixed firmly on Archer.

"Just keep your phones on. We're going to need your backup again pretty soon."

"That's it?" Theo scoffs. "That's all you're going to give us?"

"If I fucking knew the time and date then I'd

fucking share, Cirillo. You think calling you all in to help is what we fucking want?" Archer snaps, his body pulled tight with tension.

"You think we want to be here?" Nico counters.

Over the years, there's been plenty of bad blood between us. It was no secret that Damien and Archer's old man didn't see eye to eye on how our part of the city should be run. I can only assume he was the start of the Wolves/Reapers alliance. Things only got worse when Luis took over. That cunt was as corrupt and twisted as they come. But it seems that Damien is willing to put the bad blood behind him in the hope of a more united future with Archer at the helm over here and Cruz leading the Reapers. It could be a powerful time for all three of us. If we're able to work together.

Archer tells us what he does know from his moles who are living within his OG members and trying to foil their takeover plans.

When Galen first started talking about this coup, I assumed we were talking about a handful of hardcore Luis supporters who were going after Archer's new leadership of the Wolves, but the more he talks, the more it seems to be becoming more hostile than that.

This is serious, and if Archer isn't careful, the estate he loves so much could end up burned to the ground.

5

TOBY

"I get the feeling you're following me for a reason," Archer quips as I tail him out of the room after he announced he was going to take a piss.

"What gave me away?" I mutter, not giving a shit that he's sussed me out. It's not like I was hiding, I just didn't want to have this conversation in front of everyone. I don't want them to know where to find her. Not yet, anyway.

He pushes through to a bathroom but leaves the door open as he comes to a stop in front of a toilet.

"Go on then," he says, sounding more than a little suspicious about what I could possibly want.

"I need a favour," I confess as he takes a piss.

"Well, that was fucking obvious. What is it?" he asks, flushing the toilet and moving to the basin.

"Foxes is under your control, right?"

He glances over his shoulder, his eyes narrowed in confusion.

"You want a job shaking your ass for money, Doukas?" he quips, a smirk pulling at his lips.

"No. You have a new girl starting that I need eyes on."

"Ah, of course it's about a girl," he laughs smugly. "So what is it you're really asking? You want her sacked before she's even started to stop the scumbags who frequent that place getting their hands on what's yours?"

"No," I state. "I don't want to stop her from doing what she thinks she needs to do." Despite how much I really fucking want to. I would if I didn't think she'd hate me even more than she already does.

She explained to me on our waffle date about how she harboured some deep desire to be a stripper. I'm sure she never expected things to play out how they have for that dream to come true, but here we are. And I'm not going to take that away from her as well as everything else I've ruined.

"So..." Archer prompts, his brow quirked in a way that tells me he's enjoying this little interaction.

"I just want an eye kept on her. Make sure no one steps out of line, and take action on anyone who might."

"Right," he mutters.

"She's mine. Jodie Walker belongs to me, and if any of your scumbag patrons try taking a single fucking thing from her, they'll have me to answer to. As will you," I threaten, stepping closer to him and holding his eyes.

He might be the gangster from the wrong side of town, but I'm not fucking scared of him if he wants to try something. I've been taught all the dirty ways to fight and am more than capable of holding my own against him.

"Careful, Doukas. Remember who you're talking to."

"The gang leader who can't keep his own troops in line?" I ask teasingly.

"Careful. Did you want your girl protected or not?"

"Just proving a point, Wolfe. You might be the boss over here now, but you can't deny that you need us. When all this shit hits the fan, you know that we'll have your back. I'm just asking for a small favour in return. And after all, Jodie is connected to your guys."

"Oh yeah, how's that?"

"She's currently inside Jesse Madden's place, hanging out with Sara," I inform him, knowing just how important Jesse is to him.

"Right. I'll ensure my boys keep a close eye on her."

"Appreciated, man."

He nods once before taking off toward his sanctuary, but I don't miss the way he mutters, "Fucking pussy-whipped motherfucker."

Shaking my head, I walk into the bathroom and close the door behind me, shutting myself off from everyone else for just a few minutes.

I'm sure the guys are right and this is probably exactly what I need, but it's not helping me forget or be able to ignore the pain in my chest. Especially knowing that she's close. In a few short minutes, I could be at Jesse's place. They'll probably be alone too at some point, because there's no way he won't leave them to it and show his face here once the party starts kicking off.

Slamming those thoughts down, I do what I need to do and force myself to rejoin the party and pretend everything is okay.

"MR. DOUKAS." I flinch, hearing my name growled at me in an angry but familiar voice a beat before there's a loud bang right in front of me.

"Fuck," I bark, sitting upright and blinking as my surroundings begin to come back to me. "What the—"

"If you're not going to do me the courtesy of listening in my class, Mr. Doukas, then do us all a favour and go snore at home."

My eyes find the narrowed ones of my history teacher before glancing down at the massive textbook she threw on the desk beside my head to wake me.

"I'm sorry. I worked late," I lie, and she's probably more than aware of the real situation seeing as the five of us crashed in Archer's sanctuary sometime after three AM and stumbled into school, barely dressed in our uniforms after a flyby visit to our flats first thing this morning. Both Stella and Emmie ripped us all new ones for leaving them out as they drove us to school, still stinking of last night's alcohol.

"Sure you did," she mutters, swiping the book off my desk once more and stalking back to the front of the classroom where she continues talking about whatever this fucking lesson is about.

Slouching down in my seat, I ignore my need to do as she said and go home. I've had enough time off recently. I need to be here. I need to keep my grades up and get everything I need to score the uni place I want for later in the year.

Theo and I have had our futures planned for years. Our shared desire to head to Imperial College to study computing is one of the reasons I didn't finish at Knight's Ridge like I should have last year. Something about us starting together appealed to me, and I found a way to make it happen. Plus, Nico fucked up his first year here by failing everything, and I didn't want to be the only one out of the five of us to move on.

Blowing out a breath, I try to focus on what I should be doing, but I never quite get up to speed on the lesson, and before I know it, the bell is ringing for lunch. My stomach grumbles right on cue as I pack up and head toward the door.

"Mr. Doukas." I'm stopped by Mrs. Parks once more before I manage to escape. "I've taken the liberty of giving you extra homework to catch up on everything you slept through earlier. I'll expect the report on my desk first thing Thursday morning."

Snatching the papers she's holding out for me, I mutter my agreement and stalk out of the room.

"You look like death," Stella says when I catch up with her in the corridor.

"Love you too, Sis."

"I might be nicer if I got a fucking invite, or you know, if you weren't such a dickhead."

"Say it how it is, Stel."

"Have you spoken to her?"

I shake my head. "No. She'll probably slam the door in my face if I even try," I mutter.

"So you're giving up?" she asks astounded.

"When did I say that?" Her intrigued stare burns my skin. "I'm just... biding my time. Waiting for the right moment. What about you?"

"What? Have I gone back and confessed to being the one who killed her brother?"

I blow out a breath as the weight I've become used to carrying around recently only gets heavier.

"She wasn't in," she confesses. "I went over after I discovered you'd all been sent into Lovell last night. Joanne said they'd finally spoken about everything and Jodie packed a bag and walked out."

"She's staying with a friend," I admit.

"How do you know that?" she asks, her eyes widening in shock.

"How do you think? I've tracked her phone." I roll my eyes, wondering how Stella hasn't already learned our tricks.

"Jesus, you're all as bad as each other, you know that right?"

"You really think I'm letting her run away from me? Letting her forget I exist?"

Her lips part as if she wants to tell me that that was exactly what she was thinking, but she refrains from commenting.

"You really like her, huh?"

"I've got a few wrongs to right."

"Sure, that's what it's all about. Nothing to do with wanting to kidnap her and have a do-over of your dirty weekend in that cabin. Or maybe another trip to Hades."

"Seb taken you yet?" I ask, more than happy to turn this around on her.

"No," she sulks.

"Don't even think about asking me to convince him," I hiss.

"Don't worry, I've got ways of getting what I want," she says happily as we walk into the school restaurant, the scent of today's options hitting my nose and making my empty stomach growl louder.

"I don't want to know," I mutter as we join the line.

"Ah look, the rest of the idiots look about as bad as you." She tilts her chin in the direction of our table, and when I glance over, I spot Theo, Nico, and Alex looking like death warmed up. "Daemon is practically glowing. I guess he missed out on the invite too," she points out as the devil in question stalks toward our table like a younger version of the Grim Reaper.

"You should tell him that," I suggest. "I bet it'll make his day."

"Oh yeah, because he really screams 'I live for compliments and kind gestures'," she mocks before she shrieks, dragging my eyes away to see what's wrong. I soon wish I never bothered when I turn to find Seb molesting her.

"Jesus," I mutter, moving forward with the line and leaving them to it.

When I finally join the guys at the table, everyone is silent, still suffering from the night before, thank fuck.

"Well, look at you bunch of reprobates,"

Emmie announces loudly as she threads her fingers into Theo's hair and drags his head back roughly. Clearly, she's still as pissed off as Stella is about being left out last night.

"Baby C, how's it going?" Alex perks up when he spots the bubbly brunette that is Nico's little sister bouncing up to the table in her PE kit consisting of a pretty tight polo shirt and a damn near indecent white pleated skirt.

Her steps falter as she scans all of us.

"Jesus, you lot must have had a fun night."

"Don't worry," Daemon pipes up. "They didn't invite me either."

Ignoring him, she drops down beside Alex, whose face immediately lights up. I'm pretty sure he's just doing it to torture Nico. Although, this is Alex we're talking about. I doubt he'd actually turn Calli down if she were to ever take his advances seriously. Stupid fuck. There's no way I'd be putting my cock on the line like that.

"Did you want anything, Calli?" Nico snaps, keeping his narrowed eyes on Alex—or more specifically his hands that are resting on the table. "Ow," he complains when Emmie releases Theo's lips and slaps Nico upside the head.

"You just came to show off this little skirt, did you, Baby C," Alex teases, pulling his arm back.

"Drop your hand beneath the table, Deimos, and I'll cut the fucking thing off."

"Oh, big brother is touchy today," Alex taunts.

"Fuck you," Nico sulks.

Thankfully, Seb and Stella finally grace us with their presence and take over the conversation, allowing me to shut down as I eat my way through my lunch and think about all the homework I've got to catch up on.

"WHAT ARE WE DOING TONIGHT, BRO?" Nico asks as I stuff my dirty football kit into my bag after practice.

"I have no idea what you're doing but I've got a shitload of work to do, even more since Mrs. Parks caught me sleeping in history and gave me extra."

"Oh burn." He snaps his fingers like a dick.

"You're gonna need to go talk to Alex if you wanna go out and get your dick wet again."

"Who's getting their dick wet?" Alex asks, stopping at the end of the bench, ready to leave.

"Me and you tonight. You up for it?" Nico asks.

"Nah, man. Not tonight. I'm busy and shit."

"Too busy and shit for pussy?" Nico asks like he's never heard anything so ludicrous in his life.

Alex shrugs, tugs his bag higher on his shoulder and stalks off.

"What's up with him?" Nico mutters, shoving his feet into his trainers.

"No idea. Any clue as to why he's not moved in yet? Wasn't his flat finished weeks ago?"

"There's an issue with the flooring or something. Smells like bullshit though, if you ask me. You reckon his dad's got a new woman who prefers the younger model?" Nico asks, wiggling his brows in amusement.

"Nah, I doubt Alex would be up for his dad's sloppy seconds."

"Crazier shit has happened, bro."

I grunt. "You don't need to tell me that. Come on, or Stella will leave us behind," I say, throwing my bag over my shoulder and heading for the exit.

"You sure you don't want some company? We're both spending the night working too," Stella offers as we step out of the lift on our floor.

"I'm sure. I'd be miserable company anyway."

"Toby," she sighs, "I'd rather put up with your grumpy ass knowing that you're not lonely."

"I'm fine, honestly." Total fucking lie. "I'll see you tomorrow, yeah?" I say when she and Seb come to a stop by their front door.

When I turn toward her, conflict wars on her features.

"Seriously, Stel. I'm good. You don't need to worry about me."

"Seriously?" she asks. "I might not be your

biggest fan right now, but you're my brother, Toby. I don't like the idea of you being alone and miserable."

I smile at her, more than grateful for her support. "Have a good night, yeah?"

She watches me walk to my own door. I don't look back to confirm it—I don't need to. I feel her concerned stare burning into my back.

She's probably got every right to be. Hell, I'm concerned about what I'm going to attempt to do tonight.

I dump my bag in the kitchen, ready to wash later, and take myself through to the bathroom, more than ready to have a proper shower and wash off the lingering effects of last night and what mud still clings to my skin from practice.

I might not be heading out on official business, but feeling like I should probably look like I'm serious, I pull my suit on. And when I finally step back out of my front door, checking to make sure I'm not going to be caught sneaking past Stella's place, anyone would think I'd been called into work.

Nostalgia hits me as I pull up on the street outside Jodie's house. I spent so much time sitting out here, watching her unnoticed over the past few weeks that it almost feels like home.

Pulling my phone from my pocket, I check the

tracking app Theo insisted we all install a few years ago, and I wait for it to load her phone.

I downloaded the app on her phone when we were away in Evan's cabin. I didn't have time to install something a little more discreet; I just have to hope she's not OCD with her apps and notice the extra amongst the pages and pages she has on there.

I breathe a sigh of relief when it finally loads and shows that she's still at her friend's place in Lovell. She might be in the middle of an imminent war zone, but Jesse is one of Archer's best guys, and if he believes his girl is safe, then I know Jodie is too. I've seen the pair of them together more than once since they returned from Australia, and the way he looks at her, even from the distance I was watching them from, he's so fucking smitten. It's the same look Seb and Theo give their girls when they think we're not looking. Totally whipped and not even close to giving a single fuck about it.

Lucky cunts.

Not so long ago, I thought the only thing I wanted was to see Jonas on his knees with his heart ripped out of his chest. But now, that need has been replaced by just having a chance to get close to the girl who's worked her way so deep under my skin that I'm sure I'll never get her out.

I drop my head back as I allow thoughts of that motherfucker to fill my head. I should have ended him after Wednesday night. I should have gone down there after Jodie ran and put a bullet through his head. It's what I promised Mum I would do—not in so many words—but I didn't. And he's still down there.

I know why I'm putting it off.

I'm doing it for her. For the girl who grew up believing her father was a decent guy. I'm doing it so that when I finally get a chance to look her in the eyes once again, she won't only see a monster but a murderer too.

There's a very good chance she already won't forgive me, but if I were to do that on top of everything else before I get the chance to talk to her again, there would be no coming back.

Before I can talk myself out of it, I push the door open and march toward the front door, pressing my finger on the bell.

My heart is in my throat as I wait. To start with, I can't help but wonder if she knows I'm here and is ignoring me, that or she went out and left the lights on. But after a few more seconds, there's movement inside and the door is hesitantly pulled open.

Joanne's face is pale, her eyes shadowed and bloodshot.

She doesn't register who I am for a beat. Hell, I don't think she even sees me. Instead, she looks right through me.

"Joanne?" I whisper, concerned I'm going to scare her.

Finally, her eyes find mine, and the exhaustion and stress gives way to something else.

Anger and pure hatred.

"No," she barks, her hand pressing against the door on the inside as she tries to slam it in my face.

"Please, Joanne. I'm not here to cause trouble."

She puts all her weight behind the door, trying to stop me from entering. Unfortunately for her, I'm stronger. Plus, I have something I know she desperately wants.

"Just let me in. Let me explain a few things. I can help you keep your house."

She stops pushing, her eyes meeting mine in the gap of the door.

"Really?" she asks, desperation laced through her tone.

"Yes. I can fix everything. Well... maybe not everything, but... I can make it a little more bearable."

"You're the reason we're in the mess."

"Please, Joanne. Just let me—"

Suddenly, the door opens fully and she stands aside, allowing me to enter.

Unsure of where to go, I turn into the living room, a space that haunted me the first time I was here, but after everything, his judgemental stare is nothing less than I deserve.

Only, when I step into the room, I don't find the walls covered with that monster's face. They're bare. All the frames are stacked up in a box by the sofa.

"I started packing," Joanne explains behind me. "I needed to keep busy, and suddenly, I didn't find his presence quite so comforting."

"Jodie told you." It's not a question.

"I don't think she told me everything, but she told me enough to know that your presence in her life was both a blessing and a curse."

"I guess I should take that, because I deserve so much worse."

"Did he really treat you and your mum like that?"

"Yes," I state, turning back to look at her so she can see the honesty in my eyes. "And since discovering you, I'm starting to understand why he hated us so much. He was trapped with us. Everything he wanted was here, and he couldn't have it."

"I'm so sorry," she breathes, tears clinging to her eyelashes.

I shake my head. "None of it was your fault, Joanne. I'm the one who should be saying that. I went after Jodie with the intention of hurting Jonas, for punishing him for what he did to me, to my mum. And that is unforgivable. I ripped both of your lives apart while I was right under your noses when none of this was on you. You're both as innocent in all of this as I am—as I was. It was unfair of me to target you just because he loved you, Joe and Jodie the way he should have loved me... us."

"If I knew... if I had any idea..."

"There wouldn't have been anything you could have done. If anything, it probably would have made it worse." I shrug, completely believing my words. Joanne was Jonas's reprieve. He needed her. I can't imagine how intolerable life would have been if he didn't have her lightness.

"I was the one who ensured that you got nothing when he died," I confess. "I wanted you to suffer. I wanted Mum to have everything she deserved, even though he'd organised for you to have almost everything."

"She does deserve it."

I shake my head. "That may be true. But right now, she's exactly where she belongs. She's happy and with the man who stole her heart as a teenager. But you... I stripped everything from you."

A sob rips from her throat. If only she knew just how true that statement was.

"Damien Cirillo, my boss, is organising the funds you were due to be transferred to your accounts. The house will be signed over to you, and you never need to worry about money again."

"Toby no. I was never his wife, I don't deserve—"

"You do. You both do. You're the only people who are grieving someone you loved. It doesn't matter how I saw him. How my mum suffered. You must have put up with enough of his shit over the years with his absence and his refusal to publicly accept your relationship, his own children."

Finally, her first tear falls.

"I'm not here to discuss it, Joanne. Everything is already in motion. There will be no bailiffs or any more final demands. You're free to try to rebuild your life."

She nods, although the deep frown in her brow proves that she's not really accepting my words easily.

"And what about Jodie?"

"I can get her job back for her, if she wants it. But I can't do anything about the lies you've told her, or the ways I've hurt her in the past few weeks. I can only hope that one day, if I'm lucky, she'll find a way to forgive me."

"She left after I told her the truth," Joanne blurts.

"Can you blame her?" I ask as she falls down onto the sofa.

"I never really thought about it before, but since Jodie told me about your mum, about what you went through, it makes me realise just how controlling he was. How under his spell he had me."

"Don't beat yourself up over things you can no longer change," I tell her, wishing like hell I could take my own advice. "What's done is done. He's out of all our lives, and while I know you loved him, I can assure you that your future will be better this way."

She sniffles, pulling a tissue from her pocket.

"Did Jodie tell you about Joe?"

She shakes her head but guesses correctly. "It was him, wasn't it?"

"Joe was working for Jonas, yes. He wasn't the one who pulled the trigger, though."

The sob that erupts from her forces me to close the space between us, and in a move I didn't see coming, I wrap my arm around her shoulders in comfort.

"I'm sorry for all your loss, I really am."

She nods, accepting my words.

"Jodie will come around. She loves you. She just... she just needs time."

"And what about you?" she asks, her sad eyes finding mine.

I shrug. "I'll do everything in my power to get her to talk to me. But anything after that is on her. She has every right to never want to see me again."

Her eyes narrow and she reaches for my hand, squeezing gently.

"It wasn't all an act, was it?"

"No," I confess. "At first it was. The night I met her, all of it was orchestrated. But I never could have expected the woman I was going to meet. She blew me away."

Joanne smiles sadly at me. "She's incredible."

"Something we agree on," I say quietly.

"She'll come around," she promises. "I saw the way her eyes lit up when she talked about you. Hell, when she even thought about you. If you really care about her, if she really did see parts of the real you, fall for the real you, then you just need to give her time."

I sigh, not sure I'm able to believe her. Especially when she doesn't know everything that happened.

"We'll see."

6

JODIE

A groan rips from my lips as footsteps pad against the floor outside my room. A room also known as Sara's studio.

It takes her quite a few more minutes to appear, and when she does, she's smart enough to bring coffee with her.

"Morning," she sings, as if it's not fuck knows o'clock.

"Is it that time already?" I complain, dragging the duvet over my head as she flicks the light on.

"Sure is. Rise and shine, it's a brand-new day."

My chest squeezes painfully in my chest. She might see the new day as exciting new possibilities, but all I see is another day wasted.

It also marks a week since I learned the truth. And I'm still finding it hard to breathe with all the lies and betrayal hanging around me like a bad rash.

Something happened last night. When I finally crawled into bed sometime after midnight, I had loads of missed calls from both Mum and Bri. Too many for them just to be begging me to come home.

I didn't respond.

While part of me might be desperate to know, there's another part which isn't.

Concern twists up my insides, wondering if Mum's been evicted.

But then I remember the lies. The secrets.

I should just be glad that I'm away from it all. Not that I'm going to be able to run forever. I'm going to have to reenter my life soon, very soon, and I'm going to have to deal with all this shit and try to find a way forward that isn't wallowing in self-pity in my friend's studio.

Braving the light, I poke my head out of the sheet, finding Sara at her desk, waiting for her computer to wake up.

"Hey," I croak.

"I'm sorry for waking you so early after your late night. But I've got a ton of work to do and orders to get ready."

"You have nothing to apologise for. I'm the one who's in your way. And I really shouldn't have stayed up drinking with Jesse so late."

"He's a good drinking partner."

"Too good," I mutter, more than aware that my brain feels two sizes too big for my head right now.

Pushing myself so I'm sitting, I drag the duvet up as high as I can to keep the warmth and reach for my coffee, but as I do so, my phone lights up again.

"Argh," I complain, finding a new message from Bri.

"What's wrong?" Sara asks, spinning around on her chair.

"Something's happened."

"Something like what?"

"I don't know. My phone was blown up last night with missed calls. But let's be honest, it can't be anything good."

"It might be," she says with a shrug, her positive outlook on life making me want to crawl back under the sheets and never return. "You'll never know if you don't talk to anyone," she says, her eyes narrowing.

Since the moment I turned up, she's been saying the same thing. She doesn't believe that my hiding in her house is doing me any good. And while she might be right, the vodka that Jesse keeps supplying me with sure seems to make a difference.

But as the days have passed, I know what she's saying is true. As much as I might wish I could avoid the reality of everything, I know I can't. Especially now if something has happened.

If Mum has been evicted, I can't just abandon her. Yes, she lied, but that's not all she is. I can't allow one mistake to cover up the incredible job she's done of being a mother all these years. And at the end of the day, she's probably the least guilty in all of this. Jonas was a monster. If he wanted me hidden, then I'm not sure she ever would have had the power to do anything about it.

I guess I should really just be grateful that he never treated us like he did Maria and Toby.

"I know. I will," I promise.

"MORNING," I say more than a few hours later when Jesse comes strolling into the kitchen in a pair of sweats with his hand shoved down the front.

I can't help but shake my head as he grunts at me in greeting.

Even after all this time, it still amazes me that he was the one who stole my sweet, sweet Sara's heart.

His ink distorts and pulls as he moves toward the coffee machine and finally pulls his hand free. And it's when he turns his back on me that I come face to face with the evidence I missed all this time.

Across his back is a huge wolf tattoo.

I guess if I'd seen him shirtless before slotting myself into the middle of his life, then the whole Wolves thing might not have been such a shock.

"Would you be surprised if I were to tell you that there were reports of a suspicious-looking custom BMW sitting out in the street last night?"

My heart jumps into my throat at the possibility of him knowing where I am, let alone him being close.

"Uh..."

He turns to me, resting his arse back against the counter, gifting me with an unobstructed view of his abs. *Damn, Sara is one lucky bitch.*

His lips part, but I can already hear the exact words that are about to fall from him.

"I know. I know I need to talk to everyone, including him. Sara's already lectured me about it this morning."

His brow quirks at my tirade. "I was actually going to say that he doesn't deserve you. But that he's putting on a good show to try and prove us all wrong."

"By sitting out the front of your house in the middle of the night? Hardly proves anything," I scoff.

He nods, turning back toward his full mug, hiding his face from me. Something tells me his smirk only got wider. Wanker.

"What am I missing, Jesse?"

"Not much. Just that he was talking to Arch about you."

My brow wrinkles. "Why the hell would he do that?"

"They were at the Den on Monday night."

"And you're only just telling me this now?"

His lips twitch in amusement. "Oh I'm sorry, I thought you were hiding from him, not secretly stalking him."

"You're funny," I hiss. "How'd he know I'm here, anyway?" I ask, giving him the stink eye.

"Do not give me that look, Walker," he growls. I'm sure the tone would terrify many, but I've only ever seen Jesse the teddy bear around Sara, so I find it hard to even believe he could be a brutal gangster when he wants to be. I always just assumed he looked the part; I never believed he could play the part too. "I value my balls too much to risk outing you like that. Sara might look like a sweet little woman, but I can assure you, my girl has claws."

"Is that right?" the lady in question asks, sauntering into the room with an empty mug, her eyes locked on Jesse's half-naked body.

"You know it, Care Bear," he teases, eye fucking her back just as hard.

"How does he know I'm here, Jesse?" I ask before they completely forget I'm in the room.

"Fuck knows. He's Cirillo. They're ruthless fuckers. Probably tracked you."

"Tracked me?" I screech.

"What? We need to keep track of our valuable assets," he murmurs, cupping Sara's face with his giant inked hands as she steps right up to him. She looks like a mouse who's about to be mauled by a lion. "Isn't that right, baby?"

"Hmm... I always know where you are. I stalk your arse daily."

"Yeah, because you care. The only reason he wants me is for revenge. Don't you think he's already caused enough damage?"

"You think he doesn't care?" Jesse asks, his eyes meeting mine over the top of Sara's head.

"It was all an act. Fake. He played the part of the perfect boyfriend to make me fall. None of it was real," I scoff, anger beginning to lick at my insides as I remember all the good times we had that have now been poisoned by the truth.

"If you say so."

I narrow my eyes on him. "What do you know that I don't?" I hiss, getting irritated with his vague statements.

"Nothing. Just a feeling."

"You haven't even seen us together. How would you even know what was between us?"

"You're right. I don't. Probably better if I butt out."

Sara squeals as he grabs her arse and lifts her, switching their positions and wrapping her legs around his waist.

"Missed you, Care Bear," he says before claiming her lips in a kiss that makes jealousy burn red-hot inside me.

Fuck. I had that. Even if it was for the briefest time and a complete lie, I still felt like I had found something special.

It's what makes it hurt so much. In all my darkness, I really thought I had found just a little bit of light.

Sara is crying out Jesse's name even before I get to her studio, telling me that I really need to go out.

The thought sends a shiver of fear down my spine, but I know it needs to happen.

Bri only got me out of starting work at Foxes for a week, and I haven't forgotten that I promised Courtney I'd get a wax and visit a hairdresser before I started.

Dragging on a pair of leggings, a sports bra and hoodie, I tie my hair up and grab my phone and headphones.

"I'm going out for a run," I call, although I'm not sure why I bother. From the banging, grunting and groaning coming from the kitchen, they're more than a little preoccupied. Good for them. Sara should make the most of that Adonis as often as physically possible.

"Bye," I call a beat before slamming the door and jogging down the stairs. I suck in a deep breath of fresh air as I step out onto the street. But I don't let myself enjoy it for more than a second as Jesse's words from the kitchen come back to me.

My eyes scan the street, searching for his less than inconspicuous car.

He should be at school right now. I should be safe. But I already know that he's not one to follow the rules.

When I don't see anything that raises my suspicions, I put my headphones in and take off.

I don't know Lovell all that well, but I know where the main high street is, so I head in that direction, hoping the run is long enough to give my body the exercise it craves.

I come to a stop at the end of the main stretch of shops and rest back against a wall. I give myself a minute to catch my breath before pushing open the door of the salon next to me with a fake smile plastered on my face.

By some kind of miracle, I manage to book appointments in that first place for everything I need, and I walk out with the first step of my new life complete. Now, I've just got to figure out the rest.

My stomach growls, reminding me that I've only had coffee since getting woken before dawn, and the second I look up, I find a pasty shop.

Being brave and trying to pretend that I'm tackling some of my demons by even being out of the house, I follow a sign for a park with my paper bags of goodies in my hand and set about finding a bench.

I come to a stop overlooking a playground that's filled with preschool kids and mostly their mums.

I study each of them as I eat, wondering if they've got their shit together, have a husband and a happy life, if they manage to juggle careers and motherhood, or if their days are filled with their kids' smiling faces and putting all their focus on them.

I let everything else drift from my mind as my chicken slice vanishes before I even really taste it, and I reach down for my next warm bag.

I'm busy smiling to myself, watching the young kids having the time of their lives when a shiver runs down my spine.

Immediately, my back straightens and I square my shoulders.

"Shit," I hiss to myself, feeling stupid for not just rushing back to Sara's after doing what I needed to do.

My heart thunders in my chest and my skin prickles with goosebumps as I wait for the sound of footsteps on the pavement and for a shadow to fall over me.

But it never comes.

My phone burns a hole in my pocket and my fingers itch to reach for it, to demand he makes himself known and just say what he's come to say.

In the end, my willpower loses to my irrational thinking and I pull it free, unlocking the screen and finding our last conversation.

My stomach turns over as I read our last few messages.

I was so angry at him that night. I wanted the truth from his lips so badly, but I never could have imagined how the night would go.

Jodie: I know you're there.

I hesitate with my thumb over the send button, and I almost press it, but right at the last second, my phone vibrates with an incoming message that makes my breath catch in my throat.

Toby: I'm sorry.

"Not good enough," I mutter to myself.

Toby: I know it'll never be enough. Will never come close to making up for what I did, for how I hurt you. But I am sorry. My twisted need for revenge clouded my

judgement, warped what was really important.

My heart races and my hand trembles as I stare down at his apology.

I haven't seen him for a week, and despite being unable to forget a single moment of our final minutes together, deep down, I miss him.

In those few weeks, he became so important to me. He was the light in my darkness, my knight in shining armour.

My phone vibrates again, but this time with a call.

Emotion clogs my throat as I even consider hearing his voice, but when I look at the screen, I don't find the photo I took of Toby at the cabin, but instead, my cousin's bright, slightly drunk smile lights up my screen.

Swiping across, I lift it to my ear as I gather up my remaining paper bag and begin walking out of the park, away from him.

"At fucking last, Jojo. I've been going out of my mind."

"Sorry, I just needed a few days," I confess, keeping my head down, forcing myself not to look for him.

"I know, I get it. How are you doing?"

"I've booked my hair appointment, ready to

start work," I say, not really wanting to get into anything else.

"Well, that's a start," she says, relief filling her tone. "I know you're probably not going to want to hear this, but you really need to go home and talk to your mum."

"Something bad happened, didn't it?"

"What? No. What makes you say that?

"Because you were both blowing up my phone last night like the world was coming to an end. Has she been kicked out?"

"N-no, it's nothing like that. Nothing bad, I promise."

7

JODIE

Despite promising Brianna that I'd go home and see Mum, it's not until the following evening that I finally push my lingering anger aside in favour of finding out what's going on.

I barely have the key in the lock when the light comes on on the other side of the door and it's pulled open.

"Jodie," Mum breathes, immediately sweeping me up in her arms like nothing is wrong. "I've been so worried about you."

"I've just been with Sara, Mum. I haven't been far."

"I know but... I'm so sorry, baby." She pulls back and takes my face in her hands. Her tear-filled eyes look over every inch of me before she clocks my hair. "This looks incredible," she says, threading a lock of my newly highlighted hair through her fingers.

"T-thanks. That's what you're meant to do when a guy shatters your world to pieces, isn't it? Get a new do." I force out a laugh to go along with my statement, but it's more painful than anything else.

"Come in, it's freezing out here."

Taking my hand, she tugs me into the house, pulling my keys free and abandoning them on the unit in the hallway.

"You want coffee, or something stronger?"

"What do you think?"

"You got it," she says with a smile that's almost as forced as mine was a moment ago.

She leaves me at the table and immediately pulls two cocktail glasses from the cupboard before bottles of spirits line the counter.

The concerned daughter in me wants to demand to know if she should be drinking after her unhealthy relationship with the stuff since Joe's death, but I hold my tongue.

She's a grown-arse woman who is capable of making her own decisions.

She measures shots into a shaker before pulling fruit juice from the fridge to finish off her drinks.

"Here you go," she says proudly, passing the pink drink to me.

"What is it?"

"A sweet apology in a glass," she says, her eyes pleading with me to forgive her.

"Mum," I sigh, not anywhere near ready to let this all go yet. "Bri said I needed to come and talk to you."

All the air rushes from her lungs as disappointment etches into her features.

"We're not going to lose the house." My eyes widen at her statement as relief floods my veins. "And everything that Jonas left for us is sitting in my bank account."

"What? How? I thought there was nothing."

She shakes her head, and it's in those few silent seconds that reality hits.

"Toby," I breathe.

A small smile twitches at the corners of her lips, which makes me frown.

Do not tell me that all he had to do was turn up here offering our house back and she's suddenly on his side.

"He came by Tuesday night to explain everything and to tell me that he'd organised for us to have everything we deserved."

Dropping my eyes from the table, I try to process all of this.

"The house has been signed over to me, and we've got more than enough to ensure we don't need to worry about money for a long, long time."

"But why?" I whisper, still staring at the old

wooden tabletop before me. It's been sitting in this exact position all my life. It's got all our writing etched into it from where we always pressed too hard to write, small drawings that Joe and I created when we were little.

Reaching out, I trace some of Joe's childish writing from when we were kids, my chest aching with loss.

"He's not a monster, Jodie. He's just—"

"A sadistic fuck who needed to—"

"A broken little boy in a man's body," Mum interrupts.

"Christ," I mutter, reaching for my cocktail and knocking it back in one. "You really are naïve, aren't you?"

Her eyes flash with indignation, but she thankfully bites her tongue. "I know you think I'm a terrible judge of character but—"

"Jonas used to lock Toby in their basement as punishment." Mum pales at my revelation. "He controlled every aspect of Maria's life. Her treatment for a brain tumour. He forced the man she loved and her own daughter out of the country so she had to live eighteen years without her baby."

Mum swallows nervously, but her eyes don't leave mine. "That's exactly why Toby isn't like him."

"How can you say that?" I shout, the chair I was sitting on toppling to the floor behind me as I stand. "You're meant to be on my side here, Mum. He set me up for stealing from my employer. He took all our money. He watched as we grieved, as we suffered, knowing it was his fault. He... he s-showed m-me—" A sob cuts off my words and I slam my lips closed.

I have no idea why I'm hiding the fact that Jonas is alive—or at least, he was last week—from her. But something feels wrong about confessing that I've seen him.

"For all we know, Toby killed him."

"No, he'd have done it before now if it were that easy."

"Jesus, Mum," I seethe. "I can't believe you're on his side."

"I'm not on his side. I'm on yours, baby, always. I just think that he's not the total monster you've pegged him to be."

"I swear to God, there's something fucking wrong with you," I announce. "He hurt me, Mum. He ripped my heart out and stomped on it just for the fucking fun of it. You're meant to be sitting here threatening his life for causing me even more pain than I was already in. Not fighting for him. Not trying to make me give him another chance."

"I'm not trying to make you do anything, Jodie," she bites back. "I just want you to see that there are two sides to this, that you're not the only one who's hurting."

"Why do you care? You don't even know him."

"I know how much he meant to you, and I know how much he suffered, and I can't help but partly feel guilty about that. If I hadn't just sat back and accepted how my life with Jonas was, maybe I could have—"

"Guilt. Are you fucking kidding me?"

"I don't know, Jodie. I don't know how to feel. Last week I was mourning my loving partner. This week I discover that he was a monster who basically killed my son."

I gasp, not realising she knew that.

"Toby told me. He told me how Jonas turned Joe into a monster, got him to do his bidding. The man I loved my entire life did that to our own child. I don't— I didn't—" She falls back into the chair and drops her head into her hands. "And now I've lost you too, and I don't know what to do," she sobs.

My heart fractures for the broken woman before me, and suddenly I get it. She's just as conflicted over all of this as I am.

While I hate Toby for what he did, that affection, that desire is still tingling right under my skin.

The connection we shared. It was something. Something strong. And I'm not sure how I'm meant to just snuff that out like it never existed.

"I know, Mum. I know," I say, dropping to my knees in front of her and pulling her hands from her face. "We're going to get through all this. We are."

She nods, tears continuing to drop from her lashes. "I'm sorry for pushing."

"It's okay. I know you're just trying to help."

"You're always my priority, Jojo. Always. I hope you know that. I just... I want to help. I want us all to be able to move on from this, and despite never meeting him before, I kinda feel connected to him through it all."

"I'm confused too," I whisper, dropping back onto my arse. "He messaged me earlier."

Her eyes hold mine, begging me to open up.

"He just apologised." I say, ignoring the fact that he was watching me at the time. I might not have searched him out, but I fucking well knew he was there.

"So what now, baby? Are you coming home?" she asks, hoping filling her eyes.

"I start work tomorrow. I'm going to stay at Sara's just because it's closer. I'll be back next week," I promise.

"Okay," she says sadly. "I'm sorry for keeping all of this from you."

"I know," I say sadly, getting to my feet once more.

"Call me Saturday and let me know how your first shift goes."

"I will," I agree while internally wincing at

what that shift is going to entail. I don't need it anymore. We have money. But that's not the point. I want to pay my way, be my own woman.

Emotion clogs my throat and burns the backs of my eyes as I let myself out of Mum's house and into the dark night outside.

Tugging my coat tighter around me, I take off down the street. The air is filled with the scent of incoming rain, the dark clouds hanging heavy above me. Part of me craves it, but the other part knows that it'll just take me back to that night with him. A night when everything was easy, fun. When I could allow him to just take away all my pain and grief and turn it into laughter and desire.

I haven't even made it to the end of the street when I notice a set of slow-moving headlights behind me.

"Goddamn it, Toby," I hiss under my breath.

Pulling my cell out, I tap out a quick message.

Jodie: I should call the cops on your stalking arse.

Despite the fact that he's driving, his reply is almost instant.

Toby: I think you'd miss me. How's your mum?

Jodie: Trying to convince me to talk to you. I'm just trying to remember how easily manipulated she is.

Toby: Ouch. Although I think she has a point. You really should talk to me.

Jodie: You don't deserve it.

Toby: Tell me that to my face.

I move so fast that the rational side of my brain has no chance of trying to stop me. I jump out in the road and stand glaring at the man behind the wheel of the car.

He startles when he sees me standing there. He might be going slowly, but his shock prevents him from acting as fast as I'm sure he'd like and the bonnet of the car doesn't stop until it's mere millimetres from my legs.

My heart thunders, allowing me to feel its violent beat in every inch of my body. My fists curl in frustration as he throws the door open and climbs out.

"What the hell are you doing?"

"You want to talk? Let's talk," I spit.

His eyes hold mine as he rounds the car door. They're alight with excitement that I've acknowledged him, but there's also something darker within them—and not just the shadows from where he's clearly not been sleeping.

The sight of him before me renders me useless for a few seconds. The connection that has always crackled between us is still as strong as ever and confusing the fuck out of me even more than I already am.

"Here?" he growls, the deep timbre of his voice hitting me exactly where it shouldn't.

"Sure, why not? That's what you're stalking me for after all, isn't it?" I spit, finding my voice once more.

"No," he states, continuing to prowl forward, the distance between us growing dangerously close. "I needed to see you. I needed to know that you're okay. I don't deserve the chance to talk. Not until you're ready."

"So you messaged me why?"

"Pretty sure you started that, Demon."

My lips part to argue, but then I remember that he probably saw me staring at my phone about to message him in the park, and I was the one to start it just now.

When he gets so close the heat of his body burns through my clothes and into my skin, I take a huge step back.

I refuse to let him disarm me with his touch. He knows as well as I do just how powerful it is.

"I just want a chance to talk to you. In private," he adds, his eyes never leaving mine.

"And what about what I want?"

"I'll give you anything," he says, the sincerity of his words making my chest ache.

"You know, it's funny. Not so long ago, I thought you were doing just that. Excuse me."

I spin around and manage to take a step before his fingers wrap around my wrist, stopping me from escaping.

I tug, trying to free myself from his grasp, but his hold is too strong.

Nothing is said as we stand there in a silent battle of wills.

"Please, Jodie. I need you. I need—"

Wheeling around, I lift my free hand before he has a chance to notice and swing it as hard as I can. My palm connects with his cheek with a loud and painful crack, forcing his head to swing to the side.

A gasp rips from my throat as reality hits.

Holding my burning hand against my chest, I wait for him to react, terrified as to what I'm going to find staring back at me when he looks around.

"Toby," I breathe, my voice quivering more than I'd like it to.

After another two seconds, he turns his head back to me, and the streetlights above make his dark, treacherous eyes look even more terrifying with the way they sparkle.

He lifts his hand to his cheek as my body begins to tremble in fear.

His fingers brush the red angry skin there as he glares at me.

The Toby I fell for isn't the man who's staring at me right now. I have no doubt that the monster before me is the one my father trained into his perfect, brutal soldier.

"Get in the car, Jodie," he seethes, his voice low as the threatening raindrops begin hitting the ground around me.

"I-I don't think th—"

"I said, get in the car."

His fingers grip my upper arm and I gasp as pain radiates from his touch.

"Toby," I whimper as he pushes me forward.

"I won't hurt you, Jodie. But I really need you not to test my fucking patience right now," he forces out through gritted teeth.

Knowing what he's capable of, I quickly decide that the best course of action here is probably just to do as I'm told.

He rips the door open and none too gently shoves me inside as the rain gets heavier around us.

The second my arse hits the seat, he slams the door, cutting off any connection that was still crackling between us, despite his obvious anger.

The rain begins lashing around me, and in only moments little rivers run down the windscreen, obscuring my view of him as he walks around the front of the car.

I hold my upper arm, my skin burning from his touch, and gasp when he stops and turns to me.

His eyes find mine through the rain before he bends forward, pressing his palms to the bonnet.

I don't breathe as the weight of his pain and regret hits me square in the chest.

Mum was right about something. There is one very broken boy staring back at me right now.

Tears burn my eyes as I hold his stare.

What must it have really been like for him to grow up living with a monster? A monster who was determined to break him, to terrorise him, to make him feel completely worthless?

The rain grows heavier still until it's bouncing off the car, soaking Toby's hoodie and running down his face.

Eventually, he rips his eyes from mine and lowers his gaze, his shoulders dropping along with his head as he allows himself to get swallowed up by his pain.

Releasing my arm, my fingers curl around the door handle, my need to offer him comfort almost too much to ignore.

But I never open the door. Instead, I focus on that dark side of him. The side which was unable to see the truth about what we could have been and was too consumed with the need for revenge that he shattered everything we could have had.

My heart is still racing, my fists curled on my lap when he finally pushes from the car, his clothing wet through.

He marches toward the driver's side, pulls the door open, and drops inside. Cool air rushes around me, making my skin erupt in goosebumps, and a shiver runs down my spine.

The tension in the air is unbearable as he puts the car into drive and takes off down the quiet street.

A million questions dance on the tip of my tongue, but I'm not brave enough to ask them as he damn near takes the corner at the end of the street without looking.

"You probably shouldn't be driving right now," I hiss, my fingernails digging into the soft leather beneath me.

He doesn't respond, but I don't miss the way his grip on the wheel tightens and how his scarred knuckles turn white.

His speed only increases, making my heart race as he jumps light after light.

"Toby, you're going to fucking kill us," I cry when he almost takes a turn wrong which would have left us impaled in a corner shop.

"At least I'd have you by my side."

All the air rushes out of my lungs at the sincerity in his words.

Thankfully, he slows his crazy-arse driving a little after our near miss, and I manage to relax slightly.

"I know what you're doing," I state once he seems to have calmed down.

"Is that right, Demon?"

"You can't outrun it all, you know. Unless you deal with it, it's always going to drag you down."

His grip shifts on the wheel, but he doesn't say anything more as he takes a slip road toward the dual carriageway and floors the accelerator once more.

8

TOBY

My heart pounds in my chest, my entire body trembling with pent-up adrenaline, and my feet continue to press the pedal, shooting us forward faster and faster.

I've always known my car is a beast, I've just never really had a need to put her to good use before. Something I'm quickly learning was probably a mistake. The faster we fly down the road, the freer I feel. The more my anger, my frustration, my guilt washes away, and I'm just left with the contentment of having her sitting beside me. I can even pretend that she doesn't hate me as she pretends not to be enjoying the ride.

Her fingers are wrapped around the edge of the seat, but it's impossible to miss the small smile playing on her lips.

Yeah, my girl has a reckless streak in her, even if she's not aware of it yet.

"Fuck, I missed you," I breathe, just loud enough so she'll be able to hear me over the roar of the engine.

She visibly tenses, but her response isn't exactly what I was hoping for.

"Where are we going?"

"Nowhere," I confess. To be honest, I hadn't even intended on following her down the street, let alone making my presence known. But here we are, so I clearly fucked that up.

"Right, well... any chance you could take me home? I start work tomorrow and I—"

"At the bar?" I ask, already knowing the answer.

"Y-yeah," she agrees, keeping her eyes out of the window.

"You never told me which one."

"One that sells drinks," she quips under her breath.

"I'm not going to turn up and watch you all night, if that's what you're worried about."

"Seriously?" she snaps, finally twisting around to look at me.

The second our eyes connect, it's like she's knocked the air clean out of my lungs.

The urge to reach out and touch her burns

through me, and my fingers tighten around the wheel to stop myself.

She doesn't want to be here, that much is obvious, and I've already fucked this little reunion enough tonight.

My eyes are still locked on hers when she suddenly screams and launches herself at me, grabbing the wheel and twisting it beneath my hands.

"Fuck. FUCK," I bark as I catch sight of the nose of my car missing the central reservation by what must have been inches.

"Now will you just take me home?" she snaps, falling back into her seat once more and crossing her arms over her chest.

Seeing the road is clear behind, I cut across the lanes and back down toward the city.

Neither of us says another word, and all too soon, I'm pulling up outside Sara's house. I'm assuming that because she didn't tell me that I was heading the wrong way, this is where she wanted to be.

"You're really pissed at your mum, huh?" I mutter, putting the car into park.

"Not as pissed as I am at you," she snaps back, undoing her belt and pushing the door open.

"Fair," I murmur. "Wait," I call in the rush before she has a chance to close the door on me. "Can I see you again? We need to talk."

She bends down and looks me dead in the eye. I know what's going to come out of her mouth before her lips even part.

"No. Enjoy the rest of your night."

She slams the door before I get a chance to respond and watch as she runs around the front of the car, hiding under her coat as she darts for the door that leads to Sara and Jesse's flat.

"Fuck," I breathe, slumping down in my seat and tipping my head back the moment she's out of sight. "FUCK." I slam my palms down on the wheel, desperately trying to defuse some of the pent-up frustration.

I have no idea how long I sit there for, but it's long enough for Jesse to finally emerge from the flat, having looked out of the window multiple times to see if I'm still sitting out here.

Rolling my window down, I wait for him to say whatever it is he's come to say.

"You look like a pussy, sitting out here pining after her, you know that, right?"

"Like you'd do anything differently if your girl had shut you out."

"Big difference there," he points out smugly. "I wouldn't have fucked my girl over quite so badly to even have to consider dropping to my knees and begging for forgiveness."

"Whatever. If you don't have any decent advice

then…" I pull the button for the window and it starts to lift.

"You need to do something bigger than sitting out here like a grade-A stalker. You want her, prove it to her. You're sorry, prove it. You care, prove it."

"How? She won't talk to me."

"You're going to need to think outside the box here. And no, I don't mean send her flowers daily or some sappy shit like that. Show her who you really are. That you really want her in your life."

"Oh, so not much then," I mutter.

"Is she worth it?"

"Yes."

"Then I suggest you fuck off and go and figure out how you're going to do the unthinkable and get her back."

He taps the hood of the car and turns to walk away.

"Wait," I call. "How is she… really?"

"Sad. Angry. Lonely. It's like… she's in our flat, but she's not really there. I hope you know what you're doing, letting her start at Foxes tomorrow night," he warns. "That place can be—"

"I know," I confirm, more than aware of its reputation. "Archer's promised me he'll have guys watching her." Jesse's eyebrow quirks up. "And I'll be right outside."

"She'll be pissed when she finds out."

"I need her safe. Do you have any other

suggestion than fucking up her second job in only a few weeks?"

"No, not really. I just know that there's no way in hell I'd let those scumbags look at Sara the way they do to the girls in that place."

"I need to let her do what she needs to do. And if some of those scumbags end up with an eye or a finger or two missing then..." I shrug.

"Go home, Toby. Get some sleep and figure out what the fuck you're going to do."

"Thank you," I call when he manages to get a little farther away this time. He looks over his shoulder in question. "For looking after her."

He nods once in acceptance before continuing toward wherever he's going.

Pulling my phone from my pocket, I shoot off a message before taking some of Jesse's advice and heading home.

Only, I don't spend long in my flat, just enough time to change into some sweats and a t-shirt and head down to our gym in the basement, where I know a couple of people are waiting for me.

"So, you decided it was about time to finally have your arse handed to you then, Doukas," Emmie says with a smirk on her face as she straps a pair of sickly-sweet pink gloves to her hands.

"I could have you tapping out with my eyes closed, Mrs. Cirillo," I taunt back.

"Yeah, yeah. How about you actually put your

money where your mouth is, Bro. You obviously came here looking for a challenge or you'd have called the boys in."

Stella throws me a pair of gloves before the two of them duck under the ropes of our state-of-the-art ring.

If they were anyone other than my sister and one of my best friend's wives, I'd be in fucking heaven right now. But as it is, all I see is two more than willing, more than brutal opponents. And Stella's right. I fucking need this.

"Let's go then," I say, tugging my gloves on and cracking my neck to the side. "And when we're done. I need some advice."

"Ooh, so there is an ulterior motive here," Stella jokes. "I'm sure we can help come up with something. After all, we have experience of forgiving the unforgivable where you boys are concerned."

The second I step into the ring, they're on me like a fucking pair of hyenas.

Emmie's gloved fist collides with my ribs before Stella's uppercut sends my head flying back.

Pain shoots down my spine, but fuck if my body doesn't sing.

THE THREE OF us lay on the floor of the ring sometime later with our chests heaving and our skin covered in a sheen of sweat from dancing around, dodging each other's blows and landing more than just a few.

My body aches in the exact way I was hoping for when I called Stella from outside Jesse's place.

"So go on then," Stella says after long minutes of silence while we all fight to catch our breath. "What advice do you need?"

"She won't talk to me," I confess.

"And you're surprised?" Emmie asks, astounded.

"N-no. I just... I hoped she might at least want to hear me out."

"She does," Stella confirms.

"B-but—"

"She's not ready," Emmie helpfully offers.

"I get that. But I can't keep waiting."

"It's been a week," she scoffs. "She's barely even touched the surface of what you deserve."

"I know. I just—"

"Look," Stella says, sitting upright so she can look at me. "We know you wanna fix this. Wave some magic wand that will make all your lies and indiscretions go away. But that's not how it works.

"You fucked up, Toby. You fucked up big. And now you have to suffer the consequences."

"But what if—"

"No. There is no what if here. No big declaration of love gesture is going to work. The wound is too raw, too painful. I know it's not the answer you want, but it really is time. Then, if you're lucky, she'll be able to move on from the bad parts of what happened and focus on the good."

"And if she can't?"

"Then it wasn't meant to be," Emmie offers. "She served her purpose in your life, and the best thing you can do is move—"

"No," I blurt, refusing to accept that as an option.

"I'm sorry, Toby, I know this isn't what you want to hear. But it's the truth."

I nod, unable to talk around the messy ball of emotion that's clogging my throat as I consider the possibility of there being no future beyond this for us.

I abandon the girls down in the gym after they give me the truth that I deserved but equally didn't want, and I head down lower to the deepest depths of our basement where the vermin live.

I don't head for his door, but instead, the control room with the one-way glass. Finding the control panel, I allow myself to see through into his cell.

Confusion pulls at my brow as I watch him sleep on the hard bed beneath him. Was he really the incredible father that Jodie thought he was?

Was he even capable of caring? Of nurturing? Of helping to create the incredible woman I spent time with?

I guess the answer to all those questions is obvious. He might not have always been there, but he helped raise her.

The thought of her having his blood running through her veins should be enough to scare me off. The notion of her being tainted by him should terrify me. But I figure it's too late for that.

She's good. So fucking good.

The only one who's really been tainted by him is me. I'm the monster. I'm the one who caused all this. And she's right to want to keep distance between us, even if it kills me to admit.

"Why?" I breathe, pressing my head against the glass as I watch him. "Why fuck me up and give her everything? Why treat Joanne like a queen and not Mum? I get that she was unfaithful, but you were first. Why couldn't you have just let her go? Let us go? Was it all just about holding power over us, controlling us? Would you have turned that need on Jodie if you had let us go? Is it a need that's rooted so deep inside you that in a way, we were protecting them from you? Giving you people to turn your wrath on so you could love them? Because if you were, then maybe I could understand it. I'd give anything to protect her right now. Is that what you were doing? Protecting her from yourself? Giving her the man she deserved while unleashing your inner monster on us? The illegitimate child you pretended to be connected to and your long-suffering wife whom you never loved."

I blow out a breath, knowing that he can't hear me, that I won't get the answers I long for.

Yes, I could walk inside that cell and demand them of him. But experience tells me that I won't get very far.

This is the first time since that night with Jodie that I've even been down here, even acknowledged that he still existed. I should have been happy that I'd won. That I'd achieved everything I set out to. But the reality paled in comparison to how I expected to feel.

So instead of gloating that I managed to defeat the monster and bring him to his knees, I crawled back to the bedroom and let myself drown in regrets, in the pain that I caused myself as I watched the one person I truly cared about shatter before my eyes.

I press the heel of my palm against my chest in the hope it'll help squash the ache there. But it never does. The only time it's lessened since that night was sitting in the car with her only an hour ago. Having her beside me, her scent in my nose. It calmed everything inside me. Made me breathe properly for the first time in a week.

"Fuck," I breathe, slamming my fist against the glass.

The man on the other side startles, but it's not enough to wake him. And I realise just how relieved I am that I don't have to look into his eyes.

As far as I'm concerned, I never want to do it again.

There's just one problem with me doing that now. And that's Jodie.

When all of this has calmed down, will she want to see him? She knows he's alive. She knows the truth. Will she need to say that final goodbye she thought she'd been robbed?

One thing is for sure. I can no longer do it. I can't become even more of a monster in her eyes. As much as it pains me not to go through with all my plans, I just can't.

Because of her.

9

JODIE

The attention of what feels like a million eyes on me makes my skin tingle as if I've got ants crawling all over me.

In all my years imagining what this life might be, never did I think I'd feel like I do now.

I thought it would be empowering, freeing, enlightening even.

But right now, with the eyes of a bunch of old, sleazy men on me, I just feel dirty, cheap, like a complete sell-out.

Okay, so I always thought I'd be up on a fancy stage, shaking my booty in some glamorous outfit which would make me feel like a million dollars, but the reality of my current situation is very, very different.

Courtney has put me in a pair of gold knickers —she called them shorts—which show off way too much of my arse considering I'm weaving in and out of these leering men with a tray of drinks constantly in my hand, stopping me from being able to defend myself should one decide to get a little handsy. She teamed them with a bra top that at least has some padding and tassels hanging from the bottom, helping to cover me a little, and a matching pair of sky-high heels.

When I was standing in the dressing room with the other girls, I felt good. Sexy even. But the second I stepped out here, all that flew out of the window.

Add the fact that I'm the new girl to that, and I'm receiving way more attention than I'd have liked on my first night.

Some of the other girls are up on stage, dancing around the poles and looking incredible. It's where I'd prefer to be, but according to Courtney, being up there is a privilege I've got to earn. I need to prove that I can handle myself out on the main floor first. She might have explained them as the rules everyone abides by when they first start, but I couldn't help but see it as some fucked-up initiation ritual to filter the strong from the weak.

I hate it. All of it.

I keep my mind on the wages, and the tips I've currently got stuffed in my bra, but now that I've spoken to Mum and know our financial situation is okay, even the thought of how much I could make here is taking the shine out of it.

I don't belong in a place like this.

I should be at uni having the time of my life. I should be focusing on a career, a life, a future.

"Where did the boss find you from, pretty girl?" a guy wearing a greasy set of overalls sneers as I place a round of beers down on the table for him and his friends. "You look like you need some breaking in."

I bite my tongue to stop me from shooting back an insult that would probably get me fired within the first two hours of my shift here.

Although, really... do I care?

"Enjoy your evening, gentlemen."

"Oh, she's polite too. I wonder what it takes to dirty that mouth up."

My teeth grind so hard as I walk away from the arseholes that I'm surprised I don't crack one.

"Ignore Frank, he's all mouth," Courtney says when I get back to the bar with an empty tray.

"He's all dickhead," I mutter under my breath, still trying to ignore the tingling of my skin.

"Here you go, table six." She jerks her chin in the direction I should be heading and slides a tray toward me. A quick look over my shoulder tells me they're for a younger group of guys who don't seem quite as bad as the rest of the crowd tonight.

Sucking in a deep breath, and pulling up my big girl knickers, I reach for the tray and head over.

All six pairs of eyes eat up my progress, but their attention doesn't make my stomach turn over like the previous tables I've visited.

And it's not until I'm passing out the fourth beer that I get an inkling as to why.

"Thanks, doll," the guy drawls, reaching out for the glass and exposing his inked-up forearm. The sight of a very familiar wolf tattoo makes something inside me relax.

They might not know who I am, but they're Jesse's friends. Or maybe they do know who I am and he sent them to keep an eye on me.

"I thought you guys usually hung out in your Den?" I ask bravely.

"Sometimes we fancy a change of scenery, and tonight was one of those nights, doll."

"Jesse sent you, didn't he?"

His brows pull together in confusion, making my heart begin to race as I realise that I've read this wrong. "Jes—"

"No, he didn't mention that we'd find a stunning new girl handing out the drinks tonight. Nice little surprise for us though," the guy to his left interrupts, making me even more suspicious.

"Right, well... I've got work to do."

"You sure do, sweetheart. Watch your back.

There are some interesting characters in this place."

"Yeah, I'm beginning to learn that."

"You sure it's really the place for you? We'd hate to see anyone getting hurt."

The first guy cracks his knuckles as his friend says this, and I narrow my eyes as I look between the two of them.

A thought hits me, but Courtney calls my name before it has time to really flourish.

"Enjoy your night, gentlemen," I say once more and take off.

BY THE TIME my shift is coming to an end, the attention on my almost naked body hasn't lessened and my feet ache more with every step I take to the point that I swear they're bruised.

Just the thought of having to put them on again tomorrow night for my next shift makes me want to cry.

Tonight has been horrendous. Nothing like I always hoped it would be.

I feel dirty and gross, and all I want to do is go home and curl into my bed.

My chest aches with the realisation that my own bed isn't where I'm heading tonight.

Maybe I made a mistake saying I'd stay with

Sara for the weekend and I should have just put the shit with Mum behind me and agreed to go home. I can't help but feel like I'm only torturing myself at this point.

"You're walking like you've got a stick shoved up your arse," Courtney comments when I get back to the bar with a tray full of empties.

"How long does it take to get used to the shoes?" I ask through clenched teeth.

"A couple weeks. You think you're going to make it that long?" she asks deadly seriously.

"What?" I gasp, rearing back a little. "Have I been that bad?" I ask, weirdly offended.

"No, not at all. You've been great, and the punters seem to love you."

"My arse. They love my arse."

"Same thing. All I know is that your new girl appeal has been filling my till nicely tonight. But something tells me I need to enjoy it while it lasts."

"What are you trying to say?"

She blows out a breath, resting her forearms on the bar between us, pushing her tits up, much to the delight of a few guys sitting a little farther down from us.

"You're not cut out for this life, Jodie."

"I am, and I need—" I start, although I'm not sure why I'm arguing. I don't need this job. Not anymore. Not thanks to Toby. But do I want that monster's money now that I know who he really is?

"You can argue all you like, but you know I'm right."

"Let me just do the weekend. It might get better."

She quirks a brow at me as if to say 'really?' but she finally concedes. All the while, my stomach twists painfully as I silently question my sanity for asking for more of this torture.

"We'll reassess this Sunday night. If you're still here."

"I'm not a quitter," I argue, annoyed by her opinion of me.

"I'm not saying you are. If I was a bitch, I'd be telling you that you're a natural right now because of the money you've made me tonight just by hobbling around in your shoes, but I'm not. My girls are important to me. I want them happy, comfortable in their job. And you, new girl, are anything but. So I'm giving you an out.

"Go home tonight, think about it, and let me know by lunchtime tomorrow if you're coming back."

I nod, unable to argue anymore.

"Go, get out of here. Take your shoes off."

"But my shift doesn't end for twenty minutes."

"It's fine. Go. And think about what I said."

"O-okay. Thank you," I say, forcing a smile on my face.

Rolling my shoulders back, I stand tall and

walk out of the main bar, putting as little weight as possible on the balls of my feet as I head toward the back of the building and the dressing rooms.

In only minutes, I'm dressed in leggings and an oversized hoodie and I'm sighing in relief as I pull my Ugg boots on.

"Yes," I hiss, throwing the death shoes into the locker Courtney allocated me before balling up my outfit and stuffing it into the laundry basket. Definitely a perk of the job, not having to wash that myself.

Hiking my bag up on my shoulder, I walk out with my head held high.

Courtney may well be right, I might not be cut out for this job, but like hell am I going to let it show on my face.

Pushing out the side door, I'm immediately assaulted by the brisk air. The first flowers of spring might be popping up here and there, but we're still deep in the throes of winter.

Thoughts of Valentine's Day that's right around the corner make my heart sink as I make my way around the building to meet Sara, who promised to come to keep me company on the walk home.

I've never really been a big romantic, preferring no-strings hookups to meaningful relationships, but meeting Toby skewed all of that. I wasn't aware of the future I was planning—it was a subconscious thing mostly—but nonetheless, my heart ran away with me.

The wind whips around me, my ears starting to burn from the cold as I look for Sara.

Not seeing her, I take off in the direction of their flat in the hope of bumping into her.

I'm too up in my head to really pay attention to my surroundings. I'd like to think if I was of sound mind then I'd have my wits about me a little more when walking in a place like Lovell in the dead of night. But I can claim no such thing right now after recent events.

The second I step in line with the alleyway that leads around the back of Foxes, an arm darts out and drags me into the darkness.

The scent of stale cigarette smoke and whiskey fills my nose as I drag in a breath, ready to scream. But I don't get the chance, because a hot, dirty hand covers my mouth a beat before I'm slammed back against the wall. My head ricochets off the brickwork, sending a shooting pain down my neck.

My heart jumps into my throat as fear wraps itself around me, rendering my body utterly useless as I stare into the dark eyes of the man who was taunting me inside.

Frank.

Clearly, he's not so harmless after all.

"So the boss thinks you're too good for her place, huh?" he leers. "Thinks you're too sweet, too innocent for the likes of us," he snarls as red-hot tears burn the backs of my eyes.

My phone rings and the piercing sound coming from a few feet away is the first clue that I dropped it when he grabbed me.

A whimper rips up my throat, but it's cut off by his hand pressing harder against my mouth.

"Well, let's see if everyone thinks you're so fucking special after I've finished with you."

10

TOBY

I don't stop to think. I don't consider the consequences. My only focus is my girl.

I fucked up when she left the club. I didn't keep my eyes on her as she rounded the corner of the building. Instead, I pulled my phone from my pocket to write her a message.

The next time I looked up, she was gone and my heart plummeted into my feet.

Lifting my gun, I aim it right at the motherfucker's head who's standing at the other end of the alleyway.

"No, no, please," Jodie begs as he roughly turns her around and shoves her harshly against the wall, his hand immediately reaching for her waistband.

Fear like I've never felt before in my life threatens to drag me under, but I can't lose myself to it.

I've trained my entire life to stay calm under pressure. To take out our enemies before they even realise we've arrived. Now is no different.

The second he stills enough for me to take the only chance I have, I squeeze the trigger and trust in my skills.

The silencer ensures he's not alerted at the last minute, and only a heartbeat later the stupid motherfucker drops to the floor like the sack of shit he is.

Jodie twists around and screams a beat before I get to her.

"It's okay, baby. It's me."

Her eyes go as wide as saucers before her legs give out and she drops before me.

I'm more than ready, and I catch her long before she hits the ground.

"It's okay, baby. I've got you." Sweeping her up into my arms, I press my lips to her brow and take a moment to breathe her in. "I've got you."

I march out of the alleyway with her passed out in my arms, only for Sara to run straight into us.

"What the hell?" she screeches as she looks between me and her friend in my arms.

"Toby," I grunt, just in case she doesn't know.

"I know who you are," she spits. "What the hell happened?"

"The scumbag down there with a bullet in his skull was trying to rape her."

"WHAT?" she screeches.

"Come on, I'm taking you home."

"What about Jodie? And what about... *that*?" she asks, looking over her shoulder with a wince at the thought of what exactly might be hiding in the darkness.

"Jodie is in safe hands. And that will be dealt with once I can make a call."

"Who was he?"

"A fucking scumbag with a death wish."

Sara pulls my passenger door open, and I carefully lower Jodie down into the seat, hating that I've got to let her go but knowing I don't have a choice right now.

"Get in," I snap when Sara continues to hesitate.

Jodie is still out cold when I bring the engine to life and pull up my contacts.

"I've got a situation that needs dealing with," I tell Theo the second he picks up the phone.

"What have you done?"

"There's a rapist in the alley beside Foxes with a bullet lodged in his skull."

"What?" Sara hisses from the back seat, sounding utterly horrified.

"What would you have rather I did seconds before he—" I slam the words down, not liking the emotion that floods me when I'm in the middle of something. "Can you send someone to clean up?" I ask, keeping my mask in place.

"You got it, but I swear to God, Tobes, if he turns out to be an OG Wolf, we are in some serious shit."

"When aren't we?" I ask, ignoring the way my stomach knots painfully at the statement. "Just get rid of him. No one has seen me, and Jesse's girl isn't going to say anything. Are you?" I ask, holding her eyes in the mirror for a beat.

She shakes her head, her eyes wide.

"Just sort it, yeah?"

"You got it. Jodie okay?" he asks, and I can't help the small smile that twitches at my lips. Theo might be a cold, ruthless bastard, but since falling for Emmie, his soft side is showing more and more. Something I'm sure he'd hate for anyone to see outside of our little group.

"She will be. I'm taking her home now."

"Call if you need anything."

"Sure thing. Thanks, man."

"Anytime." He cuts the call before I have a chance to, and I look back at Sara once more. She's curled up in a ball, trembling in my back seat. "You okay?"

"Y-yeah."

"Right," I chuckle, not believing a word of it as I find my next contact.

"Hello?" a deep voice rumbles through my speakers.

"Jesse," Sara cries.

"Sara? What's going on? Whose phone is this?"

"Toby's. I'm in his car with Jodie. S-she was attacked outside the club."

"Fuck. Is she okay?"

"Can you get home?" I bark, cutting them off mid-conversation. "I'm taking Sara back there now. She needs you."

"Y-yeah," he says, the sound of movement rustling down the line. "I'm leaving the Den now. Who was the guy?"

"Don't know. He's dead."

"Do we need—"

"We clean up our own problems."

"All right, shit. I was just asking. I'll be ten minutes."

Sara blows out a shaky breath as I turn down their street and pull up beside the betting shop they live above.

"You're not taking her back to your place," she suddenly says, the venom in her tone taking me by surprise. "That's the last place she's going to want to be after something like this."

"I'm aware. I'm not a fucking idiot," I mutter, annoyed but understanding why she has so little faith in me.

"Just bring her inside."

"No."

"For fuck's sake, Toby. Just do what's best for her."

"I am," I growl. "Now get out. Jesse is on his way. You can trust me with her." I hold her eyes steady, begging for her to just believe me and leave me alone with my girl.

"Fine. But I swear to all that is holy, if you hurt a single hair on her head, I will come after you myself. Jesse has taught me to shoot, you know." She narrows her eyes in warning, and it takes everything in me not to laugh at how cute she looks, threatening me.

"I'll keep that in mind," I somehow manage to force out, keeping my tone flat.

"She's going to kill me for this," she mutters as she pushes the door open.

"I'll wait until you're inside."

"Stop playing the nice guy. It makes it hard to keep hating you so much."

"I am a nice guy," I argue, although I immediately cringe at trying to be the one thing I've hated being called almost all my life.

"Hmm..." she mumbles, but thankfully she takes off toward the door at the side of the building.

"Toby," a soft voice whispers beside me.

"I'm here, baby," I say, lacing my fingers through hers when she lifts her hand from her lap.

My heart tumbles at that small contact with her as she feeds my addiction, my obsession. "I'm going to take you home. Look after you, okay?"

"I missed you," she confesses, turning the air around us so thick I can hardly breathe.

"Fuck, baby. I've missed you too," I finally manage to get out, but it's too late. Her hand has already gone limp in mine, and when I look over, she's unconscious once more.

After what she just went through, it's probably for the best, but damn if I don't want to hear her voice again.

It pains me not to turn toward our side of the city and head for home. Every inch of me craves to close my flat door behind us and just keep her with me until I find a way to prove to her that I'm not the monster I showed her I can be last week.

But I'm not Theo, and I'm not going to lock her up in my castle like some damsel in distress. As much as I might want to keep her all to myself, it's not going to win me any points in the forgiveness department.

So I force myself to do the right thing, and I head toward the place where I know she'll feel at home and be comfortable when she wakes and remembers what happened.

The door opens long before we make it up the path toward the house.

"What's happened? What's wrong? Is she

okay?"

"I'm fine," Jodie mumbles as she snuggles into my chest and Joanne runs toward us in her pyjamas, her eyes wide in fear.

"What's happened?"

"It's okay," she says again, her voice hollow, void of any kind of emotion.

"I'm gonna take her up to bed. Can you make her a hot drink or something?" I ask, sensing that she needs to be kept busy.

Joanne stares at me, her lips opening and closing.

"She's okay, I promise," I assure her, refraining from telling her that things could be very different right now if it had taken me just ten more seconds to get to her.

"Her bedroom is the first on the right."

"Thank you," I say, holding Jodie tighter against my chest as I begin to climb the stairs.

"I can walk," she mumbles, although she makes no effort to actually fight me.

"I know, but you don't have to right now. Let me take the weight."

She sighs as she rests her head against my shoulder once more.

Her door is ajar when we get there, so I kick it open and march inside. I don't bother looking around at her space; I'm too concerned about the girl in my arms.

Lowering her to the bed, I place her on the edge and drop to my knees before her, taking her hand in mine.

My breath catches when I finally get a good look at the side of her face that was hidden from me in the car.

"Baby," I breathe, freeing one of my hands to gently cup her wounded cheek. It's already swollen, dried blood covering the small scratches caused by the rough brickwork she was shoved against.

The heavy makeup from her shift is smudged all over her face, darkness streaked down her cheeks from her tears.

"Don't," she whispers, twisting her face away from me and lowering her eyes to the floor.

"What do you need?"

"You to leave," she confesses.

"I can't do that right now, Demon," I tell her honestly, my hand slipping around the back of her neck and my other squeezing her hand lightly. "I'm sorry, but I... I just can't." I close my eyes tightly, the image of that cunt with his hands on her body filling my mind as rage courses through my veins.

"I need a shower. I-I smell like—"

"Okay. Where's the bathroom?"

"Across the h-hall," she says sadly, her voice cracking with emotion.

"Hey," I say, lifting my hand from hers and

turning her back to face me. "It's going to be okay. I've got you. I won't let you fall."

Her whole expression softens with my words and tears fill her eyes.

"Shit, that wasn't meant to make you cry."

She shakes her head lightly. "T-thank y-you... for saving me."

"I'll always save you, baby."

Footsteps race up the stairs before Joanne's concerned stare lands on us.

"I'm okay, Mum. Promise," she assures her, even managing to smile a little bit. "Some guy after work. He got a little... But I'm fine."

"And you're okay with Toby being here?" she asks, making my spine straighten.

Panic rushes through me, because I know that if Jodie says no right now then I'm going to have no choice but to stand up and walk away from her.

All the air rushes from my lungs when Jodie nods once, giving Joanne her answer.

"Sit with her," I say, reluctantly releasing my hold on Jodie and standing. "I'm going to get the shower running, okay?"

Jodie nods again, and I back out of the room while Joanne rushes to her side.

Joanne pulls her daughter into her body and holds her tight as Jodie's sob rips through the air and my chest squeezes hard.

Maybe Jesse was right. Maybe I shouldn't have

let her step foot in that place tonight. One thing is for fucking sure though.

She's not going back.

If she still wants to dance, strip, whatever, then I'll find somewhere safe for her to do it. Although something tells me any ideas she might have had about what the job entails have been shattered by how her first night ended.

It makes me want to go back and kill that motherfucker all over again.

Pushing through to the bathroom, I quickly turn the shower on before heading back to get my girl.

"Come on, let's wash tonight off you."

Taking her hands, I pull her to her feet before sweeping her off them once more.

"Toby," she cries in surprise.

"I told you, baby. I've got you."

Joanne watches us walk away, and when I look back, I find that her eyes are full of concern, but she's got a small smile playing on her lips.

'I've got her,' I mouth, and she nods in acceptance.

The second we're inside the bathroom, I kick the door closed and place her back down on her feet.

"Good?" I ask, but she doesn't respond. She just stares blankly at my chest.

"Jesus, Demon," I breathe, pulling her back into

my arms, crushing our chests together as I wrap my arms tightly around her.

Her breathing becomes more ragged the longer I hold her until she completely falls apart, refusing to let go until she's got it all out while the room has filled with steam around us.

Her entire body trembles against mine. Unsure if it's the lingering shock, or because she's cold, I reluctantly release her and wrap my fingers around the bottom of her hoodie.

Her large, exhausted chocolate eyes stare up at me, making my heart lurch in my chest.

"This okay?"

She nods and tries looking away, hiding from me.

"No, baby. Stay here with me, okay?"

Her eyes come back to mine, and she allows me to see the pain she's been hiding inside her.

Unable to do what I really want and take it all away from her, make her pain my own, I do the only other thing I can and start undressing her.

Darkening bruises mar her upper arm where he must have grabbed her.

My teeth grind as I fight to keep my cool, to remain gentle with her as I drop to my knees and tug her boots from her feet before pulling her leggings down.

She stands before me in just a pair of cotton

knickers and her crop top, and she totally fucking wrecks me.

"You have no idea, do you, Demon?"

She stares down at me with a deep crease in her brow.

"You have no idea just how much you own me."

Her lips part on a gasp.

"And I'm going to fucking prove it to you. Somehow, I'm going to make to see just how much you mean to me, how fucking sorry I am for what I put you through."

A violent shudder rips through her body, making reality slam into me.

Reaching out, I pull her underwear down her legs before standing and dragging her top off, leaving her bare before me.

"Get under the water, I'll be right there."

Her eyes drop down my body and she shakes her head.

"Let me look after you, baby."

Sucking in a deep breath, she nods and steps into the shower, immediately standing under the torrent of water and letting it run over every inch of her.

As quickly as I can, I strip down to my boxers. I hesitate a beat but decide better than to push them off too. I don't want her getting the wrong idea about this for even a second.

11

JODIE

I try to focus on the heat and the sensation of the water washing over me instead of the giant, messy ball of emotion clogging my throat and making it hard to breathe.

My entire body trembles. It has been since that guy grabbed me, but it only got worse when I looked down and saw him dead at my feet.

I knew Toby was there the second he stepped into the alley. I felt him. This weird sense of safety and relief washed over me despite the painful grip of the man who was trying to attack me. I knew everything was going to be okay. I knew the worst wasn't going to happen. But that didn't mean I was anywhere near prepared for what was going to come next. For what it might be like to be standing only feet away from a dead body.

My gasp rips through the air when the heat of

Toby's body burns my back a second before his hands land on my waist, making me flinch.

"It's just me, baby. I'm going to look after you, okay?"

I nod, unable to find any words for him.

His hold on me vanishes and I have to fight not to turn around, not to beg for him to come back.

Reaching forward, he unhooks the bath puff a second before the vanilla scent of my shower gel fills the air around me.

"We're gonna wash it all away," he promises me, pressing the puff to my shoulder and slowly working his way down my arm in delicate circles.

My entire body relaxes in only seconds, and I find myself leaning back against him, soaking up his strength and support.

"You're so beautiful, baby," he whispers in my ear as he continues to work the puff over every inch of me.

As he moves to my chest, my heart rate begins to increase despite all my conflicting emotions that are warring beneath the surface. It's so much easier to fall back into bad habits and allow myself to be swept away by him and the desire he elicits in my body with nothing more than his touch.

It's dangerous. It's how I managed to find myself in this mess in the first place.

If I were able to say no to him, maybe I

wouldn't have fallen so fast. Maybe I wouldn't have ended up with my heart crushed.

"I've missed you so much," he breathes, his lips brushing along the length of my shoulder as the puff dips to my heavy breasts.

A needy whimper falls from my lips as he grazes my nipple.

"You're the only thing I've been able to think about, Demon. I dream that you're beside me every night and wake disappointed. Desperate."

"Toby," I moan, barely even recognising my own voice. It's deep and raspy from my attempts at screaming while that prick covered my mouth with his hand. It's full of pent-up shock and fear, but underneath it all there's pure, unfiltered desire.

I know just how easy it would be to focus on the latter. I could leave everything else behind and just focus on him, on everything he can offer me. The escape. The release. The pleasure.

But at what cost?

I can't fall back into the trap again. I don't trust him.

How could I after what he did?

For all I know, it's not over.

He might be saying all the right words. Telling me that he's sorry, that he misses me. But how can I believe him?

"I've got you, baby."

I close my eyes and rest my head back against his and let go.

I figure nothing that can happen in here with Toby can be as destructive as what could have happened tonight.

He moves lower over my belly, and my skin erupts in goosebumps as he kisses up my neck, lingering on that sweet spot beneath my ear as he dips the puff between my legs.

"Oh God," I gasp when it gently brushes my clit.

My hips roll, my arse grinding back against him, against the solid length of him that's more than obvious against my thigh, although I can't miss the fabric barrier between us.

But he doesn't give me what I need. Instead, he continues those teasing circles down both of my legs.

His heat leaves me a beat before there's a dull thud behind me.

"Turn around," he commands, and I'm powerless but to do as he says.

My breath catches in my throat as I find him in the exact same position he was in before I fled his flat last week.

"Toby," I breathe, my fingers twitching with my need to reach out for him, to keep the connection between us.

"I know this isn't the time. But I need you to

know that I mean every single word I say to you, Jodie." Sincerity shines bright in his tired eyes, and everything inside me aches for me to give in to him.

But while my body might be on board, my head is another matter. And deep down, I can't help but wonder if I'll ever be able to get past what he did.

"I'll do everything in my power to show you how much you mean to me. I know it's crazy, I know you feel like you barely know me. But I need you, Demon, in a way I didn't even know was possible."

I hold his eyes as the water continues to rain down on me and nod. It's all I can do.

"I just need a chance, Jodie. Just tell me you'll let me explain properly one day."

"O-okay," I breathe, because I know I can't deny him that chance. Especially after what he's done for me tonight. How could I?

He saved me. He—

"You killed him," I blurt, and whatever passes across my face with that statement forces him back to his feet and he cups my face in his hands.

"He touched you. He hurt you. I'd do the same to any man who ever laid an unwanted finger on you."

"You killed him," I repeat.

"Yeah, baby. My life is... different."

A laugh rips from my lips at the word he chooses.

"But I won't apologise for it, and I won't make excuses for it. It's who I am. It's what I've been trained for my entire life. And tonight, it saved you. And I'll never regret keeping you safe."

"H-he was going to—"

"I know, baby. But he didn't. You're safe with me."

"Am I?" I ask, unable to keep the question back.

"Always. I'll never hurt you again, I fucking swear. You're the best thing in my life."

Leaning forward, he drops a kiss on the end of my nose before closing his eyes and resting his head against mine.

I feel so much in those few silent moments between us that it makes tears pool behind my eyelids. His fear for what could have happened tonight, his desperation, his regret, his pain.

"I'm gonna wash your hair."

I want to tell him no, that he's already done enough, but I can't find the strength to say the words. Because above all else, what I really need now is his touch, his closeness, his strength.

Releasing me, he grabs my shampoo and sets about doing what he said he would, his fingers working wonders on my scalp as he massages me until my eyelids get heavy and I find myself leaning into him more and more.

"Come on, let's get you out before you fall

asleep on me," he finally says softly, rinsing my conditioner out and turning the water off.

He wraps my body in a large towel before squeezing the excess water out of my hair with another.

"Why did you wear your boxers in the shower?" I ask, shamelessly staring down at the tent in the fabric.

"Didn't want you getting the wrong idea, Demon. I was caring for you, not taking advantage."

"Are you going to try to convince me you've shoved a bottle of shampoo down there then or something?" I ask, quirking a brow at him.

The smile he shoots me in return almost makes the events of the past ten days worth it. Almost.

"Nah, it's all me, baby," he says cockily. "I can't resist you."

"You seem to be doing a pretty good job," I mutter, watching intently as he pushes his thumbs into the waistband of said underwear and wrestles the sopping wet fabric down his legs, releasing his hard cock.

It's wrong, I know it is, but my mouth waters at the sight. And his smirk tells me he damn well knows it too before he reaches for a towel and covers himself up.

"Come on, Demon," he says. Wrapping his arm

around my shoulder and pulling me into his side, he steers me back toward my bedroom.

Mum is hovering in the hallway, and my cheeks burn at the thought of her hearing our conversation. Without realising it, I take a step in front of Toby, hiding his almost naked body, and more so the tent in his towel.

Mum's grin tells me that she didn't miss the possessive move, but she doesn't comment. Instead, concern swallows the amusement that was there moments ago.

"How are you doing?" she asks, taking a step forward and reaching for my hand.

"Toby looked after me."

A smile curls at her lips, and I'm reminded of just how much she seems to be on Team Toby, even after everything he's done.

"Good. So he should," she quips, looking over her shoulder at the man in question. "I've left you some clothes on Jodie's bed. They're Joe's, not..."

"Thank you," Toby says when the tension from what Mum didn't say becomes too much.

"I've made you fresh hot chocolates and left you some snacks. If you need anything, please just shout," she urges me, her eyes pleading with me to let her help me.

"We will," I assure her. "Thank you. But I'm okay. Really. Toby was there just in time. Almost like he was stalking me or something."

His hold on me tightens, only confirming what I already knew.

It also makes me realise just why those Wolves were inside Foxes. It had nothing to do with Jesse and everything to do with the man standing behind me.

"I'll be downstairs for a bit. I'm not sure I can sleep yet."

She disappears before we get a chance to say anything else, and Toby ushers me into my bedroom.

"Finally," he says, dropping a kiss on my shoulder. "I get to properly check out your bedroom."

"It's not exactly how I imagined it would happen," I mutter.

"Go sit down. Where are your pyjamas?"

"You want to go rummaging around in my drawers?"

"Like you wouldn't believe," he deadpans with a smirk.

"You're a nightmare. Over there." I point. "Third drawer down. Underwear in the top."

I sit on the edge of my bed and watch him as he looks through his options and chooses something.

"Interesting," I mutter as he drops a matching set of PJs beside me that are covered in teddy bears with 'I want a hug' printed across the chest, and a pair of my biggest, comfiest knickers. Seriously, they'd make Bridget Jones proud. He's certainly gone for comfort over style.

Dropping to his knees once more, he holds the underwear out for me to put my feet into.

"I can dress myself, you know. I'm not broken."

"Humour me. I like taking care of you. And I fear that if I'm not needed, I might just find myself out on my arse where I belong."

I stare down at him, my heart in my throat.

"Not tonight," I say honestly, finally admitting to myself just how much I need his presence, his strength to keep me grounded right now. "But you might find yourself friendly with the other side of the front door sometime after the sun comes up tomorrow."

"Ouch," he says, but it doesn't stop his smile that widened the second I told him that he could have the night. "I guess I need to up my game then, to prove to you why you need to keep me."

I smile at him but keep my thoughts on that statement to myself.

It would be so easy to agree. The way he makes me feel when we're together, it's something I could easily become addicted to again. But I need to keep my head. I have to.

His eyes burn a trail over my body when he pulls the towel free and my nipples harden under his attention. There's no way he misses it, but he doesn't make any move to make the most of the situation. He just pulls my shirt over my head and tells me to get into bed. He passes me one of the mugs full of hot chocolate, cream, and marshmallows that Mum left for us before turning his back on me and dropping his towel.

I damn near choke on a marshmallow as I take in his sculpted arse.

"You sure know how to cheer a girl up, don't you?" I mutter after fighting to swallow my mouthful.

"Anything to make you smile right now, baby," he shoots over his shoulder with a teasing wink.

As much as I might demand he stay naked for me, I don't stop him when he pulls on the sweats and shirt Mum left for him. It makes my heart ache, knowing that they're Joe's. But I'm glad they could be of use. And anything is better than forcing Toby into the clothes of the man he can't stand.

"Is it weird being here?" I ask, unable to hold the question in.

Pulling the covers back, he slips into bed beside me.

"Yes," he says honestly. "Although knowing your mum has taken all the photos down helps."

"She has?" I ask, my brows pinching.

"Yeah. She'd put them all in a box when I came to see her earlier in the week."

"Oh."

He turns to look at me, his eyes holding mine, begging me to let him in.

"I'm sorry I ruined everything about the man you called Dad. But I'm glad you grew up thinking he was a good person. That he allowed you to believe that was possible."

My lips part, but he beats me to it.

"I just want you to know that if me going through what I did meant you got a decent childhood, then I think it might have been worth it. You deserve it. You deserve more than he could have ever given you, but knowing he treated you like a princess makes me happy."

"Toby, I—"

"No. I just needed to tell you that. I'm really glad you were happy. That he loved you."

The lump that seemed to be permanently lodged in my throat earlier returns, and I lift my mug to my lips in the hope of forcing it down.

"You sent some Wolves to Foxes tonight to look out for me, didn't you?"

A small smile twitches at his lips. "Guilty."

"And you sat outside waiting for me to leave so you could make sure I got home safe." It's not a question. It doesn't need to be.

"Yes, although I almost fucked that up royally. I was writing you a message and missed you being pulled down that alley," he confesses.

"You don't want me working there?" I ask, although I already know the answer.

"It's not my place to tell you what you can and can't do, Demon. And you made it clear to me before that you wanted to dance. I have no right to stop you."

His response makes it hard to suck in the air I need.

This is why I fell so hard and so fast for him. In so many ways he's perfect. Prior to learning about the secrets he was keeping from me, he was perfect.

"What will you do when I go back tomorrow?" I ask, genuinely interested by his answer.

His teeth grind and his jaw pops. Guilt rushes through me that I'm even asking the question, forcing him to think about it as if it's really an issue when I already know I'm not stepping foot back in that place again.

"I'll find myself a table in the middle of the place and never take my eyes off you."

"And if I don't want you in there?"

"Then I'll be in the security room, watching. It's a Wolves club, and they owe us a favour."

"You don't need to worry, I'd already decided I wasn't going back before... that happened."

I'm not sure if he realised he was even doing it, but the second I confess that, a massive rush of air passes his lips.

"I don't think that life is really for me. I should probably stick to serving coffee, not alcohol."

"I can get your job back if you want," he offers. "Matt wasn't too thrilled to lose you in the first place."

"Didn't stop him agreeing to set me up though, did it?" I mutter, still pissed off about that whole situation.

"He didn't have a lot of choice."

"Even so. I won't go back there. I'll find something."

"There's no rush. You've got all the money you could need."

"I don't want his money, Toby. Even before I wouldn't have wanted it, but now... it just feels tainted."

"It is what it is. You may as well make the most of it."

"What about you and your mum?" I ask.

"You don't need to worry about us. We've got all we could need. Well... she has. I'm still working on what I want the most."

"You're smooth, you know that?"

He shrugs before I turn away from him and place my empty mug on the side. "I try. And I'll keep trying until you realise that I'm serious."

With a yawn, I slip down the bed and snuggle deeper under the covers.

My feet ache, my upper arm burns from that

prick's harsh hold, and fear still threatens right on the edges of my consciousness.

There's a huge part of me that doesn't want to fall asleep for fear that it'll all just come rushing back. But as Toby slips down beside me, wraps his arm around my waist, and tugs me into the warmth of his body, I know I have little choice. I can't fight my exhaustion or the comfort he offers me.

12

TOBY

I lay with Jodie locked in my arms for the longest time, but every time my eyelids fall, all I see is that fucking cunt with his hands on my girl, his fingers curling in the waistband of her leggings seconds before he—

I force myself to stop thinking about it once more and instead cave to my need to move, to pace, to do anything I can other than fuck her into oblivion to empty my head.

"Shit," I hiss almost silently as I pull my arms from her soft, warm body and roll out of her bed without waking her.

Aware that Joanne is still downstairs, I take myself to the bathroom for a piss and head down. Every single one of my muscles is pulled tight with tension as I descend the stairs. What I really need right now is to blow off some steam in a gym, but I highly doubt they're hiding one in a secret basement here—although knowing the man who owned the place, I guess the chance of him having a basement isn't out of the question.

"Toby," Joanne breathes when I emerge into the kitchen/diner and find her staring into what I can only assume is an empty mug. "How is she?"

"Sleeping."

She nods, pleased with that answer.

"Can I get you a drink? Coffee or something st—"

"Anything stronger than coffee, if you've got it," I answer for her.

She thinks for a beat. "I've got just the thing."

I'm left standing in the doorway as she rushes past me and heads toward the living room.

Assuming I wasn't meant to follow, I pull out a chair and take a seat. I last two seconds before remembering why I felt the need to get out of bed and move in the first place, and when Joanne returns she finds me pacing back and forth between the kitchen and dining room, my fists curling and uncurling at my sides while I silently battle the monster that always lives inside me.

I might have killed that motherfucker. But it wasn't enough.

He touched her. He fucking touched her and he was going to—

I startle when a hand lands on my shoulder.

When I turn, I find a soft, supportive smile staring back at me. In those few moments, she reminds me so much of Mum that I almost reach out and pull her into my arms. But I don't.

"Here," she says, holding up one very expensive bottle of whisky.

My brows pull together and my stomach twists painfully as I assume who that bottle belongs to.

"He was saving it. It only seems right that you get to be the one who drinks it."

She pushes it closer to me, giving me very little choice but to take it.

"Tip it down the drain if you don't want it. But it feels right."

Unable to argue, I twist the top and lift the bottle to my lips.

I lose just a tiny bit of my tension the second the rich, spicy taste hits my tongue.

I swallow mouthful after mouthful, letting the strength of the alcohol burn down my throat before it sits warming my belly.

Finally, I pull it away and lick my bottom lip.

"To the end of a monster," I say, tipping the bottle in a fucked-up salute to the sky.

Joanne's breath catches at my words, but I don't react.

Grabbing herself a glass and making her own drink, she takes a sip and turns to me.

"What really happened tonight, Toby?"

Blowing out a long breath, I decide to tell her the truth, revealing where Jodie had actually got a job and how her first night really ended.

She stands there the whole time with her mouth gawping open and the glass in her hand trembling.

"Y-you shot him while Jodie was only a foot away," she says, her eyes wide with fear. "But if you miss—"

"I wouldn't have missed. I wouldn't hurt a hair on her head."

"But— Shit, Toby. You killed him."

I shrug. It's nothing new to me.

"I was nine when I killed my first man, Joanne. The man you built a home with stood right by my side as I did it. I remember how violently my hand was trembling, but I knew I couldn't get out of it. I was terrified. The man tied to the chair was terrified. I didn't care how bad he was, how much he might have deserved it. I was a kid.

"But Jonas stood beside me and told me that I was a useless part of the Family if I couldn't do it, and that I might as well be the one in that chair if I couldn't man up and show my worth."

"You were just a child," Joanne whispers, her eyes full of unshed tears.

"In age, yes. But I was never really a child, Joanne. None of us were. We've been trained for this life from the moment we were born. It was our destiny. To protect, to serve, to conquer. I've done so many bad things, mostly to bad people," I add. "And I know what I did with Jodie is unforgivable but—"

"You don't need to explain this to me," she says, reaching out to place her hand on my forearm.

"I do. I—" I let out a pained breath. "I need you to know that I'll never hurt her again. I couldn't see past my anger, my need for revenge to see how I really felt. How she really made me feel."

"And how is that?" Joanne asks, finally taking another sip of her drink.

"I love her," I state, the words feeling so right as they roll off my tongue. "I can't imagine a life without her in it."

She nods, a small smile playing on her lips.

"I know you don't want to hear it. But I've been in your position. I fell so hard and fast for Jonas, I swear I still feel the whiplash from it. I just really hope he hasn't caused too much damage on your soul, because I want so much more for Jodie than the life that man gave me."

"I'm not going to lie, Joanne. I'm pretty fucking damaged."

"We all are," she says, her eyes focusing on something over my shoulder. "But it's how we deal with it, how we try to heal that really matters."

I nod, unable to do anything but agree with her.

"And my Jodie is going to need to figure out how to do that, and I know it hurts, but you might just have to accept that she needs to do it away from you."

"I know," I say sadly. "But I'm not letting her go."

"You're a good boy, Toby. I know all the bad stuff. I battled with it all myself over the years. I remember him coming home covered in blood, his knuckles splitting open as he scattered the kind of weapons I thought I'd only see on the TV across the counter.

"But it's not me you need to be proving anything to."

"I know, I'm working on it," I say with a sad laugh.

She lifts her arm, glancing at her watch.

"It's late. You should get some sleep."

I nod, swallowing down another mouthful of whisky. I already know there's no way I'm going to be able to sleep after the events of the night, but I can't deny that the girl asleep upstairs isn't calling to me.

When I've had enough, I upend the bottle over the sink and watch the rest of Jonas's precious whisky run down the drain, unable to keep the smirk off my face.

"You deserved better than him," Joanne says quietly behind me.

"I had my mum. She's incredible."

"I'm glad. I'd really like to meet her one day too, if that's not too weird."

"I think she'd probably be up for that," I say, placing the bottle on the side and walking toward the door that's going to lead me back to my girl.

Joanne doesn't say anything as I walk away, but I stop before I disappear and turn back.

"Thank you," I say sincerely. "Thank you for seeing the truth. For trusting me with Jodie."

"Just don't make me question it," she warns.

"I won't. She's too important to screw up again."

"I agree. Now go and make sure she's okay. I know it might not seem like it right now, but you make it all easier for her. She's just refusing to accept it."

With a nod, and a little bit of hope flowing through my veins, I head up the stairs.

I find her asleep exactly where I left her, and after clearing clothes off the chair in the corner of her room, I lower myself down to watch her.

I have no idea how long passes as I sit there with the effects of that whisky warming my body and my head full of all the things I'd love to do to the woman before me when she suddenly starts thrashing around.

One quick glance at the window tells me that

it's soon to be morning before I sit forward, ready to go to her if her nightmare gets worse.

Thankfully, she seems to calm, and I almost relax back when she suddenly screams, "No," and sits bolt upright.

Her eyes open wide and land on me as she pushes her fingers into her hair, dragging it back from her face.

"You killed him," she states, her voice hollow. "You shot him. In front of me."

"To protect you, baby," I say softly, pushing from the chair and walking to the end of the bed.

"Stop." She holds a shaky hand up to me. "Stop, please," she begs.

Dread settles heavily in my stomach once more as my eyes plead with her not to do this.

"Jodie?" I question, terrified about what is going to come next.

Her eyes fill with tears and her bottom lip trembles.

"I need you to leave," she states.

"W-what? No. No, baby, please."

She shakes her head and my heart sinks into my feet.

"I-I'm sorry. I shouldn't have asked you to stay. That wasn't fair."

Words flicker through my mind, all the things I could say to try to convince her to let me stay, but none of them pass my lips.

What's the point? I shouldn't have to convince her, and I realise there and then that rescuing her from one scumbag rapist and all the confessions I've made about how I feel about her aren't enough to make her start to forgive me.

"I'll do anything you need, Jodie," I tell her honestly as I reluctantly take a step back from the bed.

She nods and releases a long breath as it hits her that I'm not going to argue.

"I'll call you later," I tell her, already knowing that I'm going to need to hear that she's okay.

To my surprise, she nods in agreement as I bend to grab my shoes.

"If you need anything. Anything. I'm right at the end of the phone."

"I-I know." The tears she was holding finally spill over, and it damn near kills me to walk away from her when I know she's suffering, but what else can I do? "Shit, baby. Do you have any idea what you're doing to me?" I ask through the messy lump in my throat.

"I'm sorry," she whispers before I finally do what she asked for and slip out of the room.

I leave the house without looking back, without breathing. And it's not until I'm back in my car, sitting behind the wheel that I finally let it out.

"Fuuuuck," I bark, slamming my hands against the wheel as pain lashes at my insides and my eyes burn with both exhaustion and emotion. "Fuck, Fuck. Fuck."

Not hanging around for fear I might ignore her wishes and force myself back inside, I start the engine and take off.

I don't have a destination in mind. I know I should be going home, but the thought of being alone in my flat right now doesn't hold any kind of appeal, so when I get to the turning, I go in the opposite direction.

I feel nothing by the time I drive through the gates to our old home and make my way up the long driveway toward the house.

I used to dread coming here in a way I hope I never feel again.

Constantly not knowing what kind of mood Jonas might be in, and then later, just how sick I would find Mum, who was confined to her bedroom used to plague me the entire time I was away. But even with it now empty and abandoned, I can't rid myself of the fear, of the hate I felt for the man who reigned supreme here.

Pulling the car to a stop, I reach into the glove box to grab the keys and push the door open.

I could have gone anywhere in the city. Yet here I am. The place that holds all my nightmares, about to step between the walls that not long ago I swore I'd never see again. But one bad night, one more rejection from Jodie, and here I am. Seeking out the pain this place always forces upon me.

Ignoring the kitchen, the place of all my worst horrors, I head for the stairs and then to my bedroom.

The room is almost empty, void of all my childhood belongings that the shelves once held. All of that is either boxed at Galen's place or in my flat.

Ignoring it all, I head for the window and throw it wide open. Hopping up onto the sill, I climb out and up onto the roof just like I've done so many times in the past.

I was, I think, twelve when I first found this way to escape, and by some miracle, he never discovered it, never ruined it for me. The only person who even knows about it is Nico. He always knew it would be where he could find me if shit had gone wrong. Not that he ever really knew the real reasons why I felt the need to hide in my own home.

I lower my ass to the tiles and lie back as the sun begins to rise through the trees.

It's bitterly cold, my breath coming out in clouds around me, but I barely feel it. It's only pain and regrets that flow through my body, swallowing anything else in its wake.

13

JODIE

I lie staring up at my ceiling as the lingering terror from my nightmare wraps its icy cold fingers around me.

I tremble at the memory of his evil eyes boring into mine as I fought to suck in the air I need with his dirty hand over my mouth.

But then his face morphs into another, one I'm terrified of, but for a whole host of other reasons.

My chest aches as Toby's concerned eyes narrow. "I've got you, baby," he says in a voice that sounds so real even now I'm awake that it makes my skin erupt with goosebumps.

But then his grip leaves me, his stare vanishes, and he crumbles at my feet.

My body jolts just like it did in my sleep as the image of him lying there fills my mind.

Shaking my head, I blink again and again, as if it'll banish the all-too-clear pictures.

Toby is fine. He was the one who shot the gun, not the one on the receiving end of it.

But is that really any better?

He killed a man right in front of me. If I needed any more evidence about what Bri told me about him being true, then I guess that was it.

He shot someone dead. And showed zero remorse about it.

The man was trying to rape you, Jodie. Why should he show remorse?

I stay where I am, flat on my back for the longest time as the sun rises outside the window, running the events of the night over and over in my head. Each time, I linger on my final memories with Toby, and guilt tugs at me for how I freaked out and sent him away this morning.

All he did last night was look after me, protect me, tell me all the things I'd been desperate to hear.

I'd believed him, too. Every single word. And I'm torn between relief and fear for where that leaves me, leaves us.

With a sigh, I finally throw the covers off and swing my legs over the side. My eyes land on my phone on the bedside table, and I quickly grab it and shoot off two messages.

Sara first to assure her that I'm okay after

finding five messages from her. I don't even remember seeing her after Toby rescued me last night, but it's obvious from her very first message that she's more than aware of what happened.

My second is to Courtney, thanking her for the opportunity of the job but informing her that I won't be returning. I don't mention anything about what happened after my shift. The last thing I want to do is get Toby into any trouble.

Another shudder rips through me as I remember the reality of what he did last night and my part in it.

I shouldn't be covering it up. I should be on the phone with the police, telling them about the man who tried to attack me. But even the thought of doing that sends ice through my veins.

He was a monster. A rapist. He deserved the end he got. And despite all of Toby's indiscretions, he doesn't deserve to be thrown into a cell because of it. Not that I think for a second that the police stand a chance of making any kind of accusation stick to a member of the Cirillo Family. It didn't take much research on my part to understand who really owns a huge part of this city, and it's certainly not the police.

I've barely hit send when my phone starts ringing in my hand.

"Hey," I breathe, lifting it to my ear.

"Oh my God, are you okay?" Sara asks in a panic.

"I'm fine," I say, cringing at myself for the number of times I've tried to convince both myself, my mum, and Toby of that since getting back here last night.

I don't remember anything after looking down at the dead man at my feet, so I can only assume Toby had his car.

"Don't lie to me, Jojo," she warns in what I think is meant to be an angry voice.

"I-I'm..." I blow out a breath. "I think I'm still in shock mostly," I confess.

"Understandable."

"Were you... did you..." I start but fail to get my words out.

"I ran straight into Toby as he carried you out of the alley."

I nod despite the fact that I know she can't see me. "Did you know that he—"

"Yes," she says simply, calmly.

"Why aren't you freaking out about this, Sar?"

"Because if he hadn't done what he did, we would be having a very different conversation this morning. Or possibly not at all."

All the air rushes from my lungs to the point that I swear they actually deflate. "You think he would have killed me?" I whisper, not risking saying the words aloud.

"Maybe. I don't know. He clearly had no issue with... yeah," she mutters, not wanting to get into details. "If Toby wasn't there, Jojo... I doubt I'd have been a lot of help."

"He was so amazing last night, Sar. He brought me home. Took care of me. He was so sweet." Tears burn the back of my throat and behind my eyes as I put myself back in the shower with him and his gentle touch and soothing words.

"Is he still there?" she asks, and I hang my head in shame.

"No," I whisper. "I woke up and freaked out. I sent him away."

"Jojo," Sara sighs.

"I know. I just had this nightmare, and I woke up with the reality of what he did at the forefront of my mind and I—"

"Freaked."

"Yeah."

"I know it's hard. Trust me, I do. But Toby and Jesse, they grew up in a completely different world to us. The things they see as a normal reaction, we don't. He saw you in danger last night, Jojo, and he did what he knows to ensure you're safe. It's kinda romantic in a way, if you really think about it."

"He shot him in the head, Sar," I hiss, squeezing my eyes closed as the shadowed image of the dead man in question fills my mind.

"Because he was a threat to you."

"You've been with Jesse too long," I mutter lightly. "The shy little girl I met in preschool would never have approved of this."

"She was naïve, Jojo. Scared of the world. Jesse has opened things up for me. Things aren't always black and white, right and wrong. And we don't have to follow the rules. Just look at me. I shunned everything that was expected of me, and I'm happier without all those judgements and expectations for a wild life with my man."

"I've never seen you happier," I tell her. "Jesse was the best thing that ever happened to you."

"Yup," she agrees. "It's rough, raw, real, and I wouldn't have it any other way. He does things I don't approve of, but this was his life long before we met, and I'd never try to change that."

"Doesn't it scare you?" I ask, letting some of my fears out. "That man's life ended in less than a blink of an eye. That could be them."

"Yes, it could. It's something I've battled with a lot over the years. But eventually, I realised that I need to focus on what I do have right now, not fearing something which may never happen. I will never regret being with Jesse. Never."

"God, I'm so jealous of you, Sar."

She chuckles. "I'm sure there are many, many people out there who would disagree with you. My parents, for a start."

"Fuck them. Fuck all of them. You don't have to answer to anyone but yourself."

"My point exactly, Jojo."

A heavy silence falls between us and my stomach knots tightly.

"I need to talk to him," I finally say.

"Yeah, you do. And you need to be honest with him."

I nod, unable to agree through the huge lump in my throat.

"People make mistakes, especially when they're hurting. But it doesn't define who they are as a person. He cares about you, Jo. And I know you care about him too. You need to decide if it's enough. Either way, you need to be brave."

I blow out a shaky breath. She's right. I know she is. But being honest with how I really feel about him comes with so much risk, the possibility of so much pain.

I want to trust him. I want to believe that despite his upbringing and his deep-rooted need for revenge, he really is the person I got to know. The sweet guy who was doing such a good job of putting me back together after all the loss I'd suffered.

If that really is him, then can I also embrace the other side of him too?

Is what we'd found together worthy of that?

"Jo, you still there?" Sara asks when nothing but silence passes between us for long seconds.

"Y-yeah. I'm going to message him."

"Good. All you need to do is be honest. Tell him where you stand with everything right now. And remember... you only regret the things you don't do."

"I know. I know," I say, because I do.

It's basically the motto that Bri and I live by. It's what's got me into most of the situations I have with her over the years. Sara was never really one to live in the moment like Bri, but she seems to be more than willing to use it to force me into action.

"Call me later, yeah? And if you need me, you know where I am."

"Getting your brains fucked out by your hot gangster?" I quip, more than happy to turn the tables on this conversation.

"That would be it. Play your cards right and you could get yourself ruined by a bad boy too."

"One thing at a time, yeah?"

"Girl, you screwed him in a sex club the first night you met him. Chemistry and bumping uglies isn't your issue and you know it."

I bite down on my bottom lip as I cast my mind back to our shower last night and just how badly I wanted him to really touch me, to take me, to get me out of my own head.

"I'll call you later," I agree and hang up to the sound of her laughter.

Before I can convince myself otherwise, I pull up mine and Toby's conversation and tap him out a message.

Jodie: We need to talk.

Simple and to the point.

I stare at the screen, waiting for it to be shown as delivered and then hopefully read, but it never happens.

Not wanting to sit obsessing over it, I find Bri's number and hit call.

"Hey, bitch, how's it going?" she asks, her voice rough and sleepy, but happy, and I can't help but smile.

"I... um..." Something in my tone obviously clues her in to the fact that things aren't going well with me, because there's rustling and then her voice sounds much more alert.

"What's happened, Jojo?"

I blow out a breath and let it all roll off my tongue.

"Ho-ly shit, girl. That is so fucking hot."

"What?" I screech. "Bri, I was almost rap—"

"Not that bit, obviously." She cuts me off. "Toby going all hot possessive alpha on your arse."

"Are you saying that the first thing you'd do if

Nico shot a man right in front of you would be to jump him?" I ask, although I'm not sure why. I already know the answer.

"Hell yes. Although, Nico is unlikely to be trying to protect my virtue."

"Oh, he totally would," I argue.

"Meh, whatever. Brad came around last night. I've forgotten Nico even exists."

"Good night, huh?"

"Yeah, he did this new thing that—"

"Whoa, I've not had coffee yet. It's certainly too early for your kinky shit."

"Fine," she sulks. "But you're the one who's missing out."

"I'm sure I'll cope. What are you doing today?"

"Aside from resting my poor vag? I need to go into town. I ripped my trousers right up the arse at school yesterday."

"You did not," I bark, unable to get that visual out of my head.

"Sadly, it's true. Did you know the teachers' lost property is almost as bad as the kids' when you forget your PE kit? I ended up spending the rest of the day in this old granny skirt circa nineteen forty-five."

"Oh my God," I laugh, suddenly realising just how much I needed to talk to my best friend. The lightness she offers me is priceless.

"Thank fuck it's only a temporary placement.

There's no way I could ever get a full-time job there after that."

"The kids have probably already forgotten. Teenagers have better things to worry about than seeing their teacher's arse."

"I was wearing that underwear set we bought last time we went shopping. You remember the one with the—"

"Yes," I laugh, now understanding a little more why she's so mortified by this whole thing. "Why the hell did you wear that?"

"I was meeting Brad straight after work and it's been a long week, so I was hoping to get to the stress relief part of the evening sooner rather than later."

"Well, it seems like he might have worked his magic."

"He met me here, seeing as I couldn't possibly go to the restaurant in what I was wearing. We never made our reservation."

"What are you like?"

"So you're telling me you never graciously thanked your sexy rescuer?"

I blow out a long breath before telling her how the rest of our night, and morning, went.

"Jojo, how could you do that?" she asks when I tell her about making him leave.

"I've messaged him asking if we can talk. I think it's time."

We chat for a little longer before she tells me she's going for a bath to soothe her aching body and that she'll call me before shopping in case I feel up to joining her.

I lower the phone from my ear with hope filling my veins that I'm going to have a reply.

But there's nothing.

And when I open the chat, my message still hasn't even been delivered.

Concern swirls in my belly.

Jodie: I'm sorry. I was wrong this morning. Thank you for everything you did last night. x

With a sigh, I slide my phone into my pocket and head out. The scent of Mum's coffee hits me and I make quick work of using the bathroom and heading down.

The second I'm in the kitchen, she throws her arms around me and holds me tight.

"I'm fine, Mum. Really."

"I know. Just let me have a moment."

I hold her tighter as we stand there, soaking up each other's strength.

"Is Toby still sleeping?" she asks when she finally releases me.

"No, he left," I confess.

"Oh, why? Did he—" She must read something on my face. "Jojo, what did you do?"

I fall down onto one of the dining chairs as if I've got the weight of the entire world on my shoulders before relaying the story for the third time this morning.

I'M SITTING at my dressing table, putting my makeup on with Bri on loudspeaker as she leaves her flat, letting me know she's on her way to collect me for the shopping trip I finally agreed to when the doorbell rings through the house.

"You figured out how to time travel now or something?" I ask lightly, admiring the impressive job I did of my eyeliner flicks. I figure that if I'm going to spill my heart to Toby, I need some solid warpaint on.

"If only," she mutters. "Oh, maybe it's him."

My heart races at the thought of him standing on the other side of the door. That excitement only increases when Mum shouts my name up the stairs.

"It's him," Bri says, clearly having heard her down the line.

"You're coming with me," I say, standing and walking to the door.

The second I pull it open, my heart sinks,

because it's not the deep rumble of Toby's voice that floats up to me but the lightness of an unfamiliar female one.

"It's not him," I tell Bri, my disappointment obvious as I begin descending the stairs.

"He's playing hard to get," she says in my ear.

"Or actually doing as I asked." That should make me happy, but really, I wanted it to be him standing in the hallway right now fighting for me, telling me that I was wrong for making him leave, and proving everything he told me last night by totally sweeping me off my feet.

Shit. I need to put my fickle heart back in her box where she belongs.

I've never been a sappy romantic. I've always been more of an action girl. But everything seems to have changed since Toby helped me down off the stage in The Spot that night.

My eyes widen when I hit the bottom step and round the corner, seeing the girl who brought me home the night I ran from Toby's flat along with an older woman at her side.

"Bri, I think I'm going to have to cancel our shopping trip," I say despite not knowing why they're both standing there, but I sense it's important.

"Okay, sure. What's going on?"

"I don't know. I'll call you later, yeah?"

She doesn't get a chance to reply. I hang up on

her the second I've finished talking and close in on the women standing in the doorway.

"W-what's going on?" I ask, looking between them.

The girl I remember from that night holds my gaze, her eyes softening before I look to the woman beside her. The similarities in their eyes are unmistakable, and I figure it must be her mum.

"Hi, Jodie," the older woman says. "I'm Maria, Toby's mum. And this is Stella, my daughter."

My chin drops as I stare at the girl who looked after me that night. She's Toby's... sister.

Why didn't she tell me?

"Uh... hi," I stutter somewhat awkwardly.

Having my father's wife—who he abused—and his long-time lover in the same room isn't anything I thought I'd ever have to experience, but here we are.

"I'm sorry, I know this is beyond awkward, and I really hope you don't mind us just dropping in on you like this but—"

"What's going on? Is Toby okay?"

Maria's face drops and my heart plummets with it.

"We were hoping you might have heard from him," Stella says softly. "He's disappeared."

"I... uh... I messaged him hours ago, but it hasn't even been delivered," I confess.

"Shit," she hisses.

"Please," Mum says kindly. "Come in, you don't need to loiter in the hallway. Would you both like a drink? Tea, coffee, vodka?" she asks with an uncomfortable laugh.

"Vodka sounds perfect," Maria agrees with amusement.

"You're really worried, aren't you?" I say to Stella after her mum has followed mine toward the kitchen.

"We all track each other. Our one rule is that we never disconnect so we can always find everyone. He dropped off the face of the earth at dawn."

"It's my fault. I made him leave this morning."

"This isn't on you, Jodie," she says, resting her hand on my forearm. Her eyes hold mine, and unlike the last time I was in her company, I'm able to see the similarities to her brother, but more than that, I can read her concern. Both for him and me. "Are you okay? Last night must have been terrifying."

My lips part to tell her the same as everyone else, that I'm fine, but suddenly, I find the truth spilling free.

"It was. I still don't really know how I feel about it all."

"Just give it time. This life, it's... crazy. But it's also incredible. You couldn't find a group of people who care more about each other. I hope last night helped prove just what lengths he'd go to for you."

"I assume you know the truth about what happened that night?" I whisper, my cheeks heating with embarrassment that it was his own sister who helped me run, who saw me at my lowest.

"Yeah, and I kicked his ass for you when I got back."

"Y-you..."

"Don't let this face fool you, Jodie. I've been trained just like they have."

"Jesus," I mutter.

"And for the record, I'd have done exactly the same as Toby last night, should I have been the one to find you."

My lips part to speak, but I quickly find I have no words.

"We'll find him. You don't need to worry. Come on, my mum has had this fascination about meeting yours for a while."

"This is so weird," I mutter, following her into the kitchen to find both women smiling at each other.

I have the most surreal two hours of my life as Stella and I sit and watch as two women who seem to have much more in common than I ever would have predicted get to know each other.

The initial awkwardness evaporated as they

focused on the good aspects of their lives instead of the elephant in the room, which is the man who's connected them in the most unique of ways.

I start to think that Stella and Maria have plans to stay for the rest of the day when Stella's phone rings.

"Yeah?" she says to whoever is on the other end, her eyes lighting up as they hold mine.

Relief floods me.

They've found him.

"Okay, yeah. We'll head back now." She falls silent as a deep voice rumbles down the line. "Yeah, with Jodie and her mum. Yeah. Okay. Love you too."

I can't help the sappy smile that's playing on my lips as she hangs up.

"Nico and Alex have him. They're taking him home," Stella says, pushing from her chair and grabbing her bag from the floor. "You ready?" Her eyes hold mine, leaving not an inch of room for me to argue.

I still try though.

"I'm not sure that—"

"Get your shoes, Jodie. Whatever is going on, he needs you. And something tells me you want to be there for him."

I rip my eyes from hers, to Maria's hopeful ones, and then my mum's supportive ones.

"Yeah," I say, standing. "I do. Give me two minutes."

I rush from the room and up the stairs to grab what I need.

The three of them have barely made it to the hallway when I race back down.

"Ready?" Stella asks.

"Ready."

"Good. Let's go deliver you to your boy."

14

TOBY

Even as the sun rises around me, the air never seems to warm up. My breaths continue to come out in clouds around me as my body shivers in an attempt to battle the elements.

I should have grabbed a hoodie, or even the sheets from the bed—it wouldn't be the first time I've succumbed to such drastic measures in the past.

Folding my arms across my chest, I stare up at a small cloud racing across the blue winter sky.

Spring is on its way. We should be celebrating a new start. One without that abusive cunt in our lives. But his presence still seems to be lingering. Even from the depths of our basement, he has an impact on my life.

I've achieved everything I wanted. But it wasn't enough.

It makes me wonder if nothing ever will be.

Even when he is gone and finally turned to nothing but ash, my life will always be tainted with his poison.

Mum's life. Jodie's life. Joanne's life.

All of us tarnished by his need for power, to control everything around him.

My fists curl, my nails digging into my palms as I battle with the constant regrets that now fester inside me, slowly eating me alive as if I've got venom running through my veins.

Part of me thinks I should have just killed him that first night. Sent him straight to hell the night Stella put a bullet through Joker.

But then I never would have needed to find Jodie. I'd have had no reason to dig deeper into his hidden life and discover his secret family.

And right now, despite how painful all of this is, I can't imagine my life without her.

Big words, seeing as I've only known her a short time, I know. But they're the truth.

It only took one look, one touch, one word for me to realise how strong the connection was between us.

It's wrong. All of it is so fucked up.

I should walk away from her and just keep moving. Let her try to rebuild her life however she wants without me.

But I can't.

She's mine.

She's mine, and there's no way I can walk away from her.

Even if she tries to make me.

I let out a sigh and close my eyes, regretting it instantly when the image of that cunt from last night fills my eyes once more and my anger burns red-hot through my veins.

If I didn't already know that he'd been cleared away, I'd fucking go back and shoot the motherfucker again.

No one touches what's mine.

But even with images of all the ways I could have ended that sick fuck in a much less humane fashion last night and the cold assaulting my body, I somehow manage to give into my exhaustion.

But it's anything but restful as nightmares fill my mind, images of last night, of Jodie sobbing on my bathroom floor, meld with memories of my childhood.

"You disrespectful little shit," Dad groans, his fingers curling in my shirt at the back of my neck, causing it to tighten around my throat.

If I were any other kid, I might panic. But it's not the first time something like this has happened, and I'm sure it won't be the last where I fear he might just take it too far and finally just put an end to my misery.

I stumble forward, my body shutting down long

before the sight of the basement door appears before me.

There's no point fighting, begging, pleading. I've tried it all before.

I've tried everything over the years. But at some point, I realised that he actually enjoyed me fighting, suffering. So sometime around my twelfth birthday, I just gave up.

My acceptance angers him. I see it in the pulsating vein in his temple, and I can't help but get some sick satisfaction at knowing I'm affecting him in some way. Even if it is irritation.

He stops marching me along by the scruff of my neck like I'm nothing more than the unloved family mutt as he pulls the heavy door of the basement open.

Mum isn't here. By some miracle, she managed to convince Dad to allow her to have a few days away with my auntie. I'm happy for her to have some peace, but equally, I'm fucking terrified, because it leaves me here at the mercy of this monster. And his punishments for disobeying him are always worse when there's no chance of getting caught.

The second the door is open enough for me to fit through, he pushes me forward. My body moves faster than my legs and I stumble, tripping over the top step and falling into the dark abyss below.

My thigh hits the edge of the top stair first before

my shoulder slams into another a little lower down and I flip over, tumbling down into the cold, dark depths of my torture chamber.

My body aches, pain shooting down my arm, but I swallow down any groans that threaten to spill from my lips. I refuse to give him the satisfaction of knowing he's hurt me, that he's affected me in any way.

The door creaks, the light spilling from the house behind him getting dimmer as he swings it shut, plunging me into darkness.

The echo of it slamming shut and the heavy lock being twisted makes my entire body jolt as my mind slowly shuts down.

I awake with a gasp, my heart pounding at the loud bang of that door resonating through me as if it really happened.

Sucking in a deep breath, I rest my head back once more as a flock of birds fly overhead and an ice-cold breeze washes over me.

A bang hits my ears and I gasp, getting sucked back into my nightmare for the briefest second as my heart free-falls at the thought of Jonas finding my little slice of heaven in this heinous house.

There's more noise making my heart thunder in my chest as I stare at the drop in the roof that allows me to climb up here.

All the air rushes out of my lungs as a familiar head pops above the tiles.

Relief fills Nico's eyes before he drags himself up.

"You're in trouble, Doukas," he warns.

I sigh, falling back once more and letting my head rest against the unforgiving roof beneath me.

"Can't say I'm surprised," I mutter. "What do you want?" The question comes out harsher than I intended, and I wince.

But if he's at all offended by my question, he doesn't comment on it as I listen to him getting comfortable beside me.

His shoulder brushes mine as he lays down, his warmth making me shudder when he doesn't move away.

Swallowing thickly, I try to fight the emotions that swell inside me that he's found me and is putting up with my shitty mood.

"What's going on, Tobes?" he asks after his silence stretches on for longer than I gave him credit for.

I sigh, trying to find the words to properly explain where my head is at right now.

"Jonas really fucked me up," I confess.

"Nah, you're no more twisted than the rest of us, bro."

I shake my head, unsure as to whether he's looking at me or not as I squeeze my eyes tight.

"He used to lock me in the basement," I confess.

My best friend gasps in horror as I admit something I've never told him about my life before.

"T-the basement?" he stutters, a deep line forming between his brows.

I shrug, unsure of what to say.

"Why?" His horrified stare burns into the side of my face but I don't turn to look at him. I can't. Shame burns me up from the inside as I think about the things I allowed the evil cunt to do to me.

"As punishment. To teach me resilience, strength. To—"

"That's bullshit. You've never done anything in your life to deserve that kind of punishment."

"Not in his eyes. Just being born was a fucking sin."

"Jesus," he mutters as he tries to process what I've just confessed. "How long were you down there?"

"It varied. Sometimes an hour or so. Sometimes days."

"Days?" he blurts. "Why the fuck didn't you tell us any of this?"

"I couldn't," I mutter. "He held all the power, followed through on enough threats that I couldn't risk it. If he hurt Mum even more than he already was because I couldn't hack it then I'd never forgive myself."

"FUCK," he booms so loudly a flock of birds erupt from a nearby tree and scatter.

"If it weren't for him, then I wouldn't be this fucking broken," I whisper. "I wouldn't have done all that shit with Jodie. But my hatred for him fucking blinds me."

"He hasn't broken you, Toby. You're the best fucking person I know."

A bitter laugh falls from my lips.

"Don't fucking laugh it off. I'm serious. I wouldn't give just anyone the role of my best friend. It's not a position I hand out lightly."

"No one else would fucking have you," I mutter.

He barks a laugh. "I'll have you know, I've turned more than one applicant away in the past."

"You're full of shit."

"Yeah, I am. You love me for it though."

I can't help but smile, because he's right. I fucking love his brand of weird.

"What's got you going off grid and hiding up here like the old days?"

"Jodie was attacked last night after her shift at Foxes."

"Oh fuck, is she okay?" he asks in shock.

My brows lift in surprise. I kinda assumed Theo would have told the guys by now.

"Yeah. I stopped him just in time, took her home. Looked after her."

"I know you hate hearing it, but you're a good guy, Tobes. She'd be a fool if she can't see that."

"No. It would make her fucking sensible. She shouldn't forgive me."

"That's up to her, not you, don't you think?"

"I can't get the image of her breaking on my bathroom floor out of my head. It fucking haunts me day and night."

"Don't you think that maybe that's a good thing? I'd be more concerned if you'd forgotten about it already. Pretty sure that shows that you care, that you regret it. That you understand just how fucking badly you fucked up and hurt her."

I scoff at his reasoning.

"Do you think Jonas ever struggled to sleep after all the fucked-up shit he did?"

A laugh of disbelief falls from my lips.

"That sick cunt never lost a wink of sleep over that shit."

"Exactly. I know you're worried about being like him. But you're not, Toby. You care, you love hard, and you want to be a good person. You *are* a good person. It's just a hard thing to be in the lives we live. Sometimes we fuck up. Sometimes our inner monsters come out to play. But that doesn't mean that's all we are.

"Any girls who think they can handle this life need to appreciate that there are two sides to all of us. Stella's seen it in Seb time and time again. Same with Emmie and Theo. And both of them love our boys with everything they are. There's no reason why you can't have the same."

A smile twitches at my lips as I let his words roll around my head a little.

"You're a bit of a softie really, aren't you, Nic?"

He tsks. "I guess I can have my moments," he admits. "But seriously though, I've seen how happy she makes you, man. I want that for you. I want to see you smile like you do when you're with her."

Memories flood me of the time I've spent with Jodie, and I can't help but smile because he's right.

His phone pings and I look over as he pulls it out and sits up.

He shoots a message back before turning to look at me.

"Wanna get out of this hellhole?"

I stare at him for a beat.

"Thank you."

"I've got your back, man. Always." He smiles at me before his expression turns hard.

"But..." I prompt, sensing that there's more to that statement.

"But if you go off fucking grid again and make us all panic, I'll beat your arse into next fucking week."

"Pfft, I'd like to see you try."

His brow quirks as a smirk twitches at his lips. "Pull that stunt again and we'll find out."

His phone goes off again, and this time when

he reads whatever is on the screen, his face lights up.

"Booty call?"

"Hell yeah." His eyes sparkle when they find mine.

"What?" I ask, not liking the look on his face. It usually precedes trouble.

"Nothing. Come on. Alex is hanging out in the driveway, waiting for us."

"He's sitting down there?" I ask in disbelief. "Why didn't you bring him up?"

"Because this is your place. I didn't think you'd want every motherfucker knowing about it."

"Thanks, man. You're pretty fucking awesome, you know that?"

"Hell yeah, I do."

"Modest too," I joke, sliding my arse down the tiles as he drops over the edge, throwing himself back into my room a second before I follow.

"It's time to move on from this shit, Tobes. You've got too much good in your future to dwell on the past." He wraps his arm around my shoulder and drags me toward my bedroom door. "And that starts right now."

15

JODIE

"Are you sure this is a good idea?" I ask after Stella lets me into Toby's flat.

I've still got no idea where he was. All I know is that they're on their way back here and Stella thinks this will help with wherever his head is at right now.

I can't say that I'm feeling so confident, but at this point, I've got little choice in the matter.

"I'm going to take Mum home, then I'll be right down the hall. You've got my number. Call me if you need anything."

"Jesus," I mutter, getting a proper look at his flat for the first time.

It should feel totally wrong being in here after everything, but I feel weirdly comfortable amongst all his things and surrounded by his scent.

I nod, my heart pounding as nerves assault me.

Before I have a chance to argue, Stella closes the front door behind her, leaving me alone in Toby's home.

"Fuck," I hiss, clenching my trembling hands in the hope of stopping them as I walk toward the sofa.

The need to explore burns through me, but I'm already invading his privacy enough as it is.

There's a clock in the kitchen that loudly counts each second that passes as I fight to keep my nerves down. I use the ticking to ground me, and it just starts to work when there's a bang at the front door.

Keys are thrown down on the dresser before two dull thuds sound out. His shoes being kicked against the wall, maybe.

My entire body begins to tremble as I perch myself on the edge of the sofa, my nails digging into the soft grey fabric as I wait for him to appear.

This is going to go one of two ways, and I hope to hell it's the way I want and I don't find myself out on my arse in only a few minutes for Stella to find once again.

His footsteps begin to get closer and my head spins as I wait.

My stomach turns over and I worry I'm about to vomit all over his fancy floor when he emerges.

The second my eyes lock on him, all of my nerves vanish. Suddenly, my only concern is him.

I'm on my feet before I even know I've moved and closing the space between us.

"Toby," I breathe.

His face is pale, his eyes shadowed and bloodshot from exhaustion. But it's the darkness in his eyes that really guts me. The pain, the anguish. Seeing it so clearly, it physically hurts.

The connection between us crackles, its power only growing the closer we get.

His eyes hold mine, but despite all the things I can sense that he wants to say, none of them pass his lips.

Until I'm right in front of him.

"Fuck, you're really here, aren't you?"

"Y-yeah, I—" My words are cut off as his hand wraps around the back of my neck, dragging me against him and slamming his mouth down on mine.

Surprise renders me useless as he plunges his tongue past my lips.

The second it brushes mine, my body finally reacts and I wrap my arms around his neck as his hands grab my arse.

My feet leave the ground a second before my back slams against the wall, and Toby's kiss deepens.

His tongue licks into my mouth as if he's trying to brand himself on my soul.

"Jodie," he moans into our kiss before ripping

his lips from mine and kissing down my neck. "You're here."

"Yes," I cry when he sucks on the sensitive skin beneath my ear. "Oh God, please," I groan, rolling my hips against him to find some friction.

"You sure, baby? Because once that happens, I fucking swear to you that I'm not letting you go."

His words should settle in my head as the warning they're intended as, but they don't.

"I'm sure. Please, Toby."

"Fuck," he grunts, pulling me from the wall and spinning us before marching in the direction of his bedroom.

I cling to him like a spider monkey, wondering if his bedroom is actually the last place I want to be, but my thoughts soon float away as he lays me out on his bed and stands, towering over me like a god.

Reaching behind him, he pulls the shirt Mum gave him from his body in one quick and sexy move, revealing hard, toned inches of his torso for me to enjoy.

His chest heaves as he stares down at me and my eyes linger on his scar briefly before I make my way lower, finding his cock tenting his sweats.

My mouth waters and my fingers twitch in my need to reach for him.

"You're so fucking beautiful," he breathes before falling over me, his hands planted on either side of my head as he dips to claim my lips once more.

My legs lock around his back and I tug, desperately trying to drag him down on top of me so I can feel his weight pressing me into the mattress.

"Greedy little demon," he groans, kissing and nipping along my jaw as his fingers find the bottom of my jumper.

Arching my back, I help him pull it from my body before he throws it across the room. His lips immediately descend to my chest.

"Toby," I cry when his teeth graze me through the lace of my bra.

"You're everything, Jodie. Fucking everything."

He tucks two fingers into my bra and drags the fabric aside, exposing me to him. His lips are there immediately, wrapping them around my sensitive peak, making me arch off the bed when he sucks hard.

"Oh God," I cry, my fingers threading into his hair, holding him in place, needing him to keep going. "Yes," I scream when he shifts to the other side, grazing my nipple with his teeth.

His hand slips beneath me when I arch up and he unhooks my bra, allowing him access to all of me. Which he more than makes the most of, kissing, nipping, and sucking my sensitive skin until

I'm panting in need and he's thoroughly marked my body as his.

This is exactly what I needed last night. This mindless pleasure that he can offer me.

Life outside the two of us, outside of these four walls ceases to exist when we're together, and it's everything. Every-fucking-thing.

My fingers tighten in his hair when he tries to move lower, but when his eyes collide with mine, I question my sanity and let him go.

In seconds, he's pulling my jeans and knickers down my legs and tugging them free of my feet.

"Fuck, I missed this," he says, pressing his hands against my inner thighs and spreading me wide for him.

"Shit, please. Toby," I cry when he blows a stream of air down the length of me. My muscles ripple, desperate to drag something inside me—mostly his cock.

My hips grind as he remains motionless between my legs, just teasing me with what I want most.

"Tell me you're mine," he demands.

His words are like a bucket of cold water for a split second as flashbacks to the last time I was here hit me.

"I know I don't deserve it. I know you hate me. I know all of that. But fuck... I can't live without you, Demon. I'll spend every single second of the rest of my life trying to make it up to you, to prove to you how I feel about you."

My heart makes my decision for me while my head is still as unsure as it has been since fleeing this place that night.

"I'm yours," I say honestly, holding his eyes so he can read it for himself.

"Fuck, Jodie. Fuck."

Before I get a chance to figure out what to even say to that, he dives for me.

His tongue swipes up the length of me before zeroing in on my aching clit.

"Toby," I scream as he eats me as if he hasn't had a meal in months.

My entire body trembles with my need to let go, but he never lets me fall.

"Are you going to come for me, Demon?"

"If you ever fucking let me," I snap back, much to his amusement.

"I will. When you're ready."

His fingers rub at my G-spot with just the right pressure to send me heading toward the edge once more, but I already know he's not going to let me have it. I can see it in the dark depths of his eyes.

"Tell me what you want. Honestly."

"I-I want..." My words falter when he dips his head and circles my clit. "I w-want to remember how good we are together."

"And you're not doing that right now?" he asks, quirking a brow at me.

"I want all of it. I want to set the whole fucking world on fire with you."

"Fuck yes."

Clearly, it was the right thing to say, because when he dives for me this time, he doesn't let up until I'm damn near ripping his hair clean from his scalp as I scream out my release.

He doesn't stop until I'm a panting mess before him.

"You taste like heaven, baby," he says, pushing his fingers into his mouth and cleaning them up.

The sight alone makes everything south of my waist clench and the tingles of aftershocks race through my limbs.

"Toby," I whimper, nowhere near satisfied with just that.

"Greedy little demon, aren't you?"

I nod eagerly as he pushes his thumbs into the waistband of his sweats and shoves both them and his boxers down, exposing his solid length to me.

My mouth waters and I suck my bottom lip into my mouth as I remember just how he tastes, how he feels hitting the back of my throat, and the noises he makes as I bring him to his knees.

"I like where your mind just went, Demon. But this is about you, not me."

Taking himself in hand, he wraps his fingers

around the base of his shaft as he crawls onto the bed between my legs.

"I'm not stopping until your voice is hoarse from screaming my name. And then, and only then, I might let myself go."

"No," I half moan, half chastise as I register what he's saying at the same time he rubs my clit with the head of his cock. "I want you to come too."

He shakes his head, sadness washing into his features once more.

"Toby, I don't want— fuck," I scream as he thrusts forward, filling me in one swift move.

He pushes my thigh up to my chest and grinds into me in the most insane way that makes fireworks shoot off around my body.

Curling over me, he brushes his lips against mine in the sweetest of kisses as the rest of his body does filthy things to me.

"This wasn't meant to happen. I wasn't meant to fall this fucking hard," he confesses against my lips. "You weren't meant to be so fucking perfect that I'm convinced you were made for me. Made to save me. To pull me out of the darkness and allow me to see the light again."

Tears prickle at the backs of my eyes as he stares into them.

"That first night, you were so much more than I ever could have expected. I knew then that I was in trouble, but I was so fucking blinded by my need for revenge that I refused to see it, to feel it. But even before we'd stepped into Hades, you had my heart in a death grip and you had no idea."

"Stop," I beg, my heart barely able to listen to the honesty in his tone.

There's a part of me that still wants to cling onto the hate, the anger, the darkness. In some ways, it's easier because I'm in control of the hate, of pushing him away. But being drawn back in… it's fucking terrifying, because I know how much it could hurt if I'm wrong again.

"I can't. I need you to know the truth. I lo—"

"No," I cry, pressing my hand over his mouth in panic. "No. Not now. Not yet. There's so much more we need to work through than one hot fuck to get past this. I'm not ready. Please."

He nods once, and I lower my hand to his shoulder once more.

"Fine. I'll just have to show you instead."

His hips roll again and I cry out as he hits that sweet spot over and over.

"Come for me, Demon. Let me watch you fall."

His hand skims down my stomach before he pinches my clit and I go off like a fucking rocket, my nails clawing at his back in the hope of making him fall with me.

I hate the thought of him punishing himself over all this. He's already suffered so much.

"Toby, please. I need to feel you inside me," I moan, riding out the end of my release.

He thrusts forward, a smirk pulling at his lips. "Pretty sure that's exactly where I am, baby."

"That's not what I mean and you know it," I say, my voice already sounding raspy.

"Just let me have this."

He pulls out and flips me before I give him an answer, and my shriek of shock quickly follows the loud slap of his hand against my arse cheek.

"Fuck," I pant when he does it again before soothing the burn with a gentle touch that makes my skin break out in goosebumps.

He finds my entrance again, teasing me with what I really want more of.

"A bit of pain gets you so fucking wet for me, Demon," he groans as if he's hurting—which he probably is, seeing as he's refusing himself any pleasure.

16

TOBY

I push inside her once more, gritting my teeth as her warmth surrounds me, her muscles sucking me deeper as a loud moan rips from her lips.

I didn't have any intention of coming back here tonight, but I naïvely thought no one would notice that I'd turned my phone off the second I stepped out of Jodie's house first thing this morning.

I should have known better. I should have expected everyone to care enough to be worried about where I'd gone, especially after Theo knew exactly what had happened the night before.

I guess it really was only time before Nico remembered my old hiding spot.

Seeing him there was both a blessing and a curse.

Deep down, I didn't want to be alone in my misery, and his sudden appearance helped with the loneliness, but it also meant that I had to deal with the reason I was hiding up on the roof in the first place.

When he told me before we left that he had something that would make it all feel a little better, I assumed he meant the bottom of a bottle or two. Never in a million years did I think that they'd got Jodie in on the hunt, and that when I stepped into my living room I'd find her waiting for me.

Best fucking surprise of my life.

"Fuuuck," I groan as I pull almost all the way out of her before sinking back inside, absorbing every single feeling I've been craving since I fucked everything up.

"Jesus, Demon. Your cunt is fucking mind-blowing."

"Toby," she moans, pushing back against me, forcing me deeper inside her.

"Fuck yeah," I grunt, watching as she takes every inch of me.

Releasing her hip, she tenses, her pussy squeezing me tight in anticipation for what she knows is coming next.

If I weren't already riding a very thin edge of self-control then I'd hold off, but I can't. I'm done with teasing her, with teasing myself. I just want to watch her fall over and over. Watch her skin flush red as she loses herself in the pleasure she deserves so much of after what I put her through.

Crack.

She fucking howls as my hand collides with her delicate skin, and I have to fight the need to do exactly the same at the sight of her bent over before me.

My hips pick up speed as she begins chanting my name, her pussy tightening around me, threatening to make me blow, but I am determined to hold off. To show her that all that matters to me is her.

"Come on, Demon." I glide my hand down her spine and twist my fingers in her hair, dragging her from the bed and pinning her back against my chest.

My hand wraps around her throat and I squeeze just enough to remind her of the bad boy side of me that she loves so much.

"You gonna come all over my cock again, baby?" I growl in her ear.

"Yes, yes, Toby," she cries when my other hand dips between her legs, my fingers playing her clit until she shatters, her entire body trembling with her release.

I slow my thrusts before releasing her and laying her on her back so I can stare down at her as she fights to catch her breath.

Her cheeks, neck, and chest are flushed red, her lips are swollen from my kiss, and her eyes are heavy from her releases.

Fucking perfect.

"Fuck, I love—" Her eyes widen in panic. "Having you in my bed."

A soft smile pulls at her lips as I drop beside her, pulling her warm, pliant body into mine and finding her lips once more.

"Thank you," I say into our kiss. "Thank you for being here."

"I'm sorry I freaked out this morning," she whispers. "That wasn't fair after everything you did."

"It's okay," I say, hating the vulnerability that creeps into my voice.

"No," she states, her palm colliding with my shoulder and forcing me to fall onto my back. "It's not fucking okay." The fierceness in her voice makes my aching cock twitch violently. "I'm not letting you do this. I'm not."

She sits up, her eyes holding mine for a few seconds as she waits for me to argue, but when no words pass my lips, she moves, throwing her leg over my waist and dropping her hands beside my head, mimicking our position from earlier.

"What are you going to do about it then, baby?" I ask with a smirk as she grinds the burning heat of her pussy against me.

"I want everything from you, Tobias," she warns, the roughness of her voice making precum drip onto my belly. "I want all your truths, all your darkness. Every single fucking drop." I nod, more than willing to show her everything I am so that she can have one final chance to run. "But—" she adds. "Not until you've let go."

She sits up and impales herself on my cock, making us both groan in pleasure.

"I'm not stopping until you fill me with cum, hotshot," she warns, although it's hardly a threat.

"I've been forced to do worse things in my life, Demon," I quip, taking hold of her hips, unable to forego complete control.

She smiles at me knowingly as she lifts up with my help.

"I don't think so, bad boy."

Entwining our fingers, she lifts my hands over my head and pins them back against the pillow, forcing me to relinquish control.

Dipping her head, her breath rushes past my ear as she slowly rocks down on my cock.

"Just enjoy the ride, baby," she breathes in a raspy whisper.

She peppers kisses along my rough jaw before I twist my head and capture her lips with my own.

"Stop topping from the bottom," she warns, nipping my bottom lip.

"You wouldn't have me any other way," I quip, but seeing how much taking charge for once means to her, I stop fighting and let her have at it, enjoying every fucking second of it.

It takes an embarrassingly short amount of time before my balls draw up and I'm ready to finally give her what she wants.

"Baby, I need you to get there," I tell her, but from the way her arms are trembling and her pussy is clamping down on me, I know it's not a huge demand.

"I'm right with you, hotshot. Let go." Her teeth sink into my bottom lip and my restraint finally snaps. I thrust up into her roughly as my release slams into me, claiming me just like she unknowingly did all those weeks ago when I first locked eyes with her across that bar.

Her body locks up, her cunt squeezing me impossibly tight as she falls right alongside me, milking my cock for everything I have.

The second we're both spent, she collapses on my chest as we fight to calm our racing hearts.

I wrap my arms around her, holding her tightly against me, and I finally close my eyes and relax, almost immediately falling into a blissful sleep.

I SLEEP BETTER than I have since the weekend we spent in Evan's cabin, and when I begin to wake, it's with a smile playing on my lips.

Until I realise that the warm body I drifted off

holding on to is gone, and the other side of the bed is cold.

"No," I cry, sitting upright and looking around to see if she's still here. But I see no sign that she ever was here, and if it weren't for her lingering scent and the scratches that are gouged into my back from her nails, then I'd think I dreamed the whole thing. "Fuck. No, please," I quietly beg as I throw the covers off and pad toward the bathroom.

My heart sinks when I find it empty.

Pain rushes through me at the thought of her leaving after that. After she made the effort to be here waiting for me. To tell me that she was mine, to make me believe there might be a future between us.

My hand slams down on the tiles as my head hangs, the feeling of uselessness, of worthlessness that I've become all too used to over the years washing through me.

It's what I deserve. I know it is. But it doesn't stop me from hoping for more, for something better out of my life.

Grabbing a clean pair of boxers, I tug them up my legs angrily, more than ready to just fucking give up.

I really thought her being here meant something. It never occurred to me that she just wanted to hurt me.

With a sigh, I take off through my flat in search of something that will help numb the pain.

The sun set at some point during my nap, but I have no idea what the time really is. The moon lights my way as I pad toward the kitchen.

I come to a grinding halt when I turn into the open plan living room and see a figure standing in front of the windows, her silhouette illuminated as if she's an angel.

All the air rushes out of my lungs at the sight of her.

"Jodie," I breathe.

She startles and turns around.

She's wearing one of my white shirts. The front is buttoned up haphazardly, teasing me with her cleavage, the bottom of it skimming her thighs.

A smile twitches at her lips as she takes a step toward me.

Her hair is still a mess and her lips swollen. The silver light from behind her allows me to see the red marks that mar her skin from my rough touch.

"I-I thought you'd left," I whisper, still not entirely convinced she's real right now and not the angel I thought her to be only seconds ago.

She shakes her head.

"I'm not running, Toby. Not unless you lie to me again."

"I won't. I fucking swear to you."

She nods, closing the space between us and taking my hands in hers.

"I tried to make coffee, but I can't even get the machine to turn on."

I can't help but bark out a laugh.

"Baby," I whisper, relief that she's still here rendering me useless.

Leaning forward, I rest my brow against hers and close my eyes, telling myself over and over that she didn't run. That I panicked for nothing.

"I'm here," she assures me as if she's able to read my thoughts. "I'm right here."

"Go and get back in my bed, Demon. I'll get the coffee."

"That sounds like an offer I can't refuse," she quips, reaching up on her tiptoes to brush a soft kiss against my lips.

Her breasts brush my chest and my cock wakes at her contact.

"Careful, or we won't make it back there."

"We need to talk, Toby," she says, her voice deadly serious.

I swallow the lump of emotion in my throat and nod.

"I know. We will. I'm not letting you leave this flat until you know everything. Then, I'll give you one chance to run as fast as you can away from me and my fucked-up family."

She nods and takes a step back.

"Don't take too long," she says before moving toward my bedroom.

I stand there and watch her until she shoots a wicked smile over her shoulder and disappears from my sight.

"Tease," I call, much to her amusement.

I swear to God time slows down as I stand there waiting for the coffee machine while knowing she's in my bed wearing nothing but my shirt.

"Fucking finally," I mutter to myself when the coffee machine has finished. Picking up both of the mugs in one hand and the snacks I pulled from the cupboards in the other, I practically run toward the bedroom.

My breath catches when I find her resting back against my headboard, looking hot as fuck with her fingers twisting together nervously.

"You look scared, Demon," I comment, lowering the mugs to the side and dropping the packets of crisps and chocolate to the bed.

"I have no idea how bad everything you've got to tell me is. I'm terrified."

I bite my tongue, stopping me from telling her that she probably should be. The things I've done over the years, the horrors we've all seen and had a hand in... I shudder at the thoughts alone.

"I'm not going to tell you everything today. There's too much. Most of which I don't even remember until something triggers the memory.

I've been in this life a long time, baby. Done a lot of shit that would break most men. But that doesn't mean I won't tell you, because I will. All of it. But for now, we'll focus on the parts you're involved in, okay?"

She nods and I climb onto the bed, but I don't sit beside her and pull her into my arms like I crave to do. Instead, I sit opposite her so I can look into her eyes as I say all the things I need to.

Reaching out, I wrap my hand around her thigh, needing some contact with her.

"I told you a lot of it that night, but I know I wasn't in the right mindset to explain it all properly."

She nods, reaching out and covering my hand with hers.

I hang my head, preparing to drag up the past, which is going to be painful for both of us.

"You know about my childhood. Every story I told you was true. Jonas ruled our home with an iron fist. Despite knowing I wasn't his kid, he had my position in the family pegged from the day he discovered I was a boy. Clearly, it didn't matter to him that I wasn't his blood, but I was pure Greek Cirillo blood with Mum and Galen. That must have been good enough for him."

She nods. I already explained this when she asked why Joe wasn't dragged into this life. He might have been Jonas's, but with Joanne's blood in his veins, he wasn't pure Greek and he wouldn't have accepted that. I know just how seriously he took the rules about the Family's legacy. It's how I ended up in the position I was in. He thought that if he could brainwash me, I could be his perfect heir. Something I was never going to be.

"Life was shit. Mum had suffered too much already, and then to be diagnosed with a brain tumour..." I shake my head. "It was all too much. I'd been working on a way out for us for years, but I had to put it all on the back-burner while Jonas held Mum's treatment over our heads.

"He probably knew exactly what I was planning. He always found a way to know everything."

"I met your mum today," Jodie says softly. "She and Stella came to the house looking for you."

"That's why you're here." It's not a question. Jodie wouldn't have come here by herself. "Anyway, I had no idea Stella existed until she showed up at the beginning of the school year and turned our worlds upside down."

"Did you really kiss her?" Jodie asks, obviously remembering that little tidbit from my previous confession.

"Yes," I sigh. "And it's something the others are never going to let me forget. Galen, our father, pulled me off her and dropped the bomb that we were siblings. Not my finest moment."

"Oh my God," Jodie gasps into her hand. "That's mortifying."

"Yep. But that revelation was soon forgotten when she got stabbed only a few minutes later."

"Holy shit."

"We had no idea, but someone had been threatening her. Seb was a massive cunt to her when she first arrived, and she assumed it was him playing games."

"It was Jonas," Jodie states.

"He'd threatened Stella's life as a baby and forced Galen and Mum's hands, and they had to keep her safe. Galen moved with her to America. But before Mum's surgery, they came back.

"Seb, Theo and Alex were tasked to keep her safe by the boss, but it wasn't enough."

"Jonas wanted her gone?"

I nod, my heart splintering in my chest at just how close he got to achieving that goal.

"I truly didn't think it was him. The way he was going about it was so different to the way he'd controlled Mum and me over the years.

"He was clever in enlisting help, I guess. He always had an alibi, made himself look squeaky clean. But as was inevitable, he fucked up, and we all watched CCTV of him meeting Joker after he blew up the coach house where Stella was living with Seb and Theo."

"Jesus."

"We did some digging and discovered that Joker wasn't just some member of the Reapers, but Jonas's son. A son he was obviously blackmailing, controlling somehow into doing his dirty work."

"Joe idolised his dad. Always had. It's not hard for me to believe that Joe did whatever Jonas said."

"He did such a good job of covering you up, like I said before, but our PI is better. And eventually, Joe led me to you."

Jodie's eyes hold mine, the pain within them ripping me to shreds.

"I was blinded by rage, Jodie. The pain he'd caused me, my mum. Stella. He'd almost succeeded with his quest to kill her so many times. He hurt my brothers too. Everyone I loved had been tainted by him, and it needed to stop. His reign of terror needed to end.

"Once we knew the truth, we captured him and... dealt with Joker," I say with a wince, although she already knows what happened. Just not who pulled that trigger, I'm assuming.

She sucks in a shaky breath as tears fill her eyes at the thought of her brother's fate.

"I'm so sorry, Jodie."

She nods, swallowing harshly as she tries to accept the truth. "I know. It hurts, but I understand, I think. He hurt you and those you love, and you couldn't sit back and let that go."

I hold her eyes, praying that she really does

understand, that she'll be able to see the real me past all of this and not just the monster who's caused her immeasurable grief over the past few months.

"Where is he? Jonas?"

"Do you really want to know?" I ask.

She nods once.

"He's locked in a cell in the basement."

"Here?"

I nod.

"Shit. He's still alive?"

"Yes."

"Why? Why haven't you killed him? You got your revenge. I thought that was the next step." Her brows pull together as if this is the most confusing part about everything I've confessed.

"Because of you."

"M-me?"

Shifting forward, I take both of her hands in mine.

"You shouldn't be here right now, Jodie. You should have got yourself as far away from me as possible. The things I've done, the things I've told you about. Y-you shouldn't—"

"I'm more than aware," she whispers.

"But I couldn't do that to you. I couldn't go down there after you left like I'd planned to. I couldn't rip the chance away from you before we'd talked properly, before I gave you the option to—"

"The option to what, Toby?"

I shrug, hating even the suggestion of allowing her anywhere near him, but knowing that it's what she deserves.

"To see him."

She sucks in a sharp breath, her eyes widening with shock.

"Y-you think... you think I'd want to see him after everything you've told me?"

Ripping the covers away, I slide my legs beneath her knees and wrap her trembling body in mine.

"I don't know, baby. But I wanted you to have the option. I've taken so much from you. You deserve to make your own choice about him."

She rests her head against my chest and sighs. "I don't know whether I'm horrified or grateful."

I can't help but laugh, the insanity of all of this on top of my exhaustion making it hard to take seriously.

"You are legit fucking insane, you know that, right?"

"I'm more than aware, Demon. But what I want to know is, can you put up with my crazy brand of fucked up?"

She pulls back and looks up at me with her huge chocolate eyes, and my heart skips a beat.

"I think I could probably give it a go."

A smile twitches at my lips. "You have no

fucking idea what you've just agreed to, Demon. Wait until you meet all the others."

I claim her lips in a kiss that leaves us both breathless.

"Surely they're not any more terrifying than your sister. Did she really beat you up for hurting me?"

"Yes. She's a fucking bad-arse. Never agree to get in a ring with her. She's brutal."

"Can't say I'm in a rush to do that."

"If you want some training though, she'll sort you out. Emmie, too."

"Who's Emmie again?"

I smile down at her as my heart sings that she's trying to make sense of my crazy world.

"I love you, Jodie." The words fall from my lips without instruction from my brain, and I curse myself the second I realise I've said it when she specifically asked me not to. "Shit, I'm sorr—"

"Don't. Please don't ever apologise for being honest and telling me how you feel."

"Okay. Can I show you too?" I ask with a smirk.

"Yeah, I think I'd be okay with that. Although, didn't you bring coffee?"

17

JODIE

I groan in contentment as I stretch my legs out and tighten my hold on Toby's waist.

"Morning, baby," he damn near growls, and it makes my entire body erupt in tingles.

"Hey," I whisper, looking up at him.

I'm pretty sure that any sane person would have run last night. After he explained once more about Jonas and how I found myself smack bam in the middle of his life, he went on to tell me a little more about the life he leads, although I'm sure he kept the stories on the lighter end of the spectrum. As much as I might want to know every dark and dirty secret he holds within him, I'm also grateful that he didn't just spew it all.

I know who he is now. He's let me see into some of the darkness he hides in his soul. I figure I don't need everything. Not right now, at least.

"Hey, Demon." The smile that curls at his lips makes my stomach tumble and my heart soar. "How are you feeling?"

"Uh... thoroughly fucked," I say lightly.

He barks out a laugh that echoes around the room, and my own smile grows at the happiness I find on his face.

"That wasn't exactly what I meant, but I'm glad I was able to achieve it."

My cheeks heat as I think back to the events of the previous night. To our little fuck fest before he started confessing his truths that was really only a starter for what the rest of our night held.

"It was a pretty epic night."

He nods, staring down at me where I rest on his chest as if I belong.

"You didn't run," he says, cupping my cheek and caressing my skin with his calloused thumb.

"You thought I would?" I ask, hating that his doubt in me hurts despite the fact that it's exactly what I did do last time. I thought I'd made my intentions clear last night. Clearly, though, Toby's insecurities about where my head is at still reign strong.

He shrugs. "I think it's pretty obvious that you should."

"Meh, I've never really been one to follow the rules."

"Thank fuck for that," he laughs, flipping us so

I'm beneath him and the thickness of his hard cock presses against my thigh.

"You still want more?" I tease, rubbing against him.

"Damn right I do. I can't get e-fucking-nough, baby."

Dragging my nails up his back, I moan as he shudders and groans in need.

"Good. Me neither. Remind me why I didn't leave again."

He dips his head to my neck and makes me cry out, sucking on the sensitive skin beneath my ear.

In only minutes I'm panting for him and he's pushing inside me once more.

"Oh shit," I gasp in shock. "That's..." He stares at me in horror at the prospect of hurting me. "Tender," I confess.

"Fuck. I'll stop."

He pulls back and I quickly move, digging my heels into his lower back.

"Don't you dare," I growl, holding him in place with every ounce of strength I have. "Just take it slow, yeah?"

His eyes hold mine, the darkness within his blue depths making my heart ache for him, but then they crinkle at the edges and the softest smile plays on his face.

"You want me to make love to you, baby?" he asks.

He rocks his hips gently, his cock stroking all the right places deep inside me, and a moan falls from my lips.

"Toby," I groan, wrapping my hand around the back of his neck and dragging his lips down to mine. Ignoring my morning breath, I push my tongue into his mouth, searching out his own as he continues to rock into me with the most teasing of movements.

I lose sense of everything as we move together. It's a whole new level of intensity, which is saying a lot after everything we've been through.

Each roll of his hips and stroke of his tongue builds me higher and higher until I'm riding right on the edge of my release.

Just before I fall into oblivion, there's a bang somewhere outside the room, making Toby tense before a female voice shouts.

"Yo, big bro. You shown Jodie what you're really made of yet?"

"Motherfucker," he grunts into our kiss a beat before ripping his lips from mine. "Fuck off, Stel. We're busy."

"Sorry, Bro. I got plans that involve your girl. I can totally wait though. Take your time, enjoy yourselves."

"Oh my God," I hiss. "Is she for real?"

"Unfortunately, yes. I think in her weird

sisterly way, she's just glad I'm getting laid," he deadpans.

"Toby," I gasp. "We can't have sex while your sister is out there."

"Oh, Demon, I've still got so many things to tell you about my life and the crazy shit we've experienced. Trust me, this is nothing."

He thrusts into me with a little more force than previously, but any pain I first felt when we started is long gone now, replaced with nothing but pleasure.

"Oh God," I moan, my nails clawing at his back.

"Louder," he demands, pistoning his hips.

"This is fucked up," I cry, clinging onto him as he really goes to town.

"Welcome to my world, baby."

He sits up and drops his hand between us, circling my clit with a dizzying pressure that sends me flying off the cliff and screaming out his name only three thrusts later. His fingertips dig into my hips as his final few movements turn brutal before he spills himself inside me with a loud growl.

"Fuck yes," he grunts, folding himself over me and claiming my lips once more.

"You're welcome, Jodie," Stella calls from somewhere in the flat.

"Fucking hell, this is mortifying."

"Imagine walking in to find one of your best

friends knuckles deep in your sister with the rest of your mates watching."

"No," I breathe, unable to believe his confession.

"She's got a lot more torture coming her way for the shit I've had to put up with since she and Seb got together. Be warned." His eyes sparkle with amusement, which makes my insides sing. He looks so fucking happy, and after the horrors he's been forced to live through, I can't help but be relieved for him.

"I don't like the look in your eyes right now, Tobias," I warn.

"I think you're going to love it, Demon." He finally pulls out of me and pushes himself from the bed, immediately leaving me feeling cold and lost without him. Although, I must admit, watching him walk naked across the room almost makes up for it.

I lie there with my muscles twitching from the intense release, listening to him in the bathroom and wondering what the hell his sister has planned for me.

I sit up when he finally emerges, drinking in every bare inch of him.

"Keep looking at me like that and she'll be forced to listen to another round."

"And you say I'm the demon," I quip as he pulls a pair of clean boxers up his legs.

"Here," he says, throwing a second clean pair at me, quickly followed by a shirt. "Take your time, use whatever. I'll go see what she wants."

He drags a pair of sweats on and rips the door open.

Too intrigued to know what his sister thinks is so important that she needs to sit and wait, I rush to the door to listen.

"Here he is," she says lightly. "You look happy."

"And you look uninvited," he shoots back.

"Ouch. And here I was thinking I was owed a thank you for delivering your girl safely for you."

"I guess you're right. Thank you," he says, his voice suddenly quieter, and I can only imagine that he's pulled her in for a hug. I internally cringe. He must smell like sex, seeing as he hasn't showered yet.

Giving them some privacy, I head back to Toby's bathroom and set about cleaning up and washing the scent of our hours of exertion off my body.

I pull on the clothes Toby gave me after washing every inch of me with his shower gel, take a huge breath, and step out of the bedroom to discover what's really going on.

Stella's eyes light up when she sees me, but Toby is faster, rushing to my side and pulling me into his arms.

"Mmm, you smell insane."

"You are insane. Both of you," I say, glancing around him and looking at Stella.

She just shrugs. "Tell us something we don't know. Now," she says, pushing from the sofa. "You've had your time with your girl. Now I'm going to get to know her properly."

"Oh no, you're not—" A door opens behind us and voices fill Toby's flat.

"Oh my God," he groans. "Stella, what have you done?"

She smiles innocently at Toby before snatching me from her side as a crowd of people spill into the room.

I recognise Nico instantly, but not the other three guys or the two girls that file in behind him.

"Go change and grab your stuff," Stella instructs.

I look at Toby, my brows pinched in concern. "I don't have clothes or—"

"We've got you covered, go on."

"Stella," Toby warns.

"Chill, Bro. We promise to bring her back to you in one piece."

"I can't believe I'm letting you force me into this again," the brunette with the heavy dark makeup says with a pout.

"Oh shush, you love it," Stella says. "Jodie, that's Emmie and Calli. Welcome to the Cirillo princess club."

Calli beams at me while Emmie continues to scowl.

"Ignore her. That's not a thing."

"Can I make more jackets?" Calli asks excitedly, rubbing her hands together.

"Oh my God," Emmie whines, throwing her hands up in defeat. She soon gets distracted though when one of the guys steps up to her, wraps his hand around her throat and whispers something in her ear. She immediately relaxes and leans in to kiss him.

"Come on, kiss Casanova goodbye. We'll be back in a few hours."

Toby draws me into his body, and I wrap my arms around his neck.

"Your friends are crazy," I say, loud enough so they can all hear.

"I did warn you," he says with a smirk before brushing his lips against my cheek. "I'm sorry," he whispers in my ear. "I'll make it up to you later."

"It's really okay. I'm looking forward to getting to know them all better."

"Don't say I didn't warn you," he says, capturing my lips in a toe-curling kiss that makes everyone around us immediately stop talking in favour of cheering. "You'd better go before she drags you out." When I look over, I find Stella standing with her hands on her hips and a soft smile playing on her face.

The second I step away, the boys descend on Toby, teasing him about having a girl before they all fall down on the sofa as if they're here to stay.

"Let's go, we've got facials and massages with our names on them," Stella announces.

"And you're sure I can't stay here and play Xbox with the guys?" Emmie asks.

"Nope. Suck it up, Mrs. Cirillo. We're having a girls' afternoon and welcoming Jodie to the pack."

"Mrs. Cirillo?" I can't help but ask.

"Grab your stuff, we'll explain everything and give you all the gossip I'm sure Toby failed to."

I shake my head at the three of them and quickly rush down to Toby's room to pull on yesterday's clothes and grab my bag.

This might be a little spur of the moment, and I might have been longing for a day with Toby, but I can't deny the butterflies that are fluttering around in my belly at the prospect of diving deeper into his world and being accepted amongst his group of friends.

18

TOBY

"What the actual fuck was that?" I ask the second my front door closes, leaving me with the guys while the girls steal Jodie from me.

"Don't look at us, man," Seb says, holding his hands up in defeat as Alex and Nico battle to the death in the new zombie game they downloaded a few minutes ago. "It was all Stella's doing. She thought that Jodie might need a breather from you or something."

"Charming," I mutter.

"How's she doing?" Theo asks.

"Overwhelmed, I think. All of this, Friday night, me... it's a lot to process."

"Motherfucker. Bro, that was fucking brutal," Nico barks, throwing his controller down on the sofa cushion where it bounces onto the floor.

"Stop being a fucking pussy," Seb snaps,

swiping up the controller and setting up another game against Alex.

"So is it finally time to put that cunt in our basement into the ground or what?"

My head snaps to the side at his words, but all he does is shrug and take a pull on the beer someone apparently brought with them.

"What? It's long fucking overdue, if you ask me."

"Not sure I ever remember asking you," I spit.

"He's got a point though, bro," Theo adds. "You've got a good thing going with Jodie. Don't you think it's time to finally cut ties and move on?"

"I will. I just… he's her dad, man. I hate him more than anything, I want him as fucking worm food more than you can imagine. But there's no way in hell that I deserve a second chance with her. If I put a bullet through his skull, she'll never forgive me."

"Have you asked her?" Seb pipes up. "Now she knows the truth, she might feel differently about daddy dearest."

"I've told her that I won't do anything until she says so."

"Bro, you're giving this chick too much power," Nico scoffs.

My eyes collide with Seb's and then Theo's amused ones.

"She has all the motherfucking power, arsehole.

Tell him," I say, pointing from my two whipped friends to my stupid one. "I'm going for a shower."

"Good call. You smell like pussy, man," Alex pipes up, proving that he was actually listening while whipping Seb's arse. Something tells me that he's practised this game prior to downloading it here. Competitive cunt.

"Careful, bro. You sound awfully jealous about that fact. You spent the night with your hands all over a controller, didn't you?" I taunt.

"Fuck you. I'll beat your arse when you come back smelling like a man again."

"Pretty sure I smell perfectly manly right now after a night of fucking my girl senseless."

"Cunt," Alex mutters.

"Aw, bro. One day you'll find a woman who doesn't run at the first sight of your tiny cock," Nico teases.

"It's not small and you fucking know it. I vividly remember you telling me just how tight I made that filthy blonde we pulled a few weeks ago when I slid right into her arse while her cunt was full of you."

"Okay," I say, throwing my arms up. "I don't need that fucking visual in my head."

"Nah, man. You're just jealous I wasn't out tag teaming with you," Nico says with a shit-eating grin.

"You spoken to Brianna recently, Nic?" I ask,

knowing for a fact that she's ignored the couple of messages he's sent her.

"Sorry, who?" he asks, his brows drawing together as he tries to play it off.

"You're a fucking idiot."

"Oooh, Brianna," Alex sings. "Sounds exotic. She single, yeah?"

"Fuck you. You couldn't handle her even on your best day."

"I'll be fucking sure to give it a good try though."

I can't help but laugh as Nico's jaw pops in frustration.

"I'll give you her number," I offer sweetly, digging the knife in a little deeper.

"Don't you fucking—"

"Nico, man. You're looking really fucking whipped by this mystery girl right now," Theo says with a smirk.

"Nah, she's just got a fucking fantastic pussy, that's all."

"Ah," Seb pipes up. "I didn't think you were that fussy."

"Fuck you." Nico throws a punch into Seb's shoulder which ends up with Seb forgetting about the game he was in the middle of as the two of them tumble to the floor.

"Animals," I mutter lightly as I take off toward my bathroom, leaving the two of them grunting and groaning as they fight and Theo and Alex offering words of encouragement.

Grabbing my phone that I find half kicked under the bed, I wake it up to find a whole string of messages from both Stella and Mum. I guess I shouldn't be surprised after I took off yesterday.

Opening Stella's conversation, I quickly read through her messages checking in on me and making sure that I'm treating Jodie properly before shooting her a quick message in return.

Toby: You'd better look after my girl.

Toby: I haven't told her about Joker. I wanted to talk to you first.

I knew it was wrong of me not to tell her exactly who ended her brother's life yesterday when I was explaining everything, but that's not just my story to tell. If Stella envisages a future friendship with Jodie, then I think it's important that she's involved in revealing that truth.

Next, I find Mum's contact and hit call.

"Thank God you're okay."

"I'm sorry I worried you, Mum," I say, falling back on my bed and breathing in the scent Jodie left behind on my sheets.

"I always worry, you're my baby. How is everything now?"

"It's... good," I say, unable to fight my smile. "Things are good."

"You and Jodie work things out?"

"We've started to, yeah. Things are so complicated."

Mum laughs down the line, the sound making everything suddenly seem so much more possible.

"You've certainly not gone for easy with your choice here."

"When have we ever gone for the easy option?" I ask, thinking of everything our lives have consisted of so far.

"I really like her, Toby."

All the air rushes out of my lungs at Mum's words. I had no idea that I needed her approval with my relationship with Jodie, but knowing I have it, I realise what a weight was pressing down on my shoulders.

"Is it not really weird knowing who her father is?" I ask with a wince.

"Does it bother you?"

"Honestly?" I ask.

"Always, baby. That's how this works, remember?" I bite back my knee-jerk response to comment on the fact that she's covered up so much from me over the years, especially where my sister is concerned. But it's too late for all that now. It's in the past, and I understand that all she was trying to do was protect everyone.

"Jodie is... She's her own person. She's nothing like that poisonous snake, and I think I'm happy to forget that he ever had a hand in her making."

"I thought the exact same thing when I met her yesterday morning. She's her mother's daughter."

I nod as emotion begins to clog my throat.

"God, this is so messed up, Mum," I whisper.

I know how I feel about Jodie. So does she, now I've blurted it out. But that doesn't mean that this isn't a huge ugly mess.

"Toby, have you taken a step back and really looked at our lives? They are one big mess," she says lightly. "This is nothing new. And if I've learned anything over the years... you've got to follow your heart, baby. It's the only thing that's really important in all of this."

"Yeah, I'm seeing that."

"Nothing else matters. If you find happiness, no matter in what form, I say hold on tight and enjoy the ride."

Silence falls between us for a beat before I push up on my elbows.

"Thanks, Mum."

"I haven't done anything," she laughs.

"You've done more than you could possibly know."

"What are you doing talking to me, anyway? You should be enjoying time with your girl."

"Stella's stolen her and taking her to a spa with the girls."

"Oh, where was my invite?" she jokes.

"I'll leave that for you to deal with," I mutter.

We chat for a few more minutes before she lets me go and I finally head through to my shower to reluctantly wash Jodie's scent off my skin.

Thankfully, the guys have stopped fighting when I get back to the living room and they're all happily arguing over where Nico should be hiding if he stands any chance of beating Alex, who still has the controller.

Pulling the fridge open, I pluck out five fresh beers and take them over with a couple of bags of crisps.

My arse has almost hit the sofa cushion when my buzzer goes off.

"I messaged the devil," Theo says. "Looks like he might be willing to play today."

Shaking my head at him, I head over to let Daemon in. Since we all moved into this building, he's been hanging out with us a little more. I'm not sure if that's because he really wants to or just because we remember to invite him more, knowing he's close. Either way, it's nice to spend more time with him. We were all tight as kids, although he never really clicked with any of us. But I always felt bad when we all seemed to move in a different direction from him.

"Hey, man. How's it going?" I ask when I pull the door open and find him leaning against the wall opposite, half asleep. "Shit, rough night?"

"Something like that," he mutters, pushing forward. "Theo said—"

"Come in. You know you never need an actual invite to hang out, right? If you need—"

"I know," he cuts me off, but I'm not convinced that's because he really does know.

"So what's going on then? Anything we need to know about?"

He shrugs. "Spent all night in Lovell on surveillance."

"Boss really is taking all this shit seriously, huh?"

"With good reason, I think."

"Oh?"

"I have no evidence, but I've got a bad feeling."

"Great. Just what we need," I mutter as he follows me through the flat. "Beer?"

"Hell yeah," he mutters before dropping down beside Theo and immediately getting down to business.

Things have been weird between them for a few years now. Ever since Daemon dived headfirst into the Family instead of focusing on school, I think Theo's felt a little pushed out. He wants to be the boss, the big man as heir, but Daemon generally has more of a clue about what's going on. But recently, Theo seems to have chilled about it all a little. Possibly Emmie's influence, who knows? But it's nice to see them getting along and working together better these days.

Daemon isn't a threat to Theo's position. Yes, he's a fantastic soldier, but he's not a leader. Their skillsets are completely different, and if they do manage to continue to figure it out, together they will be fucking dangerous.

"You look fucking wrecked, man," Alex helpfully points out, finally dragging his eyes from the TV for a second.

"Yeah, thanks," Daemon mutters, stealing his beer from the coffee table.

"Hey, that's— Oh, you fucking motherfucker," he spits as Nico whoops in celebration as he's finally booted from his winning streak.

"Bro, you're meant to be on my fucking side," Alex snaps at his twin, who cheers Nico on.

"Uh... whoops," Daemon says innocently, lifting Alex's beer to his lips with a smirk. "You never were a good loser. Some things never change," he mutters.

"What the fuck are you talking about? I never lose," Alex sulks.

"Evidently," Daemon deadpans as Theo rips the controller from Alex and sets up another game.

The six of us fall into easy conversation about life, school, football, girls, until Seb gets a message from Stella letting us know that they're on their way back and to be ready.

His face lights up like a fucking Christmas tree as he taps out a response.

"Don't even fucking think about it," I warn, seeing his filthy intentions swirling around his eyes.

"No idea what you're talking about, man."

"You're not fucking my sister in my flat," I seethe.

"Yeah, yeah. We'll see what happens when you're distracted with your own girl."

"Wait," Daemon pipes up. "Toby's got a girl?"

"Oh mate," Alex laughs. "You're gonna fucking love this one."

"Jesus Christ," I mutter, scrubbing my hand down my face, knowing that I'm not going to love what's about to fall from his lips.

"She's Joker's sister."

Daemon stills for a beat as that information settles.

"She's your fucking sister?" he barks. "I'm all for a few kinks, man, but don't you think that's taking it a bit far?" he asks, dark humour sparkling in his eyes.

"She's not my sister," I sigh. "We share no blood, nor knew each other existed."

"Didn't stop you with Stella," Seb deadpans.

I sigh heavily, more than aware that I'm going to be on the receiving end of this shit for years.

"Completely different situation."

"Hey, I'm just glad it's not my fucking sister," Nico barks, his focus still mostly on the screen. "Cos I'd really fucking hate to kill any of you motherfuckers for touching her."

I swear to fucking shit, Daemon actually tenses opposite him, but it's quickly forgotten when Alex happily announces, "She's fucking banging hot these days though, man. You could hardly blame us."

The controller in Nico's hand goes flying across the room, colliding with Alex's temple only a few seconds later.

"What the fuck did you just say, Deimos?"

"You fucking heard me. And if it makes it any better, I'll totally let you molest my sibling."

"Fuck you," Daemon spits.

I watch the two of them closely, more than ready to jump in if this starts escalating.

"I ain't having his filthy hands all over me."

"You'd love it and you know it," Nico taunts.

"A little too much cock and muscle for me, but thanks for the offer, man. If I'm ever that desperate, I'll be sure to let you know."

19

JODIE

I throw my head back and laugh as sweat runs down my skin from the blistering heat from the hot stones in the corner of the sauna.

Turns out, Stella really had thought of everything. Waiting in the car for me was a bag with a bikini that fit me like it was made for me, a towel, cover up, and even a clean set of clothes for later that she's already confessed to getting Mum involved with.

Leaving Toby behind might have not been a part of my plan for today, but I don't think it could have turned out any more perfect. These women are... incredible. I've barely spent a few hours with them, but their strength, their passion, and above all, their love for their little family damn near takes my breath away. Oh, and also, they're freaking insane.

"Oh my God," I gasp, trying to catch my breath from laughing so hard at their stories that my sides hurt. "I didn't think it was possible, but you actually make my life look fairly normal."

"Girl," Stella says with a smirk, "there is nothing normal when it comes to us."

"You're all certifiable," I blurt.

"Hey, now. I take offence to that," Calli says, fighting a smile. "I was normal until these two hellions crashed into my life."

"You weren't normal, Cal," Emmie argues. "You were just a good little princess all locked in her castle, waiting for her prince charming."

"And look what I got instead," she barks, gesturing to both Stella and Emmie. "Two violence-obsessed nymphos. You're both basically the guys but with boobs."

Both Stella and Emmie glance at each other before falling about laughing once more, the bucks fizz we've been drinking since we first got here clearly having as much effect on them as it is me.

"You wouldn't have us any other way," Emmie says, and Calli just shrugs.

I shake my head as I look at the three of them. I barely know them, but I'm not sure that I've ever felt like I fit in somewhere quite like this before. I feel weirdly at home. The only other times I've felt it is when I'm with Toby. It's unnerving, but not unwelcome.

"Okay, I think I'm done," Calli says, pushing from the wooden bench opposite me. "I need to cool off and eat."

"Same. And despite sweating my arse off, I need a pee," Emmie says, walking out after her.

I slide to the edge of the bench, more than ready to follow and get out of this dry heat when Stella's voice stops me.

"You two go on. Jodie and I need to talk for a bit."

The three of them have some kind of silent conversation that I'm not able to decipher before Calli and Emmie push through the door, allowing a rush of cool air to flow over me.

The second we're shut back inside the sauna, a ripple of tension goes around the small room that wasn't there before.

"W-what's going on?" I ask suspiciously. The feeling of belonging I was revelling in not so long ago has just been completely ripped away, leaving me on edge and anxious for what Stella has to say to me. I want to say that it's just a 'don't hurt my big brother' warning, but something tells me it's a hell of a lot more serious than that.

I hold her eyes as she pulls her silver hair back into a fresh ponytail, and I wait for her to gather her thoughts.

She looks like a freaking model sitting there in her aqua bikini, muscles and curves all slick from the intense heat. I have no doubt from what I've learned so far that if Seb were here, he wouldn't be able to keep his hands off her.

"There's something Toby hasn't told you yet, and it's something that I think you need to hear from me," she says, but despite the concern I can see in her blue eyes, her voice is steady, the set of her body confident.

"O-okay," I breathe as my heart begins to pick up speed.

"I... um..." That first hesitation from her makes my entire body jolt. Her confidence about whatever this is isn't as shatterproof as she might like it to seem. "I was the one who killed your brother, Jodie."

All the air rushes out of my lungs as if she's just shot me. Silence ensues, and the atmosphere between us becomes so thick it's hard to even think about breathing.

My head spins, images of Joe and me as kids filling my mind. His goofy smile, his stupid fake laugh that used to drive me insane. His secret geekiness that he didn't ever want to show anyone outside of our family. How much he cared. How he'd pull me into his arms when I was sad and just make everything that little bit better. His strength. His determination, even when it was to do something that none of us agreed with. Or at least that was what I thought. Now I have to wonder if

Da— Jonas was behind the huge change in him that saw him joining the Royal Reapers and turning into a man I barely even recognised.

"Jodie?" I barely hear Stella's soft voice or the extra heat of her body as she moves closer to me. "Jodie. It's okay. Look at me."

Her burning hands land on my cheeks, and I'm dragged back to reality as I stare into her eyes. Eyes that look so much like a pair I'd happily drown in forever.

That realisation brings me back as my tears free fall over her fingers and my body trembles.

Her lips part to say something, but no words fall free.

"I... I want to tell you I'm sorry. I am sorry. I'm sorry you're hurting because of that monster. I'm sorry you've lost your brother, your father—even if he was a mirage. I'm sorry you got messed up in all of this. But Joker, he... he tried to kill me, Jodie. More than once. He hurt those I love more than anything else in the world, and I can't be sorry for protecting my family."

Pain rips through me. The sheer depth of my grief that I still battle on a daily basis threatens to consume me as her eyes implore me to understand. To understand and not to hate her for it.

"Deep breaths, yeah?" she whispers when my breathing becomes so erratic I can't help but wonder if I'm about to collapse in a sweaty, hyperventilating heap on the floor. "This probably wasn't the best place to have this conversation," she mutters to herself, realising her mistake with the lack of decent fucking air.

The seconds tick past, and eventually, I get my breathing back under control and my body begins to stop trembling, but even after Stella releases my face, she doesn't move back. Instead, she drops her hand to mine and squeezes it in support.

"I'm not a bad person, Jodie. None of us are, not really. But this life is dangerous. It's dog eat dog, and if we don't stand up for ourselves and those we love, then it'll all crumble around our feet. I need you to know though," she adds before I get a chance to say anything, "that you're a part of that now. You're one of us, even if you decide that all of this is too much and you walk away. I know how you feel about him. I saw it in your eyes that night I took you home, and I see it even stronger today. You might question it... a lot... but you're exactly where you belong with all of us. It might have been messy, and painful, and all shades of fucked up, but I believe that the two of you were meant to meet out of all of this. That motherfucker might not have given Toby much over the years other than pain and torture, but at the end of it all, he brought him you.

"I haven't been around Toby all that long. I don't know him as well as I should. But the difference in him since he met you, even when his intentions weren't entirely pure, was unmistakable.

"You're it for him, Jodie. I know it."

She pauses for a beat and looks down at her hand holding mine.

"Toby's not like the others. He's not a player like Nico and Alex, like Seb was," she adds with a roll of her eyes. "They've all got him pegged as the nice one because he's never really been a fuck 'em and chuck 'em kinda guy. But that's not true at all. He just wants... more. Something..."

"Kinkier," I blurt without even realising it.

Stella barks out a laugh. "Yeah, I didn't see that one coming either, don't worry. What I meant was that he's after something meaningful, not just some quick thing to blow off steam. He's welcomed you into his life because he wants you to stay. We all want you to stay. But we also understand how... unconventional this is.

"What he—"

"Enough," I say, cutting her words off immediately. "You don't need to convince me of anything here, Stella. I'm..." I suck in a breath, knowing that one day I might very well regret this decision, but not letting it consume me. "I'm not going anywhere."

Stella blows out a breath of relief that I don't think she even knew she was holding.

"He told me he loved me last night," I blurt.

"He does."

"It's crazy. It's—"

"Our lives. Things are intense in this part of the world. But we all understand. Seb was vile to me when I first moved here, but he's almost the most incredible person that I love with everything I am. Emmie and Theo, well, they're just fucked up. You wouldn't fit in if you weren't just a little bit crazy."

I can't help but laugh.

"The things those boys do when they're hurt and angry... they can be brutal. It's how they've been taught to handle shit situations. It takes a very special kind of girl—or guy, if any of them decide to swing that way—to be able to see through all of that, to see the big hearts they're hiding beneath their steel armour."

"I see it. I see it in you too," I confess.

A smile twitches at her lips.

"My training may have been less... hands-on than theirs, but I like to think I'm just as dangerous."

"Just as dangerous?" I ask, my brows shooting up. "Girl, with that body, you are way, way more dangerous than the boys. They never stood a chance with you and you know it."

She chuckles at my words.

"I'm not expecting you to forgive me... ever. But do you think we might one day be able to put the past where it belongs and find a way to move forward? To be friends?"

I fall silent for a beat as tears burn the backs of my eyes once more.

"The Joe that I grew up with, that I loved, died a long time before Joker did. Jonas got to him. Poisoned him. I didn't really understand what happened before, but I'm seeing it now.

"Do you know why he did it?"

Stella shakes her head. "I don't know the truth, no. But I agree with you. I believe that Jonas had filled his head with promises of this insane future, probably a powerful position beside him at the head of this Family, and your brother just ate it all up."

"It's just so unlike him."

"People do strange things for money and power, Jodie."

I nod, beginning to understand that statement more than I ever thought I would.

"I'm sorry too," I whisper. "I'm sorry that people I thought were decent human beings hurt you. You didn't deserve any of that."

"Maybe not," she says, "but it brought us right here, didn't it?" She bumps her shoulder against mine. "And I don't know about you, but I wouldn't want to be anywhere else in the world."

"Oh, I don't know. I could quite happily be on

some tropical island right now," I joke. "The company would be the same, though."

"I learned long ago that home isn't a place. I've been moved time and time again. Home is where your heart is. And mine belongs with those boys, one more than others, but all of them all the same."

"They're really quite something, aren't they?"

"They sure are. The girls are pretty fucking awesome too." A wide smile splits across my face. "Come on, I'm sweating my tits off." She grabs my hand and pulls me out of the sauna toward where Calli and Emmie are sitting on the end of two loungers with a massive plate of fresh fruit between them. But Stella doesn't slow down.

"I need to cool down. You in, Jodie?"

"I don't know what—" Before I can figure out her intentions, she picks up speed, dragging me along with her, and hauls us both into the pool, causing a massive splash in our wake.

My scream is cut off when I go under, my arms and legs flailing to get back to the surface.

"Oh my God, you're crazy," I bark right as two more bombs go off around us and the three of them come up laughing with wide smiles and excitement sparkling in their eyes.

BUTTERFLIES ARE HAVING a freaking riot in my belly as I sit in Stella's passenger seat as she drives us back toward their building.

"I hate to admit it, but I'm actually starting to like going to the spa," Emmie says from the back seat.

"Yes," Calli sings while Stella barks, "I fucking knew we'd break you eventually."

"Yeah, my skin is all soft and shit. Theo's gonna love it."

Calli makes a gagging noise. "Less talk about fucking my cousin, please," she requests, just like she has done multiple times this afternoon.

Emmie chuckles, letting me know that she's doing it on purpose, and I decide I should really join in.

"You should just be glad it's not your brother. I've seen his white arse railing—"

"Enough," she blurts.

"He really is quite an animal too. The way he made, Bri—"

"Oh my God, stop please," Calli begs, much to all our amusement.

"I like you, Jodie," Emmie announces. "You're like the missing piece to our puzzle."

"Thanks. You're not so bad yourself," I say, shooting her a wink over my shoulder.

"Do you think there could be anything serious

between Nico and your friend?" Stella asks me a little more seriously.

"Nah. Brianna is about as big a player as he is. She's convinced the only thing men are good for are their cocks and tongues and fingers."

"She's not entirely wrong," Emmie jokes.

"Sounds just like the female version of my pig of a brother. If I have to hear him say that a girl is only as good as her pussy is tight, I'm gonna vom on his feet."

"Pretty sure they could be the perfect match," Stella says, ignoring Calli.

"Oh, they totally are. Sadly, I think they're both too stubborn to see it."

"You should invite her to hang out with us, see if we can intervene."

"Nico does not need us playing matchmaker, Stel," Emmie says.

"I know. But how funny will it be to watch him fall at her feet?"

"Okay, yes. I would fucking pay to see him called to heel by his woman."

A round of laughter rings through the car before I turn back to look at Calli.

"So what about you then? I know the ins and outs—literally—of these two's relationships. You got anyone on the go?"

Calli's cheeks blaze with heat, but her eyes are like ice as she silently pleads with me to drop it.

Interesting.

"Nah, I'm not interested in those idiots."

"She's still hanging on to her V-card, aren't you, Baby C?" Stella teases.

"Don't fucking start," Calli warns.

"There's nothing wrong with waiting."

"Oh, I know. I was moaning about the nickname."

"You love it."

"Hmm..." she mumbles.

"You've been texting someone though, haven't you, Cal?" Emmie pipes up.

"Oooh, why don't I know about this?" Stella asks, shooting her friend a look in the rear-view mirror.

"Because it's nothing," Calli says. "What are your plans for Valentine's?" she asks, trying to deflect the conversation.

"I'm hoping there might be a trip to Hades in my future," Stella confesses. "I'm desperate to check the place out. Is it as good as I'm imagining?" she asks me.

"It's pretty insane, yeah."

"I want in too. You reckon Theo will let me tie him up?"

"Hell no, he's way too much of a control freak," Stella laughs.

"Oh, I don't know. I'm quite good at turning him around to my way of thinking."

"I'm sure the promise of a good blowy might help," I add.

"Hmm... is a double date in a sex club on Valentine's too cliché?"

"How the fuck should I know? I let a stranger take me there as a one-night stand."

"And look how well that turned out. Drama aside," Stella says, finally pulling into the underground garage beneath their flats.

"You're not tempted to move in then, Calli?" I ask, knowing she doesn't have a place here yet.

"I'm happy where I am right now. Far, far away from my brother and his overactive cock."

"I guess having the basement with its own entrance to yourself means you can sneak guys in and out pretty easily," I say, still hella intrigued about what she's hiding.

"I'm yet to find out, but my parents are hardly ever home so it shouldn't be an issue. Hell knows Nico got away with all sorts of shit down there."

My hands are trembling by the time we step out of the lift and walk toward Toby's flat.

"Are you nervous?" Stella asks.

"Yeah, and excited," I confess. "This... hanging out with you guys, meeting his friends—family—it's a big deal."

"You don't need to worry about the boys on the other side of that door. We've got them well under control," Emmie announces as Stella lets herself into the flat to the sound of shouting and cheering.

"What the fu—"

We round the corner to find the guys wrestling in the middle of the room, the dining table pushed aside to give them all space.

"Demon," Toby announces, causing Alex and Nico to pause as he jumps over them and sweeps me off my feet. "Mmm... you smell divine," he says, nuzzling my neck, making me giggle like a schoolgirl.

He backs me into the wall and twists his fingers in my hair, dragging my head back so I have no choice but to look into his eyes.

"They didn't scare you off then?" he asks. His tone is teasing, but his eyes give away his real concern.

"It was touch and go for a while, but I'm hungry so I thought I should make the most of the takeout they've promised me."

"Argh, Toby," I cry when he latches onto my neck, sucking on my skin until it starts to burn.

"You're a demon," he groans, grasping my jaw with his free hand, keeping me pinned to the wall with nothing but his hips.

"Exactly as you like me," I manage to get out before his lips slam down on mine.

I hear the boisterous cheers from his friends for about three seconds, but then his tongue sweeps against mine and I forget about everything including my goddamn name in favour of handing myself over to him.

I have no idea how long we stay there in our embrace, our bodies locked together, but eventually a deep, male, "Get a fucking room," breaks through my haze.

"Aw, you missing my girl, Nico?" I ask, shooting him a teasing look over Toby's shoulder.

"Uh… who?" he asks, his brow creasing as he fakes confusion.

"You're a shitty liar."

I look around the living room where everyone has collapsed on the couch—Stella into Seb's lap and Emmie into Theo's—before I stop on a new face. Or… not a new face, a very familiar one to another in the room.

"I think the fizz was stronger than I thought. I'm seeing double."

Toby laughs, putting me back on my feet as Calli emerges from his kitchen with drinks for the girls.

"Help yourself, Cal," Toby grunts.

"I already did, thanks," she quips, placing the beers on the coffee table seeing as both Stella and Emmie's lips are otherwise engaged right now.

"I'll take one of those if you're offering, Baby C," Alex says.

"I wasn't. Shift your arse over." She kicks him in the shin and his brows shoot up.

"Naw, come snuggle with your favourite boy."

She snorts a laugh but obviously decides against fighting him and falls down at his side. Although she's stiff as a fucking board as he wraps his arm around her shoulders and pulls her into his side.

"You smell good enough to eat, Baby C," Alex announces after dropping his nose to her hair.

"Put your mouth anywhere fucking near her and I'll—"

"So I'm assuming Alex is a twin," I say to Toby, ignoring Nico's threat to shove something so far up Alex's arse he'll never be able to remove it.

"Daemon," Toby says loudly, causing Alex's double to look over. "Jodie, Daemon. Daemon, Jodie."

He nods in greeting as I quickly take in the differences between them. Physically, they're almost identical, but their aura is totally different. Daemon's eyes are also darker, more mysterious, and he looks a hell of a lot tenser than his twin does right now as he continues taunting Nico.

"Your friends are—"

"Dickheads, but I love them anyway. Come on." Toby takes my hand and drags me toward the group. He falls into a space beside Emmie and Theo and drags me onto his lap.

"So what are we eating? I'm starving," Alex asks.

"Dude, you just ate two massive bags of crisps," Seb points out.

"Yeah, I'm a growing boy." He leans into Calli and loudly whispers. "I'll show you which bit grows later if you want."

Nico growls in irritation.

"Nico, bro. You're gonna give yourself an aneurysm if you carry on. Alex isn't gonna fuck your sister."

"In front of you," Alex adds just to continue poking the bear. And from the way Nico's face turns damn near purple with irritation, I've got to say I understand why they tease him so much, even if it is a bit mean.

20

TOBY

"You're making it really hard to leave, Demon," I growl as she tightens her leg that's thrown over my hip.

"Did you ever think that maybe that was my intention?"

"I offered to stay home," I remind her, rolling on top of her and nuzzling her neck.

"I know," she breathes, "but you need to go to school."

She presses her hands against my chest in a poor attempt to force me up.

"I'm sure you could teach me a few things, Demon."

"Oh, I don't know about that. You're the one with all the freaky shit."

"You love my freaky shit."

She shrugs, a downright filthy smile playing on her lips.

"Go to school, Tobias. I can't miss you while you're still here."

"You promise you'll be here when I get back?" I ask, brushing my nose against hers and almost stealing a kiss.

"Promise. If you're a good boy, I might even be right here, as naked as I am now."

"Fuck, Jodie. I'm going to be hard all fucking day now," I confess, rubbing the head of my solid cock through her folds, coating her in my cum that's spilling out from only a few moments ago.

"I think..." I start but pause when I circle her clit and her wanton moan rips through the air. "I need to fuck all this back inside you before I leave."

"Toby," she cries when I thrust forward, letting her velvet walls surround me once more.

Safe to say, but by the time I'm pulling my blazer on and hooking my tie around my neck, I'm thoroughly late.

"If I don't get the grades I need from here on out, I'm blaming you," I tell her as she follows me wearing nothing but one of my shirts.

"Then I guess I need to work on my motivational skills."

"Oh yeah? And what might they look like, Demon?" I ask, spinning back around to her once I'm at the door.

She thinks for a minute. "Blowjob for every A."

"That does sound appealing, but I think you can probably do better than that."

"Hmm... I'll think something up when I'm rolling around your bed today while you're sitting in class."

She steps up to me and cups my junk through my trousers.

"You're bad," I growl, wrapping my hand around her throat and holding her captive.

"You're worse," she teases.

"Okay, I really need to go. You've got everything you need, right?"

"Sure do," she agrees.

"And you remember how to use the biometric scanner to get in and out?"

"Yes, Mum," she drawls. "I've got it covered. Now go, before you're even later and end up failing. Forever is a long time without coming down my throat, Tobias."

"You drive a hard bargain. I'll see you later." I steal one more kiss before ripping the door open and forcing myself to walk away from her.

Originally, she wanted me to take her home. But after a little discussion, and an orgasm or two, I turned her around to my way of thinking. There's just something so fucking hot—so fucking right—about the thought of coming home and finding her here.

I look back down the hallway as I get to the lift, wishing she was standing there watching me, and continue to fight with myself not to just stay with her.

I know she's right. I could very easily let my feelings—my obsession—for her consume every second of my life. *Again.*

But deep down, there's this real fear that she's going to run. That the last few days have been nothing but a tease for something I can't have.

It's all just been too... easy, and I'm waiting for the other shoe to drop.

She took the news about Stella shooting Joker too well. She's fitting into my life, my friends, my entire fucking world entirely too easily. And nothing ever is that simple.

My fists curl as the lift doors open before me and I squeeze my eyes closed as I try to convince myself that leaving her right now is the right thing to do.

I've got her tracked, I'll know if she leaves and where she goes. Something she's more than aware of, and amazingly hasn't asked me to stop.

I just... I can't force aside that something is wrong. But I swallow it down as I step into the lift and put some more distance between us.

"BRO, YOU LOOK FUCKING WIPED," Seb says when he's the first to find me in the common room at lunch.

I decided against sitting in the restaurant like we usually do and just grabbed a sandwich so I could hide in here. Maybe get some sleep, because he's not wrong. I haven't exactly got much rest since I found Jodie in my flat on Saturday afternoon.

"Things with Jodie that good, huh?"

"Yeah, that's the problem."

"Uhh… how is getting laid until you can't keep your eyes open a bad thing?" he asks, dropping onto the sofa beside me.

We're in the very back corner of the common room, hidden behind a few rows of bookcases. There's usually a group of book nerds surrounding it, but I made the out-of-character move to pull rank over them when I got here not so long ago so I could make use of the solitude. That's more of a Nico or Alex move, and probably why they looked at me for a good minute as if I'd just sprouted an extra head. But they soon figured out that I wasn't joking and was a big enough threat to their remaining time at Knight's Ridge that they quickly grabbed their stuff and fucked off.

I stare at him for a beat, the need to talk to someone who understands all this crazy shit burning through me.

"It's… I can't…" I blow out a breath as he smiles in amusement at me.

"She's fucked your brain right out of you, hasn't she?"

"What is she doing, Seb? Why, after everything, is she still willing to be anywhere near me?" I ask, deciding to just go for it and bleed out all over him.

"Because despite all that, she fucking cares, man."

"But why? After everything I did, she should be running in the opposite direction."

"Yeah, right alongside Stella and Emmie, but they're still here too."

"Stella told her about Joker."

"Yeah, she told me."

"And Jodie is okay with it. She's barely said a word about it."

"She's probably just trying to get her head around everything. Deal with it all. This situation, us… we're a lot to take."

"Yeah, I just don't get it."

He stares at me for a beat, shifting in his seat, showing me just how uncomfortable he is having this heart to heart with me. I'm grateful that he doesn't back away from it.

"How quickly did you know that she was it for you?"

My lips part to answer, but no words come.

"The first night you spoke to her? Before that, when you were just stalking her?" He must see something in my eyes that gives him the answer he's looking for. "So you fell for her before she even knew you existed, yet you're doubting that she can fall for you after spending a few weeks together?" He quirks his brow at me.

"But all the things I've done—" I start.

"We don't fall in love with people's actions, Toby. We fall in love with the person, their hearts."

My chin drops at his words, all the air rushing from my lungs.

"Thank fuck, because I sure don't deserve Stella otherwise."

"Shit, Seb. That's—"

"Deeper than you were expecting?" he asks, clearly knowing just how out of character his words are.

"Well... yeah."

"You're sitting here feeling like no one could possibly understand, but you're missing the fucking point. I've been there. I am there. Theo too. Do you think we've not had the exact same fears that you're having right now?

"Both of us fucked up beyond belief with our girls. But they saw past it. They dug beneath the bullshit we show the rest of the world, and they found the scared little boys living deep inside who desperately just want to be loved like we believe we can't be.

"Yeah, you fucked up. Is that what you want me to tell you? But that doesn't define you, Toby. Your past, your mistakes... they're not the most important things when it comes to Jodie. She wants what's in here." He leans over and pats my chest. "And despite all the shit with Jonas and Joker, there's a fucking good heart in there, man."

Emotion clogs my throat as I stare at him.

"Trust her. Trust her to know what she wants. Trust her to deal with this in her own way. Not everyone out there is like us. They don't all go off killing their enemies or anyone who's hurt those they love. As hard as it might be to believe, some people actually sit back and think things through, process things properly, and come to sensible conclusions.

"You've shown her so much. Too much to have processed already. She's going to be working through all this shit, this grief, for a long time, I'm sure. No different from me." His eyes lower for a beat as he thinks of those he's lost. His dad, his mum, his little sister.

"Grief is... unique. Every single person deals with it differently. But who's to say that just because she's grieving, she can't fall in love? That she can't see beneath the armour you wear every day to the real person who's existing beneath?

"If she wants you to stand by her side while she figures all this out and puts herself back together, then why the fuck are you questioning that?

"If you really love her, take every fucking chance you can get, because trust me, it's fucking worth it."

I blink back the emotion that's threatening to make itself known.

"You really love her, don't you?" I ask.

Seb's brow creases in confusion as I turn the conversation on him. "Stella? Yeah. Yeah, I fucking do. She's... everything.

"Trust me, I understand exactly what you're feeling right now. I battle with it most days, thinking that she deserves so much more than this, than me. But ultimately, she's chosen this. And I have to believe that if she didn't want it, she'd let that fact be known. Probably painfully so. You need to do the same."

I suck in a breath as I roll a handful of words around my head that I don't want to say.

"And what if she changes her mind?"

"Then it'll hurt like a bitch to let her go, but at least you'll have had that time with her. You tried. You gave it your all. What more can you really ask for?"

"Fuck," I breathe, falling back into the sofa cushions.

I might have my eyes closed, but I sense when we're joined by another.

"What's going on?" Theo asks, coming to stand in front of us.

"Just giving our boy some advice on his love life."

"From how they were molesting each other last night, I'm not sure they've got all that many issues," he quips. But when I open my eyes and look at him, I see it. I see the same torment lingering in his dark depths that Seb just explained.

He glances at the floor before dropping to his arse and resting his forearms on his bent knees opposite us.

"Welcome to the club, Tobes. It's fun, but hell… it's a real head fuck.

"No one can tell you what's right or wrong when it comes to love and relationships. Just fucking look at me." He holds up his left hand. "I'm fucking married."

"Okay, so maybe I should be less concerned about the speed of all this when you say things like that."

Theo chuckles. "Enjoy the ride, Tobes. There's no pressure, no expectations. You want her, just do fucking everything in your power to keep her."

"And make her scream," Seb offers. "Often."

I shake my head, a smile playing on my lips as I look between the two of them.

A huge weight lifts off my shoulders, one I didn't truly appreciate the heaviness of.

If the most important people in my life are behind me—behind us—then what the fuck am I even questioning it for?

MY LAST LESSONS of the day and then football training fucking drag. Knowing that she's inside my flat, possibly naked and waiting for me, meant that every second felt like an hour.

By the time I walk out of the showers after practice with a towel around my waist, my patience has just about run out.

"Someone's on a promise," Nico jokes as I try dragging a pair of sweats up my still wet legs, failing miserably and ending up on my arse on the bench.

"Better than what you're on," I tease. The boss messaged both him and Theo earlier to call them in tonight. Things are heating up in Lovell, and I've got a feeling shit is about to hit the fan. I just really fucking hope they're not planning on doing anything tonight, or any fucking night, and screw up my time with my girl.

"It's not all bad. Meeting with the boss, then I'll head down to the basement, see what girls are working tonight."

"None that will want to be within a square foot

of you," Theo joins in. "You're just jealous, bro. Toby, Seb and I are all going home later to our women, and you haven't even got so much as a goldfish waiting for you."

"Fuck you, I could have a whole harem of women waiting in my flat if I wanted."

"Sure, I don't doubt it. It's just a shame there's only one you really want, huh?"

Nico barks out a laugh that is nothing but fake before dragging his hoodie over his head, flipping us all off he blows out of the locker room, leaving us all laughing in his wake.

"We need to meet this chick that's got him all tied up. She must really be something," Alex muses.

"She is," I say with a smile. "She's Nico with a banging body and a smarter mouth."

"Don't let your girl be hearing you say that, Doukas," Seb teases.

"There's no competition. Nico is welcome to his firecracker."

"My point still stands. I want to meet her."

"So you can drive him to the brink of insanity flirting with her just like you do his sister?" I ask with a smirk. As amusing as it might be, watching him teasing Nico with Calli, we all know he's playing with fire. I'm also not entirely sure if it's all completely innocent and purely for poking the bear. There's something in the way he looks at her that makes me wonder if he'd more than willingly take things further with her. I mean, I get it, she's hot. That little girl who used to annoy us with her Barbies and threaten us with glitter sure did grow up good. Even more so now she's got Stella and Emmie as bad influences. I might not be interested in going there, but I can sure see the appeal.

"Yeah, maybe. I'm always up for entertainment," Alex says, rubbing his hands together.

"So that's all it's about with Calli then?" Seb asks, clearly on the same page as me.

"Damn right it is," Theo barks, not willing to even consider the possibility that Alex might actually be interested in his cousin.

"It could be worse, man," I say, trying to defuse the situation as Theo continues to glare at Alex.

"How?" Theo spits.

"You could still be fighting off that Italian fuck," Seb reminds him.

"It could be a Wolf," I offer.

"None of them are that fucking stupid. We've already proved what happens when they go anywhere near her."

"So what are you left with?" I ask. "She's going to end up with one of us," I say, not meaning literally one of the five of us, but someone within the Family.

Theo's teeth grind as I'm sure he pictures a few

of the faces of the younger members of the Family we work with. I can't deny, I can't really come up with a good candidate out of the lot of them. Maybe Alex isn't so bad.

"She can just stay single forever," he finally says, reaching for his bag and throwing it over his shoulder. "Get cats or something."

"Fucking hypocrite," Alex mutters as Theo stalks off.

Both Seb and I turn our eyes on him as he bends over, pulling his socks on.

"What?" he snaps, sensing our attention.

"Do you actually like her?"

"Calli? Nah, I'm just yanking their chains. I need some kind of fucking entertainment around here while you're all off fucking your girls."

I watch him for a few seconds, trying to figure out if he's bullshitting us or not, but in the end, I give up. I've got somewhere much more appealing to be than standing having this discussion in our stinking locker room.

I drive home like a bat out of hell, and in record time, I'm pulling up in our underground garage and heading for the stairs. The lift is probably faster, but the thought of standing there just watching the numbers climb puts me off, and I head for the stairs.

My lungs hurt and my legs are like jelly by the time I've got to the penultimate floor where our flats are, but I don't let it slow me down as I race toward my front door and press my hand to the scanner.

I rush into my living room, my eyes darting everywhere as I search for her.

"Demon, where are you hiding?" I call, excitement stirring in my belly.

Not finding her, I turn toward the bedrooms.

"Are you naked in my bed, baby?" I growl, my cock hardening at the thought of finding her laid out on my bed, waiting for me.

Shit, I damn near drool, and I rush forward.

But the second I fly around the doorway, I come to a grinding halt.

And everything comes crashing down around me.

21

JODIE

I had every intention of getting up and heading to Mum's so that I could grab some things. I wasn't planning on moving in with Toby, but I figured a couple of days to continue talking was probably a good idea. It's not like I had anything better to do.

I know that to everyone else, this thing between us looks too easy. And I guess a part of it is. Falling for Toby, being with him, and allowing him to take some of my weight, my grief, my worry, is easy. It's so natural it almost feels like he's always been a part of my life. But then there's this whole other ugly part of us, something that I barely even know how to process let alone attempt to deal with.

My head and my heart seem to be at constant war right now.

I want to be with him. The way he makes my heart race, my skin tingle, and butterflies erupt in my belly is like nothing I've ever experienced before. But am I just setting myself up for a massive fall?

Is it all too good to be true?

Can I really see past everything that's happened?

Does love really always win?

I lingered in his flat, poking deeper into his life by looking into his cupboards and trying to find anything that might help convince me that I'm crazy for even thinking this is possible and forcing my hand to turn my back on the whole thing.

But I found nothing.

In fact, I discovered a whole heap of things that just convinced me more that the boy I first met, the sweet, caring, loving guy really is who he is. I found a box at the bottom of one of his wardrobes with birthday cards from his mum and friends over the years. In there were other sweet keepsakes, like drawings done by small kids. Toby doesn't have any younger siblings aside from Stella, so I can only assume they're his friends' little brothers and sisters. I even found his childhood teddy sitting up on a shelf beside a photo of him and his mum.

Everything I discovered just made me fall harder, which only confused me more.

It wasn't until I was descending through the building, standing alone in the middle of the lift and staring at the lower ground levels that everything hit me at once.

I spilled out of that enclosed space with my heart in my throat and tears cascading down my cheeks.

I had a car key that Toby said I could use today clutched tightly in my hand, and the only thing I could think about was running away.

And that's exactly what I did.

I don't even remember the journey across the city. I have no idea how I—or the car—made it here in one piece, but thankfully we did.

Even hours later, my heart aches, my head spins and my eyes burn with the tears that I've shed for everything I've lost.

But just as I said to Stella yesterday, those men I'm grieving aren't the men I've actually lost. It's a massive head fuck, knowing that the good memories I have of both my dad and my brother have now been tainted by reality.

I sit on a bench overlooking a play park that Joe and I spent many, many hours at as kids. It's only a few streets over from our house. We used to play here from sunrise to sunset, often completely losing track of time, ensuring our days ended with Mum coming to find us with a furious expression on her face.

Joe always took the blame. He was older and happily took the responsibility for our screw-ups.

It's so hard to imagine that little boy ending up so brainwashed that he would try to kill someone. But as unbelievable as I might think it to be, I know it's true.

I saw the change in my brother first-hand. I saw the darkness set in, his need for violence that I never understood. It was so at odds with the boy I'd grown up with, but it leaves me with no doubt that he did what Stella explained to me yesterday.

I might not have known the truth about my father, but I know how much Joe idolised him. He used to look at him like he literally hung the moon in the sky. I did too, to a point, but Joe was besotted. All Dad had to do was ask him to jump and he'd immediately ask how high. It shouldn't really be a shock that Dad set up his final fall. I can only hope that he really thought it would have a better outcome, that they would win.

That thought sends a violent tremor down my spine, because if they did win, then Stella wouldn't be here right now. Toby and Maria would be the ones grieving. Toby's entire family would be grieving. And haven't they already been through enough?

What would have happened next? Toby has said that Jonas's game plan was about power. So who would he have gone after next? Who would the next part of his plan end up hurting?

The faces of Toby's friends flicker through my

eyes, and I can't help but wonder where they all fitted into Jonas's sick and twisted games.

My body trembles with the cold, and I wrap my arms around my legs tighter in the hope of both warming myself up and holding myself together all at the same time.

I have no idea what time it is, but I know I need to move. But being here… it makes me feel closer to that little boy I once knew, to that life I once had.

A sob rips from my throat as I watch a couple of kids making the most of the last few minutes of light on the slide.

I took it all for granted. I thought I had the perfect life, and while it's turned out that that is far from the truth, I wish now that I stopped even just once more to tell Joe how much I loved him, how awesome I thought he was.

It probably would have made very little difference in the grand scheme of things, but at least I would have known that he was aware of how much he meant to me.

"I'm sorry, Joe," I whimper at the sudden despair of feeling like I've let him down somehow, that I could have done something along the way to stop the chain of events.

"None of it is your fault."

My entire body jolts at his words, at the deep rumble of his voice, and my breath catches.

Have I really been here that long?

"Toby," I breathe, twisting to look back at him over my shoulder.

He looks wrecked, his face pale, his lips pressed thin, but in his eyes there's relief. So much fucking relief that it makes my chest ache.

"Shit. I'm so sorry, I—"

He shakes his head as he rounds the bench I'm sitting on, and I finally uncurl myself and place my feet on the ground.

"Shh," he soothes, reaching out and pulling me into his body.

He holds me tightly as my body trembles in his arms.

"I've got you."

His soft words only make the torment inside me worse, and I crumble once more. The only difference from the rest of this afternoon is that I've got someone to hold me up.

I have no idea how long we stand there for, but by the time I pull back from his chest, the sun has finally set and the kids in the playground have gone.

Taking my hand, Toby tugs me down on the bench and wraps me up into his warm body.

"Talk to me, baby. Tell me what's going on in your head."

And so I do. I dive as deep into my happy childhood memories as I can. I talk about Joe, and Jonas, until my mouth is dry, my throat is sore, and my heart hurts so much that I'm sure someone has pushed their hand straight into my chest and ripped it clean out.

Toby is silent, soaking up my stories of happier times. He's the pillar of support I needed in order to fully dive into this. And although I know my stories must be hurting him, he doesn't react in any way but to encourage me, to hold me up, and stop me from completely crumbling at his feet. I don't think I'll ever be able to explain to him just how grateful I am for that.

Aside from the obvious, he's always been like this. He's always known exactly what I've needed and given me this solace, despite his own pain, to allow me to grieve. It's how I know that he really is this sweet, caring guy. Time and time again, he's pushed his own demons and nightmares aside to just help me deal with my own.

By the time my memories begin to dry up and my guilt sets in from not remembering any more, I'm shivering from the cold.

"Come on, baby. I'll take you home."

I don't say a word as he pulls me to my feet. I can't. I'm numb and lost in my childhood memories, desperately trying to search the depths of my mind for those I've forgotten.

The second we're in the car, Toby turns the heat to its highest setting and in only minutes, hot air is filling the space around me, although it does little to warm my heart. That feels like it's been wrapped in a layer of ice that's never going to thaw.

I barely register the direction we're heading in until the car slows to a stop on a very familiar street.

"W-what are we..." My words trail off as Toby kills the engine and turns to look at me.

Reaching out, he takes my hand in his and squeezes as his eyes search mine.

"This is fucking killing me, Jodie. I need you to know that this is literally the last fucking thing I want to do right now, but equally, I know it's right.

"Everything I said to you this weekend is true. I fucking love you, Demon."

I thought I'd run out of tears over the past few hours, but just those few words from him and they spill over once more.

"I never could have imagined all of the things I'd feel for you when I started learning about who you are or even the first night we really met. But I do. I'm so fucking gone for you that I don't know what to do about it. I'm addicted to you, fucking obsessed with you. And I know it's not healthy."

"W-what are you s-saying here?" I stutter out as fear wraps itself around me.

"What I'm saying, Jodie, is that I want this. I want you. So fucking badly I can barely think about anything else. But I'm not the important one here. I fucked this up with you before I even knew who you were. And you're going through so much right now, much of which I've caused.

"You need time to deal with all that. I need you to be sure that this is—that I am—really what you want."

"Yes, Toby. It is. You are."

"And if that is true, then it will still be the same in a few weeks once you've had a chance to really get your head around everything."

"A few weeks?" I breathe. My bottom lip trembles and my heart shatters as realisation of what he's telling me settles in my head.

"This has been... incredible, crazy, intense. And fast. And the truth behind us even meeting is a lot to take. I get that, I do. And I need to give you the time to come to terms with that.

"The last few days have been amazing, but today I've realised that I've swept you up in this life, and finding you this evening was just proof of that.

"All my life, I've been pegged as the nice one, and I've always resented it. But the past few months I've shed that persona and I've discovered that I've hated it even more. I want to be that good person again. I want to be the nice one, and I want to be worthy of you."

"You are, Toby. You are so sweet and so caring. You have no idea how much you helped me overcome all of this before you—" I slam my lips closed, stopping me from addressing what happened that night in Toby's bathroom.

"And I want to be that person again, and the best way I can figure to do that is to give you time. Once all of this has settled and you've had time to process it, if you want to come back to me then I'll be waiting with open arms. And if you decide it's all too much, that you can't forgive me, forgive Stella, then I'll walk away and let you move on with your life."

An ugly sob rips from my throat.

"I don't want that," I argue. "I want this, I do."

"Then we'll have it, baby. Just take this time. Mourn your losses, do whatever you need to do so that I know you're making the right decision."

Unable to argue with his point, I let out a heavy sigh.

"You're..." I pause, unable to find the right word to describe everything he is. "Everything."

He shakes his head. "I'm not, baby. I'm so far from that right now it's laughable. But I want to be. I want to be your everything."

I nod, sniffling unattractively.

His eyes leave mine, catching on something over my shoulder.

"You should go in. Your mum's waiting for you."

My heart twists painfully at the thought of

walking away from him, but before I get to say anything, he seems to read my mind.

"We're not over, Jodie. Not unless you want us to be. I'm right at the end of the phone. I'm here for whatever you need. But I refuse to drag you into my life, into this relationship until you've had time to really come to terms with everything."

"I hate this," I admit. "But I also understand it. Today has been hard."

"I know, baby," he says, cupping my cheek and wiping my tears away with his thumb. "But things are going to get better, I promise."

"Thank you," I whisper and he frowns, not understanding why I would need to say those words. "Thank you for being honest with me this weekend, for telling all the ugly and painful parts of your life."

"There's one more thing," he confesses.

"Oh?"

His eyes close for a beat, letting me know that whatever is going to come next will hurt, and I attempt to prepare myself for the blow.

"My scar," he whispers. "The one on my chest," he clarifies.

I remember him shunning the subject when I tried to talk about it before I knew the truth about his life. Now I know who he is, I have a whole host of new ideas about how his skin has been damaged in such a way.

"You were shot, weren't you?"

He nods. "Seb and I both took a bullet one night last year in our attempts to protect Stella."

"Shit," I hiss, all the air rushing from my lungs as I read between the lines. "It was Joe," I state, reaching out and pressing my palm to the scar high up on his chest.

"Yeah."

"He could have killed you. He could have killed all of you."

"He could have. But he didn't."

No. He was the one who ended up dead.

"What are you going to do about Jonas?" I ask, remembering what he said about not doing anything until I've decided if I want to see him or not.

"My offer still stands. He'll remain alive until you make a decision. Speak to your mum about it. If she wants to see him, then I can arrange that too."

"I will," I promise.

"Go inside and warm up, baby. I'll message you when I get home."

"Yeah?" I ask, feeling a little better about this whole thing with just those few words.

"Yeah. I'm not going anywhere if you don't want me to."

"You're incredible, Toby."

He shakes his head, but he doesn't argue.

"I don't deserve you, but if you let me, I'll spend the rest of my life trying to be worthy."

My lips part to respond, but he beats me to it.

"Go. And if you need me, you know where I am."

His eyes hold mine, and it breaks my heart that he's suddenly unsure around me.

Reaching out, I wrap my hand around the back of his neck and pull his lips to mine.

Our kiss is full of pain and longing, but thankfully, I don't taste a goodbye on his lips, and I swear to God that he can't on mine either, because this isn't the end, it's just… we've hit pause to do the right thing.

"I'll talk to you soon, okay?"

"I'll be waiting, baby. Go and do your thing."

He smiles at me, although it doesn't meet his eyes before I find the strength from somewhere deep inside me to push the door open and climb out.

I open the door, spotting a shadow moving in the hallway through the crack, but I don't step inside until I've forced myself to watch Toby drive away. And when I do stumble inside, I fall right into the arms of the woman waiting for me.

"Shh, baby. It's going to be okay."

22

TOBY

The past week and a half have been hell. Pure fucking hell. But I stand by my decision to drop Jodie off at her mum's last Monday night. And as it is, even if I hadn't done that, it isn't like we'd have actually spent any time together. If I haven't been at school, then I've been working. We've spent more time than ever in Lovell this week, and quite frankly, I'm getting fucking fed up of wasting my time over there. Nothing is happening despite the threats from the OG crew. So far, they seem to be all mouth, and it's getting on my last fucking nerve.

At least I had to work Valentine's night. It somewhat kept my mind off the fact that I should have been in a nice restaurant, giving my girl another one of the best nights of her life.

I had it all planned, all booked.

But it all went to shit, right along with the rest

of my life when I decided to do the right thing and give her the space she deserved.

"Hey, Bro. How's it going?" Stella asks, inviting herself into my flat.

We've got an hour before we've gotta head back to the estate. I'm surprised she's not busy wearing Seb out before we head to battle—or not, which is probably more the case.

"Yeah, it's... going," I mutter, putting my phone to sleep and dropping it to the sofa beside me.

I haven't heard anything from Jodie since first thing yesterday morning, and it's fucking killing me, not knowing that she's okay or where her head is at with all this.

"Still no news?" Stella asks, scruffing up my hair before she rounds the sofa and drops down on the end.

I shake my head.

"She'll come back to you, Tobes. Have faith."

I did have faith last week. But as the days have passed, it's been waning. Our conversations are getting less and less, and it's terrifying me that she's on the verge of pulling the plug. That our time apart has just proved to her that she doesn't need me and my twisted way of existence in her life.

"Only time will tell."

I glance up just in time to see guilt flicker through her eyes.

"What?" I ask, not willing to let her keep her secrets if they've got anything to do with Jodie.

"I saw her last night."

Anger surges through me. "And you're only just telling me this now."

"She didn't call me to talk about you," she assures me.

"So what did she want to talk about?" I ask, although the answer is obvious.

"What do you think?" She quirks a brow at me. "She just wanted to hear more from my side on the whole situation."

"How did she seem?"

"Good. She looked..." I hold my breath, unsure as to whether I want her to say that she looked good without me in her life or that she looked like she was missing me. "Good. I think she's been sleeping better, resting. Processing."

"G-good. That's... good."

"She did tell me something interesting though, which I'm assuming you don't know." I quirk a brow at her. "Did you know who Nico hooked up with Valentine's night?"

"His right hand, as far as I'm aware," I mutter.

"I mean, knowing Nico, he probably made use of his own palm too, but no. Turns out, he had a booty call. A kinky booty call where he left his Valentine tied to the bed. Jodie had to go rescue her."

"Fuck off," I bark, not believing what I'm hearing. "Nico spent Valentine's with Brianna and hasn't said a word about it?"

"Apparently so. Bri was pissed."

"I can imagine. He's so fucking whipped by her."

"I desperately want to meet her."

"I think you'd get on like a house on fire. If Jodie comes back to me, maybe I'll let it happen."

"Let it, pfft," she scoffs. "Jodie and me are like this," she says, crossing her fingers. "My new sister-in-law will introduce me to her bestie."

"Don't tempt fate, Stel."

"She's coming back to you. Trust me."

"So she did say something," I urge.

"Nope. I could just sense it."

"Fucking clairvoyant now, huh?" I ask, pushing from the sofa and pocketing my phone.

"Where are you going?"

"Heading upstairs to see our resident Casanova. I'm sure you can make yourself useful before we have to leave. I bet Seb is lonely right now."

"He's showering," she says, following me toward the door.

"He's naked and you're here with me. What have you done with my sister?"

"I'm more than happy to storm in and let him fuck my brains out against the shower wall. It sure wouldn't be the first time," she says, amusement filling her tone.

"You're a ho, little sister."

"Aw, you love me really, big bro."

"You know I do."

Wrapping my arm around her shoulder, I drop a kiss to her temple before delivering her back to her flat and then jogging up the stairs to Nico's penthouse.

Pressing my hand to the scanner, I let myself in and race toward the living room right as a shrill female voice I recognise fills the flat.

"That's it. You're such a fucking bad boy." I snort a laugh, knowing all too well that I'm not about to walk in on Nico balls deep in some girl.

"You fucking know it, baby," he grunts before a loud moan rips through the air.

"Spending some personal time with your favourite girl?" I ask, shamelessly walking in on him with his preferred porn star still taking it up the arse on his massive flat screen. He quickly tucks himself back into his sweats and wipes himself down with his discarded shirt.

"If you wanted to watch, Tobes, you only had to ask. I know it's been a dry few days for you. Get me good and drunk and I might even let you take advantage of me."

"I ain't that fucking desperate," I mutter, falling onto the other sofa, confident I'm not about to get his jizz stains on my arse. "Anyway," I say, pinning him with a serious look. "Were you ever going to tell me about your Valentine's night?"

"Well, the fact that I haven't told you thus far probably answers your question."

I shake my head at him. Nico always kisses and tells, so the fact that it's been over a week and he hasn't so much as uttered a word about it tells me more than I think he wants me to know.

"I can't believe I was home, lonely and miserable and you were having it off with my girl's best friend and you didn't even tell me."

"I fucking knew she'd spill," he mutters. "Can't fucking trust chicks."

"She didn't tell me actually, Stella did."

"Oh great." Getting up, he heads for the kitchen and pulls a beer out of the fridge.

"We're working tonight," I remind him when he cracks the top and damn near drinks the whole thing in one go.

"Why the fuck do you think I'm drinking? Another night in Lovell babysitting Archer and his fucking minions. Jesus, can life get any more fucking boring?"

I stare at him as he paces back and forth.

"So it's got nothing to do with Bri—"

"Don't," he spits. "Don't say her name."

"Dude, you've got it fucking bad."

"Fuck off have I. It was one night of fun. That's it."

"You mean *another* night of fun. One you didn't tell me about. Which is weird, because you usually tell me the ins and outs of every girl you hook up with, literally."

"I was thinking of you, actually. I didn't want to rub it in your face when things are weird with Jodie."

My lips part to respond, but I quickly find that I'm at a loss for words. That kind of consideration is out of character for Nico, but for once, I find that I don't want to call him out on it.

Maybe he's bullshitting me and trying to cover up his feelings for Brianna, or maybe he is being genuine. It doesn't really matter.

"So what's the deal tonight, then? Same shit as the rest of the week?"

"Apparently so. Theo and I tried telling the boss that we should just go after the OGs and get this fucking over with, but we were told quite clearly that this isn't our fight. We're just the support act."

I can't help but laugh. I bet that went down like a sack of shit with Nico.

"Shit could be worse," I mutter, thinking of some of the bullshit jobs we've been sent out on over the years.

"Could it? I need some fucking action, man.

I'm gunning for a decent fucking fight and they're not taking the bait."

"It'll happen. They're playing the long game, waiting for us to think it's not going to happen. And when we show weakness, they'll strike. They know they stand less of a chance of taking the Wolves over if they've got us on side. They're not stupid."

He stares at me, and I swear I can see the fucking cogs turning behind his eyes.

"You're right."

Pulling his phone from his pocket, he swipes the screen, finds a contact and marches toward his bedroom as he puts it to his ear.

"I'm going to shower. Be ready."

I salute him as he disappears down the hall.

"Theo," he barks when the call connects. "This is fucking happening tonight. I'm sick of waiting."

He pauses.

"Yeah. Yeah, so what I'm thinking is..."

A door slams and his thoughts are cut off. It's probably for the best, because Nico's plans never are the most fucking sensible.

JUST OVER AN HOUR LATER, the five of us are in Theo's car on the edge of the Wolves territory, waiting for the nod that something is about to kick off.

Usually, we'd already been in sight by now, parked up at the Den and making our presence known. I just really hope these two know what they're doing, because I could really do without the wrath of the boss if this goes tits up tonight.

"What the fuck are we actually waiting for?" Seb barks after we've been sitting here in the dark for thirty minutes. "If I knew tonight was gonna be this shit, I'd have taken my girl's offer of continuing what we started in the shower."

I roll my eyes at him, knowing full well that he's just trying to get a rise out of me. There's no way Stella didn't march back into their flat and tell him exactly what we talked about.

"Dude, if we're forced to sit here much longer, I'll come fucking join you," Alex mutters.

"You'd be so fucking lucky," Seb barks. "I'm sure Calli is all cold and lonely tonight. You could keep her company."

From my spot in the back of the car, I watch as Nico's fists curl on his lap and his jaw tics with frustration.

"We're waiting for Daemon," Theo tells us, ignoring Seb's attempt to bait the both of them.

"Waiting for him to do what exactly?"

Theo's eyes meet mine in the mirror.

"I thought you all wanted this over."

"Well, yeah but—" My words are cut off when his phone rings through the speakers.

"Yeah," he barks when the call connects.

"They're on the move. Get your arses to the Den."

"You got it. Thanks, man."

"What did he do?" Alex asks.

"Nothing much. Just poked the hornet's nest a little," Theo says, starting the car. "Something we should have done days ago."

"Ready to party, boys?"

Seb cracks his knuckles. "Fuck yes. Let's wipe these old motherfuckers from the face of the earth and get home to our girls."

My heart sinks at his words.

If fucking only.

23

JODIE

"Hey, this is a nice surprise," Bri says as she finds me loitering outside the school she's currently working at like a creep.

"I thought we could go for coffee," I say with a smile. "I feel like I've hardly seen you. You know, aside from saving your arse last week."

She cuts me a scathing look. "What happened to never talking about that again?"

"You really think that's going to be possible?" I can't help the smile that splits across my face as the image of her tied to that hotel bed and cursing a million painful deaths on the guy who put her there fills my mind.

Fair play to Nico, though. If his plan was to leave her with a lasting impression and a reason for revenge in order to see her again, then he hit the nail right on the head.

She's gunning to wrap her hands around his throat for leaving her to the mercy of whoever she was brave enough to call for help.

I've been desperate to tell Toby what our best friends had been up to, but for some reason, I kept it back when we've chatted since, preferring to focus on us. The same couldn't be said for when Stella agreed to come over last night for a chat. The whole situation just fell from my lips, much to her amusement.

I knew that I needed to not only work through this whole situation with Toby, but that I also needed to process her part in all of it, and I really appreciated her making the effort to come and talk to me. Although I can't deny that it only made me miss Toby more.

What he did last Monday night wrecked me. But I understand.

I was a mess. My grief, my confusion, my overwhelming feelings for him... they had all collided and were sending me on a collision course to self-destruction, I'm sure.

I couldn't see it.

But he could.

And he was right. Although hard, I've needed this time.

Mom and I have talked. Properly talked. About the past, what her life was really like and the things she experienced over the years with Jonas. She's fully explained her reasons for being okay with him having another woman, and although I don't necessarily agree, I do understand. She may have been treated better than Maria in all of this, but she's still been manipulated by a master all the same.

We discussed Joe until we were both sobbing, emotional messes as we tried to dissect where everything went wrong with him. But even after hours of trying to pinpoint the moment, I don't think one specific event was the turning point. Knowing what I know now about Jonas, I can't help wondering if he had this plan all along, if his manipulation of his son started from the very first day he was born.

It's also allowed me to think about him. The man who stole my heart when I thought it was too broken to even feel anything. But I quickly realised that this time wasn't about focusing on all that good, on the way he picked me up and held me together. It's about the bad. About the man who has my father locked in his basement, the man who only walked into my life because of the blood running through my veins. Of his plans for vengeance using me as a pawn in his game to hurt the man who spent his life hurting him in return.

Time and time again, I've tried to put myself in his shoes, tried to imagine how I would have reacted after all those years of abuse. But I can't. I can't, and don't think I ever will fully comprehend just how much he's suffered. And another surprise visit from Maria the other day only confirmed it.

Mum had mentioned that they were in contact, and when I first heard her downstairs, my heart jumped into my throat and I panicked, locking myself in my bedroom. I didn't want to have to listen to her tell me how wonderful her son was, basically all the things I already knew. The issues we had ran deeper than anyone but the two of us could understand. Although Maria and Stella came hella close.

But eventually, I pulled up my big girl pants and headed downstairs. And fuck, am I glad I did.

She never once tried pleading Toby's case for him. We just talked openly and frankly about our lives, our pasts, our experiences, and it helped me to understand the place Toby was coming from before we met.

When she left, it was with concern filling her eyes and fear written all over her face for where this was going to go with Toby. But still, she never said a word or tried to convince me of anything. And I liked her all the more for it.

Bri follows me to a coffee shop a few streets down from her school and finds us a table, dumping her overloaded bags onto the floor before falling into the chair dramatically as I stand in line and laugh at her antics.

"So," I say, lowering her coffee and a muffin I feel like she probably needs in front of her. "What's new?"

She lets out a heavy sigh.

"Nothing. I've been too swamped with work for anything exciting."

"So no more hotel rendezvous with he who shall not be named?"

"No," she spits. "And there won't be. Ever again." I hold her eyes, waiting for the truth to come out. So far, she's held her tongue but I know there's more to the story than she let on that night. "I was lonely, okay?" she blurts.

"So was I. You could have come and hung out with me."

"No offence, Jojo, but it was V day. I'd had a date with Brad and was on a promise to have my brains thoroughly fucked out of me. A night watching bad rom-coms with you wasn't going to cut it."

I want to argue with her, try to convince her that I would have been a fun date, but really, I wouldn't have been. I wasn't in a good place, and I certainly wouldn't have been good company.

"Fair enough," I mutter, taking a sip of my coffee.

"I just knew he'd give me what I needed after Brad bailed."

"Why'd he bail?"

"Work or some bullshit. I don't know, and I don't really care. It just proved that I've been right about keeping him at arm's length if he's going to let me down on the most important night of the year."

"That's a bit harsh. He seems like a good guy," I argue. Admittedly, I've never met the dude, but from what Bri has told me about him wanting to make things serious between them, I have to think he is one. It takes a certain kind of guy to willingly want to tie down my cousin, so he must have something good about him at least.

"Have you seen him since?"

She shakes her head. "I've been too busy. He's like a fucking dog with a bone though, trying to make it up to me."

"Just let him. He'll give you what you need and then some if he's really sorry."

"I agreed to see him Saturday night. If he doesn't bring his A-game, then he's fucked." She rips a piece of muffin off and throws it into her mouth. "Oh my God, I needed this," she mutters appreciatively. "How are things with you, anyway? Seen Toby yet?"

I shake my head.

Sitting forward, she reaches across the table and takes my hand in hers, squeezing tight.

"You'll figure it out. I've got faith in you."

"You're on Team Toby too?"

"Nope," she says quickly. "I'm on Team Jodie

Deserves to be Happy. I want you to do what's best for you. And I'll stand by your side the whole way. I mean, if you do choose him, I might just hurt him the next time I see him after all the bullshit he pulled, but I'll be nice after that."

"I love you, Bri."

"Love you too, Jojo."

"So how's school and shit?" I ask, happy to change the topic of conversation and focus on her.

"Oh yeah, you know. I'm in one of the roughest schools in the city. It's all fun and games when there's a very high chance that every kid I'm teaching has a fucking knife in their pocket."

I wince as the seriousness of that situation settles in my head.

I know the school she's at has a bad rep, but shit. The thought of her risking serious harm while she tries to instil some knowledge into the youth we're surrounded by is fucking terrifying.

"Can't you get a better placement?" I ask.

"I've only got a few more weeks and I'll move again. Final school," she says, her eyes lighting up with excitement.

"You're going to be applying for jobs soon, right?" I ask, recalling her saying that the vacancies get released pretty early in the year.

"Yep, won't be long and I could be a full-fledged teacher with my own little gaggle of reprobates to whip into shape."

"Maybe don't mention the whipping in your interviews," I suggest with a laugh.

"Yeah," she says with a wince. "Probably for the best."

"Any idea where you're going next?"

"Nope. They haven't released them yet. I'm not too worried. It can't get much worse than where I am. Unless they throw me into Lovell Academy. That place is the fucking pits of hell."

"You are aware that you've probably just tempted fate, right?"

"They wouldn't, surely? After these past few weeks, I'm due some good karma."

"I'll keep everything crossed for you."

"What about you?" she asks, pinning me with a look. I knew the question was coming but even still, I don't really have an answer.

I shrug. I've spent the past week or so trying to figure out what I want out of my life, and not just in regard to Toby, but also my actual life. Uni, a career, a future.

This time last year, I thought I knew exactly what I wanted. I was well on my way to getting my place at the uni I'd dreamed of for years, and I had everything to look forward to.

Now, the thought of moving away, of leaving Mum, Bri, Sara, Toby, and starting my life over is the last thing I want.

It's why I've spent an insane amount of time on

the phone this week as I try to figure out my options with my deferred place.

Thankfully, my grades mean that I can almost have my pick of universities, but I don't even know if I want it anymore. Years of studying, stress, deadlines. But then, what's the alternative? Another job in a coffee shop with limited possibilities to further my career?

I always wanted the world. I was motivated, dedicated, and determined. But since losing Joe, learning the truth about my father, I've never felt so beaten down.

"I don't know," I confess. "I've got options. I just don't know what I really want."

"I wish I had the answers for you, babe," Bri sighs.

"I'm trying to take it one day at a time and just hope everything falls into place, but it's hard."

"I know." She gives me a sympathetic smile.

It's easy for her—she's always known exactly what she's wanted to do. She's lived and breathed being a teacher from as early as I can remember. But while I knew I wanted uni, a career, I've never really pinpointed the exact thing I wanted to spend my life doing. My plan was always to get my business degree, hopefully discover the avenue I wanted to go down, and then find a job that would allow me to do my MBA as well.

But now... who the hell knows what I'm going

to do?

"What about on the job front? You found anything?"

"I've got a couple of interviews lined up for next week, but nothing of any excitement. Another coffee shop, a restaurant." Thankfully, now I don't have the issue of being fired for stealing hanging over my head, I've had a little more luck. I'm relieved, because there's no way I'm going back to Foxes. A shudder rips through me at the thought. I think my days vying to be a stripper are well and truly dead. Just another thing to mourn, I guess.

"What are your plans for the night?" Bri asks once we've both finished our coffees and contemplate leaving.

"Just gonna head home and hang with Mum, I guess. Unless you want help marking those?" I ask, nodding to the huge bag of papers she needs to go through.

"Wouldn't wish that on my worst enemy, Jojo. You go home and chill. Maybe have some hot and steamy phone sex with that man of yours," she teases.

"Things haven't been like that," I confess.

"No? But the chemistry between you usually burns bright enough to bring the fucking city down."

I can't help but laugh. "I didn't say it wasn't there, Bri. We've just not gone there."

"Well, maybe you should. Bring a little excitement back into your life. I bet he'd love to see you at work with that vibrator I got you for Christmas."

"You, Brianna Andrews, are a bad influence."

She beams at me. "And that's exactly why you love me."

Our first coffee soon turns into three and a panini each, and when we finally walk back out of the coffee shop toward the Uber that we ordered to take us both home, the sun has long set.

"Shit, what time is it?" I ask, pulling my phone from my bag and gasp. "Bri, why didn't you say anything? You've got loads of work to do."

She steps up to me and cups my cheek with her free hand.

"None of it is more important than making you smile, Jojo."

A grin twitches at my lips.

"I don't want you falling behind because of me and my drama."

"It's totally fine. Come on, it's freezing, and neither of us have willing guys to warm us up when we get home."

"I beg to differ. I think we've both got more than willing ones."

She barks a laugh as we climb into the back of the Uber and I roll my eyes as Bri immediately starts flirting with the driver.

"So, what are you going to do about Nico?" I ask, more than curious about what she's planning for revenge.

"Right now, nothing. But I have every confidence that the perfect opportunity will present itself soon enough."

"He's going to regret the day he ever met you, isn't he?"

Bri laughs, but I can see the devil smiling back at me in her eyes.

"Oh, I don't know. I wouldn't go that far. I'm sure he'll get some enjoyment out of it. He's a bit fucked up like that."

"Pretty sure they all are," I mutter.

In only minutes, we're pulling up outside Bri's flat and she's smacking a wet kiss on my cheek as she says goodbye.

"Laters, bitch," she calls seconds before slamming the door behind her.

"Your friend is... interesting," the driver says as we both watch her bound up the stairs toward her front door.

"Putting it lightly," I quip.

Thankfully, he falls silent after that comment and doesn't expect a full-on conversation from me as we head toward home.

We're just about to turn down the street when my phone starts ringing.

"Hey, how's it going?" I ask the second the call

connects with Sara.

"H-hey. What are you doing tonight?"

"What's wrong?" I ask, immediately hearing something I don't like in her voice.

"I… um… something is going on here and Jesse has gone and… I don't know. I'm probably overreacting but—"

"I'm coming right now. Give me a second." Lowering my phone, I poke my head between the seats. "Can we make a diversion to the Lovell Estate?" I ask sweetly.

"Sure thing, just update our journey."

"Okay, awesome. Thank you so much."

"Hang on, Sar. I'm already in an Uber. I've just got to change my destination," I tell her before opening the app and doing what I need to do. "Talk to me, tell me what's happening."

"I don't know, that's the problem. I'm scared, Jojo."

"It's okay," I assure her, although I can't deny that the fear in her voice doesn't make my stomach knot with worry. Because if something is happening in Lovell, then I have no doubt that Toby and the guys are going to be in the middle of it.

I remember all too well the state of him the last time things kicked off in the estate with the Wolves, and I know from what he's told me that they're expecting things to get worse rather than better.

"I'll be there in a few minutes, and I'm sure Jesse will be fine."

"Yeah, I know. I'm just overreacting. I know. I just… I can't lose him, Jojo. I can't."

"I know, babe, and you won't. That stubborn fuck isn't going anywhere but right by your side, okay?"

She quietly agrees down the line, but my words have done little to console her. I just hope whatever is going on isn't going to give her, us, any real reason to worry.

As I get deeper into the estate, the sight of smoke filling the sky and the bright orange of flames in the distance makes my stomach knot.

Panic and dread flood me. Thoughts of Jesse, of Toby and the guys make my blood turn to ice.

"Jesus, that looks—"

The car rocks, the ground beneath us jolting as a loud explosion booms around us making me squeal in fright.

"I'm not sure this is a good idea, sweetheart."

"I don't have a choice. You either take me or I'll walk from here," I warn.

He blows out a breath but thankfully keeps driving while chaos seems to ensue just a few streets away.

Please, God. Please don't force me to say goodbye to anyone else.

24

TOBY

Everything was weirdly quiet as Theo parked up his car a short distance from the Den in the hope that it would be safe. But the second we invited ourselves into Archer's headquarters, we discovered that things weren't as peaceful as the streets led us to believe.

Archer, Dax, and Jace stand around a door in the floor of the main room that I had no fucking clue even existed as their Wolves pass weapons up the stairs that descend into darkness.

"You ready for this, Cirillo?" Archer barks, his face hard and his eyes fierce as he prepares to fight at long last for what's rightfully his.

"You fucking know we are. Backup's on its way," Theo agrees.

"Good. They've already started hitting our

businesses over on the west side, and they're heading this way."

"Your businesses?" I ask despite the fact that I heard every single word he just said perfectly.

"Yes. I'll let them take a few, allow them to think they're going to win this thing. We'll take them fucking down before they start hitting the east.'"

My eyes fly to Jesse, who's standing at the very top of the stairs, passing guns to a guy who's laying them all out on the table for another to check and load.

His eyes are hungry, desperate to fight for the gang he swore into years ago, but I also see the fear in them. I know as well as everyone else that his girl lives above one of the Wolves' betting shops on the east.

"We'll stop them before they get past this part of the estate," Archer states, clearly reading my silent conversation with Jesse.

A ringing phone pierces the tension hanging in the air. Archer swipes his screen and lifts it to his ear.

"Yes," he barks as I take the gun Alex hands me along with more ammunition than I'm going to be able to carry. "Fuck. Fuck. Yes, we're on our way."

All eyes fall on him for a beat, but he doesn't let it dampen his determination. Instead, his shoulders widen and his chest puffs out.

"Time to go boys. Let's take them down for fucking good."

A round of agreement ripples through the large room full of men as more come rushing in behind us. Most are Wolves, but there are a few of us mixed in with them.

"Who owns this fucking estate?" Archer booms over the ruckus of everyone reaching for weapons.

"The Wolves rule this fucking Den," they all roar back, making the hairs on the back of my neck stand on end before they let out the most almighty howl that I'm sure actual wolves would be impressed with.

My eyes collide with Nico's just in time to see him attempt to cover his laugh of amusement.

"We should have a tagline, dude," Alex says with a twinkle in his eye.

"Fuck off," Theo barks as someone comes to stand with us. "I'm not howling like a fucking animal in the hope it'll make someone scared of me."

"He's right," our latest addition agrees. "The devil is always more effective when he moves quietly in the dark. No one ever sees you coming that way."

"Daemon," Theo greets with a nod, the corner of his lips twitching up.

"What the fuck did you do to get this party started, bro?" Alex asks.

"Make your moves quietly and in the dark, bro." Daemon winks before shooting his brother a rare smile. "Ready to go put some Wolves in the ground?" he asks, danger and death oozing from his every pore.

"Just make sure you're pointing that rifle at the right fucking Wolves, Deimos," Archer says, clapping Daemon on the shoulder.

"You doubting me, Wolfe?"

"Wouldn't fucking dream of it."

Archer stands before everyone and casts his eyes over his crew, who are all standing in front of us.

"This is our fucking estate, and we fight with everything we have to ensure it stays that way. Those corrupt fucking bastards belong with their cunt of a leader."

He continues to explain his plan for how we're going to take them down and reclaim his hold on this estate.

We all listen, more than willing to take his lead on his own patch, but there's no doubt in my mind that how we execute this will be on our terms.

Once he's happy everyone knows where they're going, he starts up another round of howling before he leads his crew out. Dax and Jace take up their positions right behind him, along with Jesse and the rest of his boys.

"Ready?" Theo asks.

"Like you have to fucking ask, man."

We let the Wolves head out and into the thick of the fight for their territory before we follow, our role to stand back and take them out from a distance.

Fucking fine by me. Although I can't deny that I could really do with getting my hands dirty.

Daemon, who has apparently been working with Archer closer on this than any of us realised, leads us in the opposite direction to where most of the Wolves go and toward an abandoned high-rise.

"This building has the best view of the valley. From each side, we should be able to take out those cunts without them even knowing we're here. I hope you've been practising your shots, boys."

"Fuck you, Deimos. You know we're good for it," Seb hisses, clearly offended that Daemon doesn't think he's got it in him to suddenly become a sniper.

"Toby, Seb, go to the west. It's where the OGs are coming from if our intel is right. Alex, Daemon, take the south. Nico and I have the north covered," Theo instructs.

"East?" I ask, aware that that's where Sara and Jesse's place is. I can only fucking hope he's got her out of there tonight.

"You two can move around once they've cleared from the west."

My heart races and adrenaline surges through

me as Seb and I take the stairs first, the footfall of the others behind us pounding through me.

"Come dawn, all will be calm in Lovell," Theo promises before we all split up.

Seb and I find ourselves in a room with a good vantage point of the valley, and the sight of the flames licking high up into the sky from the businesses the OGs have already claimed makes my stomach twist.

"I really fucking hope they know what they're doing," I mutter as we watch the chaos that's raining below us as another explosion rocks the building we're in, and a dark cloud of smoke plumes into the night sky.

"Fuck me. No wonder this took some planning," Seb mutters as yet another explosion echoes through the air.

"This isn't going to be as easy as Archer thought, is it?"

"He just needs to remember who trained those twisted motherfuckers. But he knew Luis better than anyone, so if anyone can topple what are undoubtedly his plans, then it's Arch."

"I hope you're right."

"I trust Emmie's judgement."

"Fair enough."

"She thinks Arch has what it takes, so we just gotta hope a little peace is heading our way."

"Look out," I say as I spot movement at the end

of the street before gunfire explodes beneath us and the darkness is illuminated with bright orange. More and more buildings are engulfed by flames as explosions go off like dominoes until one final overpowering one literally rattles the floor beneath me.

"Was that—"

"Move your arses now," a deep voice booms through the building, confirming what we already knew.

"They fucking knew we'd be here," Seb shouts as we run back toward the stairs. Smoke begins to plume up from the ground floor.

"Fuck. We need to get out of here before it goes up.

It only takes a couple of flights of stairs before the smoke becomes so thick around us it becomes hard to breathe. But we don't let it stop us.

The temperature increases with every step we descend until the flames become visible.

"This way," Theo barks from behind us. "There's a fire escape."

I turn around, relieved to find the others all standing there, covering their mouths.

We race after Theo, who rushes forward and into another flat before heading to the window and climbing straight out.

The ladder doesn't take us right to the ground, but the jump we need to make is a hell of a lot better than running through a fucking inferno.

"I didn't fucking sign up for this," Nico barks as he lets go of the ladder and tumbles to the ground only seconds after Theo.

I don't have time to think about how much it looked like it fucking hurt as a surge of heat floods the room behind us.

"Fucking move," Daemon barks, and I jump through the window with him and Alex hot on my tail as the building begins to lose the fight against the fire behind us.

A loud crash sounds out as I hit the ground, and my legs buckle beneath me as I'm thrown across the road from the explosion.

Pain blooms down my entire right side from where I hit the building opposite the one we thought we were safe in as shouts and gunfire get louder around us.

"Is everyone okay?" Theo asks, and when I look up, I find him, Nico and Daemon staring down at where me, Seb and Alex are laid out on the fucking tarmac.

"Yeah," I grunt, rolling onto my good side and sucking in a breath as I prepare to stand.

Glancing over, I find Seb and Alex in a similar position with pain etched onto their faces.

"Shit," Nico barks as the crack of gunfire gets louder. "Move."

Sucking in a breath, I gather every ounce of strength I have to start running. An unrelenting grip wraps around my upper arm, and when I look over, I find Nico dragging me along with him into a dark alley a few buildings up.

"Holy fuck," I pant, bending over and pressing my hands to my knees as I try to catch my breath.

My heart is a fucking runaway train in my chest as my hands tremble with adrenaline, which I'm pretty fucking sure is stopping me from hurting as much as I should be right now. I hit that building hard.

"You guys okay to keep going?"

I follow Theo and Nico's line of sight, my eyes landing on Seb, Alex and Daemon. They've got blood and dirt covering them, but I thankfully can't see anything serious. And thank fuck they're standing.

"Yeah," they all agree before giving each other a look.

"We're good," Daemon says. "Let's fucking finish this. Those motherfuckers aren't taking anything else."

We pull our guns, ready to help fight for Archer's ownership of this estate, but right before we head back out to where the OGs are getting closer, my phone ringing cuts through our heaving breaths and the sound of gunfire.

"Shit," I hiss, knowing with the first note of the ringtone that it's Jodie. "Fuck."

"Answer it," Seb says, guessing who it is from my reaction. "We've got you."

My hand trembles as I pull my phone from my pocket.

If she's been on social media or talked to Sara, then she has to know we're in the middle of this. I haven't exactly shied away from telling her the truth about our involvement here.

"Jodie," I bark, the roughness of my voice giving away the shit situation we've just come from.

"I'm with Sara," she cries down the line. "The betting shop is on fire. We're stuck. Jesse isn't answering." The panic in her voice sends an ice-cold shiver down my spine.

"Fuck. I'm coming, baby. I'm coming, okay? Do anything you can to get out."

"I'm scared, Toby," she confesses quietly as Sara screams in the background.

"I'm coming right now."

I'm already running before the call has even cut.

"Toby, what the fuck are you doing?" Theo calls.

"Jodie is with Sara. They've hit the bookies. They're stuck."

"Motherfuckers," Nico hisses.

"We'll cover you and be right there," Theo agrees. "We'll get her."

"Fuck," I mutter as my legs pick up speed. Any pain I'd felt before is now long forgotten as I focus on my girl.

Bullets fly around me as I run out into the street that's now completely ablaze. But I don't look back. I put every ounce of trust I have in my brothers to ensure I get out of this so I can get to them.

Get to her.

25

JODIE

My heart thrashes in my chest as I stand beside Sara at her living room window as the sky in the distance glows orange.

Reaching out, I take her trembling hand in mine.

"I love him, Jojo, but I hate this. I hate this so fucking much," she whimpers.

"Jesse will be fine," I assure her, wishing that I could say it with a little more confidence. "They'll all be fine."

My phone rings in my pocket and I rush to pull it out, hoping it might be Toby telling me that he's far, far away from all of this, but I know it's wishful thinking.

"Stella, what's happening?" I bark. I'd called her not long after I first got here and calmed Sara down in the hope that she might have some answers.

"I have no idea. I haven't heard from any of them. I'm watching their trackers though, and they're in the valley."

"Oh my God," I whimper, and Sara's eyes go as wide as saucers as figures dart across the street beneath us.

"Shit, Jojo. What's happening?" Sara asks quietly, her voice cracked with emotion and panic.

"From what I can tell on social media, they're attacking all the Wolves' businesses. Where are you?" Stella explains.

"Above a bookies," I confess.

"Owned by the Wolves?" Stella implores.

"Sar, is the betting shop owned by the Wolves?" I ask. But deep down, I already know the answer.

She nods as her tears spill over once more.

"Okay, you need to get out of there. Send me your address, and I'll come to pick you both up and bring you back here."

"Y-you can't do that. It's not safe."

"I don't have a choice, Jodie. If anything happens to you and I knew and did nothing, Toby would never forgive me. Now send me your address. I can be there in like, twenty minutes if the roads are quiet. I'm putting my shoes on right now. Send me the address."

"Okay, okay."

"Oh my God," Sara screams as a bright orange flash fills the room.

"What's happening?" Stella barks in my ear as I turn back toward the window, staring down in horror at the car that's just gone up in flames right out the front of the shop below.

"Sar, we need to get out of here. Right now," I say, my voice quaking with fear.

"Shit, shit." She looks around at her home, her eyes wide as realisation hits her.

"Get out. I'm coming for you."

"Okay." I hang up and push my phone into the back pocket of my jeans. "Come on. Grab anything you desperately need, but we need to go now."

"Y-yeah, okay."

I pull my boots on as Sara runs to her and Jesse's bedroom.

A loud roar rips through the air before the floor beneath me moves and the contents of the kitchen cupboard behind me rattle. More than a few things hit the floor, many smashing and making an ominous thud.

"What was that?" Sara asks as she comes running back toward me with a bag thrown over her shoulder.

"I don't think we want to know."

The orange glow from the window is only getting brighter the longer I stand here, and I'm afraid that we're too late and the shop beneath us is already ablaze.

There are more building-trembling bangs along with loud pops that I swear are gunshots, but I try to push that thought aside. If I allow myself to believe there are men out there shooting, then I'll never convince myself to leave. And that might just be a worse idea than getting shot at, if what I fear is happening beneath our feet is reality.

"Come on," I say, grabbing Sara's hand and dragging her from where she's frozen on the spot.

The fact that the door handle is warm when I wrap my hand around it doesn't register with me. But it sure as fuck does the second I open the door and a surge of heat hot enough to singe my skin barrels into us, followed by angry, hungry flames that are already engulfing the entire hallway and stairs down to the exit. In a rush, I swing the door closed. But deep down, I know it's pointless.

"Holy shit. Fire escape. We need to use the fire escape," I shout, desperately trying to keep my cool. Sara lost her grip on reality a long time ago. One of us needs to keep a clear head.

"I-it doesn't work," she cries behind me as I drag her across the flat to the door at the other side of the living room.

"What?" I roar, not wanting to believe her words.

"It's stuck closed. Has been for months. The landlord was meant t-to—"

There's a loud crash behind us, but I'm too terrified to turn around and see what it is as I continue toward the door despite Sara's words.

Even if it is stuck, we need to try. We have to try. I refuse to die up here with her tonight.

"If we throw all our weight into it, we might get it open," I say, sounding way more confident than I feel.

"O-okay," Sara whimpers, not looking like she's got a whole lot of strength to give.

"Think of Jesse, Sar. He's out there now, fighting to get back to you. You have to do the same to get to him, okay? There just so happens to be a door standing in our way."

As we stand there, the scent of burning gets stronger and stronger, and when I risk a quick glance back, I see the smoke beginning to spill under the front door.

We really need to get out of here now.

"Okay, after three we'll throw all our weight at it."

Sara nods.

"We've got this, okay?"

"Yeah," she agrees, but I don't believe a second of it.

"Three, two—" Another crash rattles through

the building before a loud bang comes from outside. Another car, maybe. Who knows. "One."

Together, we slam our bodies into the unlocked door, but just as Sara feared, the thing doesn't so much as budge.

"Fuck. Let's go again," I demand.

"It's not going to work," Sara whispers, turning around and looking over my shoulder. Her eyes widen in shock, and the fear I'm trying to stave off so that I can think rationally threatens to consume me.

"Jodie, I-I—"

Unable to stay still, I turn toward what Sara's staring at, and the second I do, all the blood drains from my face.

"Holy fuck," I breathe as I take in the sight of the flames practically melting through the front door and quickly engulfing the flat.

"Can we get out of any of the windows?"

"Only the bedroom ones," she admits, and my eyes fly toward the bedroom doors that I can barely see for the smoke. "But we'd jump out to the main street where the cars are blazing and the men are shooting."

"Jesus. Fuck." My entire body trembles with fear and my breathing starts to get more laboured as the oxygen in the room begins to be replaced by smoke. "We've got to try the door again. It has to open." Sara nods, and we spend the next few minutes throwing everything we have at it. Despite it creaking and groaning against our weight, it never opens more than a few millimetres, just teasing us with the breathable air outside.

One glance back over my shoulder tells me that time is running out.

My lungs burn with the smoke I inhale with each breath, and one look at Sara's pale face tells me that if we don't find a fucking miracle right this second, then we're not going to make it out of here.

"Once more."

"And then what?"

I don't get a chance to answer, because there's a loud, terrifying crash, and when I turn around, I discover that almost all of the kitchen has collapsed into the shop below.

"Oh my God, Jodie," Sara screams before embarking on a coughing fit that has fear clawing at my chest, making it even harder to breathe.

"This last one will do it," I say between coughs of my own. "Come on. Give me everything."

"It's not going to help, Jodie. We need to get down. We need to find air."

I stare at her hopeless expression, my heart plummeting to my feet. She's right. We're stuck. We both sink to the floor in the hope of escaping the thick, suffocating smoke, utter hopelessness consumes me.

Sara pulls her phone from her pocket and hits

call on Jesse's number. But when it goes to voicemail, her cries of despair cut through me like knives.

Following her lead, I pull mine free and find Toby's number.

"Please, please, please," I beg silently as it connects and starts ringing.

"Jodie." Just the sound of his voice sends a rush of relief through me before some more of the flooring falls and I'm dragged back to our terrifying reality.

"I'm with Sara," I say, trying desperately hard not to let him know just how scared I am. "The betting shop is on fire. We're stuck. Jesse isn't answering." There's a beat of silence as I'm sure I hear gunfire on his end.

Holy fuck, we're all going to die tonight.

"Fuck. I'm coming, baby. I'm coming, okay? Do anything you can to get out."

"I'm scared, Toby," I confess quietly as Sara screams beside me, reaching for my hand and squeezing tightly.

"I'm coming right now."

The line goes dead and my head begins to spin.

No. No. I need air. I need... Fuck. I need anything but this fucking hopeless situation.

"Toby is coming. He's going to get us."

"How?" Sara asks weakly. "There's no way in and no way out."

She clings to me, her tears soaking my hoodie and her body trembling violently.

"If you get out of here and I don't, tell Jesse I love him, yeah?"

"Shut up, Sar. We're both getting out and you can tell him yourself. You'll see. You're too good to go out like this."

"I'm sorry, Jojo. I never should have called you tonight. I'm so fucking sorry."

26

TOBY

My lungs burn and my legs ache, but I don't let any of the pain in my body stop me from running through the streets toward Jesse and Sara's flat.

The gunfire that was so dangerously close behind me when I first emerged from that alleyway has all but faded, but I have no chance of forgetting the rioting that's happening around me.

The air smells like destruction and death, and the sky is still glowing orange from the flames engulfing the estate.

Archer was convinced they would leave this part of town until last, that they'd hit the rest of their businesses first. But it seems their intel was fucked, because as I run, all I can hear is the fear in Jodie's voice.

I'm coming, baby. And I'll run through the flames of hell to make sure you're safe.

My body is on the verge of giving up on me as I round the corner and my eyes collide with the worst sight I've ever been forced to witness in my entire life.

The bookies' is totally ablaze, the flames flickering higher than the building. The windows of the flat above have been blown out, the entire place a fucking inferno.

"NO," I scream, surging forward as I dig up a reserve stock of energy from somewhere. "JODIE," I bellow, hoping like fuck that they've managed to get out. That by some miracle they found a fucking way to escape.

"JODIE," I scream once more, not giving a fuck if it turns any of our enemies on me. If she's in that building, then they might as well just gun me down right here.

I'm vaguely aware of a car pulling to a screeching halt behind me, but I don't look back. I'm too busy trying to figure out a way to get into that building.

"Toby," someone shouts, and familiarity rushes through me. "Toby, don't you fucking dare even try it."

A small hand wraps around my upper arm, but I don't let it stop me, ripping myself free of the grip and charging forward.

The crumbling and creaking of the building

giving in the heat of the flames engulfing it assault my ears, but I refuse to acknowledge what that means. Because it can't happen. I can't lose her. Not now, and not like this.

"Toby, please, stop." Finally, the voice registers, and I spin around, finding my sister staring back at me with tears cascading down her cheeks. "Please don't try to go in there."

"She's in there, Stel. I can't leave her to—"

There's a loud bang, and the entire side of the building collapses right before our eyes.

"JODIE," I bellow.

"No, Toby. No, please," Stella screams, her nails digging into my arm through my ripped shirt, but it's not enough to stop me. I take off running, using the massive hole in the side of the building to enter the inferno.

Tugging my tie off, I rip my shirt open and pull the fabric over my face as I try to find a way to get to the top floor. But it's not necessary. The entire flat has fallen through into the shop.

A whimper hits my ears, and I search frantically for where it might have come from.

"Jodie? Make another noise, baby. I'm right here," I try to shout as the smoke billows from the burning embers of what once used to be the betting shop.

The weak sound hits my ears again, and finally,

I catch sight of a person beneath all the dust and rubble.

"Baby," I breathe, forgetting about covering my face and rushing toward her.

"Toby," she whimpers, and my heart shatters, my eyes burning from the smoke and the strength of the emotion that washes through me as I start pulling the rubble off her. Everything I touch burns my hands, but I don't care. I just need her safe. I just need her in my arms.

Time seems to stand still as I fight to dig her out and the fire continues around us. The heat of the flames burns my skin, but it's a small price to pay if I can get her safe.

Sirens hit my ears, and I fucking pray to anyone who will listen that they're coming here first. *The entire fucking estate is on fire, but please, for the love of all that's holy, come here first. Come and get my girl.*

"I'm going to get you out of here, baby. I fucking promise you," I tell her as I lift the final bit of plasterboard from her legs and sweep her into my arms.

Just as I pull her from the floor, part of the wall that she was sitting against crumbles and my heart jumps into my throat, knowing that it would have landed on her.

"Sara," she breathes. "You need to get Sara,"

she whispers, her voice raspy and weak, her body limp in my arms as I navigate through the rubble to get us out as flashing blue and red lights begin to replace the glowing orange filling the street.

The second I emerge from the building and the smoke around us clears, Stella comes rushing forward as a fire engine and an ambulance come racing down the street.

"Oh my God. Is she okay?"

My lips part and I'm about to assure her that Jodie was talking when her body suddenly gets heavier in my hold, and when I look down, her eyes are closed.

"No," I cry. "Jodie, come back to me, baby. Jodie."

A shadow falls over us and when I look up, I find a paramedic standing before me with his arms outstretched.

"Let me," he says softly but firmly, and I have no choice but to hand my girl over to another man in the hope that he can bring her back to me.

I stumble forward and collide with Stella. Her arms wrap around me, her sweet scent finally overtaking the death that's filled my nose since the building we were in earlier went up around us, and I finally break as I cling to her.

"I can't lose her, Stel. I fucking can't."

"You won't. This isn't her time."

And all I can do as we stand there, clinging to each other as chaos breaks out around us is pray that she's right.

Toby and Jodie's story continues in RECKLESS DYNASTY

HATE YOU PROLOGUE

Tabitha

I stare down at my gran's pale skin. Her cheeks are sunken and her eyes tired. She's been fighting this for too long now, and as much as I hate to even think it, it's time she found some peace.

I take her cool hand in mine and lift her knuckles to my lips.

"It's Tabitha," I whisper. I've no idea if she's awake, but I don't want to startle her.

Her eyes flicker open. After a second they must adjust to the light and she looks right at me. My chest tightens as if someone's wrapping an elastic band around it. I hate seeing my once so full of life gran like this. She was always so happy and full of cheer. She didn't deserve this end. But cancer doesn't care what kind of person you are, it hits whoever it fancies and ruins lives.

Pulling a chair closer, I drop onto it, not taking my eyes from her.

"How are you doing today?" I hate asking the question, because there really is only one answer. She's waiting, waiting for her time to come to put her out of her misery.

"I'm good. Christopher upped my morphine. I'm on top of the world."

She might be living her last days, but it doesn't stop her eyes sparkling a little as she mentions her male nurse. If I've heard the words 'if I were forty years younger' once while she's been here, then I've heard them a million times. She's joking, of course. My gran spent her life with my incredible grandpa until he had a stroke a few years ago. Thankfully, I guess, his end was much quicker and less painful than Gran's. It was awful at the time to have him healthy one moment and then gone in a matter of hours, but this right now is pure torture, and I'm not the one lying on the hospital bed with meds constantly being pumped into my body.

"Turn the frown upside down, Tabby Cat. I'm fine. I want to remember you smiling, not like your world's about to come crashing down."

"I know, I'm sorry. I just—" a sob breaks from my throat. "I don't know how I'm going to live without you." Dramatic? Yeah. But Gran has been my go-to person my whole life. When my parents get on my last nerve, which is often, she's the one who talks me down, makes me see things differently. She's also the only one who's encouraged me to live the life I want, not the one I'm constantly being pushed into.

That's the reason I'm the only one visiting her right now.

When my parents discovered that she was the one encouraging my 'reckless behaviour', as they called it, they cut contact. I can see the pain in her eyes about that every time she looks at me, but she's too stubborn to do anything about it, even now.

"You're going to be fine. You're stronger than you give yourself credit for. How many times have I told you, you just need to follow your heart. Follow your heart and just breathe. Spread your wings and fly, Tabby Cat."

Those were the last words she said to me.

HATE YOU CHAPTER ONE

Tabitha

The heavy bass rattles my bones. The incredible music does help to lift my spirits, but I find it increasingly hard to see the positives in my life while I'm hanging out with my friends these days. They've all got something exciting going on—incredible job prospects, marriage, exotic holidays on the horizon—and here I am, drowning in my one-person pity party. It's been two months since Gran left me, and I'm still wondering what the hell I'm meant to be doing with my life.

"Oh my god, they are so fucking awesome," Danni squeals in my ear as one song comes to an end. I didn't really have her down as a rock fan, but she was almost as excited as James when he announced that this was what we were doing for his birthday this year. Although I do wonder if it's the music or the frontman who's really captured her attention. She'd never admit it, but she's got a thing for bad boys.

I glance over at him with his arm wrapped around Shannon's shoulders and a smile twitches my lips. They're so cute. They've got the kind of relationship everyone craves. It seems so easy yet full of love and affection. Ripping my eyes from the couple, I focus back on the stage and try to block out that I'm about as far away from having that kind of connection with anyone as physically possible.

I sing along with the songs I've heard on the radio a million times and jump around with my friends, but I just can't quite totally get on board with tonight. Maybe I just need more alcohol.

"Where to next?" Shannon asks once we've left the arena and the ringing in our ears has begun to fade.

"Your choice," James says, looking down at her with utter devotion shining in his eyes. It wasn't a great surprise when Shannon sent a photo of her giant engagement ring to our group chat a couple of months ago. We all knew it was coming—Danni especially, seeing as it turned out that she helped choose the ring.

Shannon directs us all to a cocktail bar a few streets over and I make quick work of manoeuvring my way through the crowd to get to the bar, my need for a drink beginning to get the better of me. The others disappear off somewhere in the hope of finding a table

"Can we have two jugs of..." I quickly glance at the menu. "Margaritas please."

"Coming right up, sweetheart." The barman winks at me before his eyes drop to my chest. Hooking up on a night out isn't really my thing, but hell if it doesn't make me feel a little better about myself. He's cute too, and just the kind of guy who would give both my parents a heart attack if I were to bring him home. Both his forearms are covered in tattoos, he's got gauges in both his ears, and a lip ring. A smile tugs at the corner of my mouth as I imagine the looks on their faces.

My gran's words suddenly hit me.

Just breathe.

My hand lifts and my fingers run over the healing skin just below my bra. My smile widens.

I watch the barman prepare our cocktails, my eyes focused on the ink on his arms. I've always been obsessed by art, any kind of art, and that most definitely includes on skin.

I'm lost in my own head, so when he places the jugs in front of me, I startle, feeling ridiculous.

"T-Thank you," I mutter, but when I lift my eyes, I find him staring intently at me.

"You're welcome. I'm Christian, by the way."

"Oh, hi." A sly smile creeps onto my lips. "I'm Biff."

"Biff?" His brows draw together in a way I'm all too used to when I say my name.

"It's short for Tabitha."

"That's pretty. So... uh... how do you feel about—"

"Christian, a little help?" one of the other barmen shouts, pulling Christian's attention from me.

"Sorry, I'll hopefully see you again later?"

I nod at him, not wanting to give him any false hope. Like I said, he's cute, but after my last string of bad dates and even worse short-term boyfriends, I'm happy flying solo right now. I've got a top of the range vibrating friend in my bedside table; I don't need a man.

Picking up the tray in front of me, I turn and go in search of my friends. It takes forever, but eventually I find them tucked around a tiny table in the back corner of the bar.

"What the hell took so long? We thought you'd pulled and abandoned us."

"Yes and no," I say, ensuring every head turns my way.

"Tell us more," Danni, my best friend, demands.

"It was nothing. The barman was about to ask me out, but it got busy."

"Why the hell did you come back? Get over there. We all know you could do with a little... loosening up," James says with a wink.

"I'm good. He wasn't my type."

"Oh, of course. You only date posh boys."

"That is not true."

"Is it not?" Danni asks, chipping in once she's filled all the glasses.

"No..." I think back over the previous few guys they met. "Wayne wasn't posh," I argue when I realise they're kind of right.

"No, he was just a wanker."

Blowing out a long breath, I try to come up with an argument, but quite honestly, it's true. My shoulders slump as I realise that I've been subconsciously dating guys my parents would approve of. It's like my need to follow their orders is so well ingrained by now that I don't even realise I'm doing it. Shame that their ideas about my life, what I should do, and whom I should date don't exactly line up with mine.

Glancing over my shoulder at the bar, I catch a glimpse of Christian's head. Maybe I should take him up on his almost offer. What's the worst that could happen?

Deciding some liquid courage is in order, I grab my margherita and swallow half down in one go.

I'm so fed up of attempting to live my parents' idea of a perfect life. I promised Gran I'd do things my way. I need to start living up to my promise.

By the time I'm tipsy enough to walk back to the bar and chat up Christian, he's nowhere to be seen. I'm kind of disappointed seeing as the others had convinced me to throw caution to the wind (something that I'm really bad at doing), but I think I'm mostly relieved to be able go home and lock myself inside my flat alone and not have to worry about anyone else.

With my arm linked through Danni's, we make our way out to the street, ready to make our journeys home, and Shannon jumps into an idling Uber while Danni waits for another to go in the opposite direction.

"You sure you don't want to be dropped off? I don't mind."

"No, I'm sure. I could do with the fresh air." It's not a lie—the alcohol from one too many cocktails is making my head a little fuzzy. I hate going to sleep with the room spinning. I'd much rather that feeling fade before lying down.

"Okay. Promise me you'll text me when you're home."

"I promise." I wrap my arms around my best friend and then wave her off in her own Uber.

Turning on my heels, I start the short walk home.

I've been a London girl all my life, and while some might be afraid to walk home after dark, I love it. I love seeing a different side to this city, the quiet side when most people are hiding in their flats, not flooding the streets on their daily commutes.

My mind is flicking back and forth between my promise to Gran and my missed opportunity tonight when a shop front that I walk past on almost a daily basis makes me stop.

It's a tattoo studio I've been inside of once in my life. I never really pay it much attention, but the new sign in the window catches my eye and I stop to look.

Admin help wanted. Enquire within.

Something stirs in my belly, and it's not just my need to do something to piss my parents off—although getting a job in a place like this is sure to do that. I'm pretty sure it's excitement.

Tattoos fascinate me, or more so, the artists.

I'm surprised to see the open sign still illuminated, so before I can change my mind, I push the door open. A little bell rings above it, and after a few seconds of standing in reception alone, a head pops out from around the door.

"Evening. What can I do you for?" The guy's smile is soft and kind despite his otherwise slightly harsh features and ink.

"Oh um..." I hesitate under his intense dark stare. I glance over my shoulder, the back of the piece of paper catching my eye and reminding me why I walked in here. "I just saw the job ad in the window. Is the position still open?"

His eyes drop from mine and take in what I'm wearing. Seeing as tonight's outing involved a rock concert, I'm dressed much like him in all black and looking a little edgy with my skinny black jeans, ripped AC/DC t-shirt and heavy black makeup. I must admit it's not a look I usually go for, but it was fitting for tonight.

He nods, apparently happy with what he sees.

"Experience?" he asks, making my stomach drop.

"Not really, but I'm studying for a Masters so I'm not an idiot. I know my way around a computer, Excel, and I'm super organised."

"Right..." he trails off, like he's thinking about the best way to get rid of me.

"I'm a really quick learner. I'm punctual, methodical and really easy to get along with."

"It's okay, you had me sold at organised. I'm Dawson, although everyone around here calls me D."

"Nice to meet you." I stick my hand out for him to shake, and an amused smile plays at his lips. Stretching out an inked arm, he takes my hand and gives it a very firm shake that my dad would be impressed by—if he could look past the tattoos, that is. "I'm Tabitha, but everyone calls me Biff."

"Biff, I like it. When can you start?"

"Don't you want to interview me?"

"You sound like you could be perfect. When can you start?"

"Err... tomorrow?" I ask, totally taken aback. He doesn't know me from Adam.

"Yes!" He practically snaps my hand off. "Can you be here for two o'clock? I can show you around before clients start turning up. I'll apologise now for dropping you in the deep end, we've not had anyone for a few weeks and things are starting to get a little crazy."

"I can cope with crazy."

"Good to know. This place can be nuts." I smile at him, more grateful than he could know to have a distraction and a focus.

My Masters should be enough to keep my mind busy, but since Gran went, I can't seem to lose myself in it like I could previously. Hopefully, sorting this place's admin out might be exactly what I need.

"Two o'clock tomorrow then," I say, turning to leave. "I'll bring ID. Do you need a reference? I've done some voluntary work recently, I'm sure they'll write something for me."

"Just turn up on time and do your job and you're golden."

I walk out with more of a spring in my step than I have in a long time. I'm determined to find something that's going to make me happy, not just my parents. I've lived in their shadow for long enough.

I look myself over before leaving my flat for my first shift at the tattoo studio. I'm dressed a little more like myself today in a pair of dark skinny jeans, a white blouse and a black blazer. It's simple and smart. I'm not sure if there's a dress code—D never specified what I should wear. With my hair straightened and hanging down my back and my makeup light, I feel like I can take on whatever crazy he throws at me.

With a final spritz of perfume, I grab my bag from the unit in the hall and pull open my door. My home is a top floor flat in an old London warehouse. They were converted a few years ago by my father's company, and I managed to get myself first dibs. They might drive me insane on the best of days, but at least I get this place rent-free. It almost makes up for their controlling and stuck-up ways... almost.

Ignoring the lift like I always do, I head for the stairs. My heels click against the polished concrete until I'm at the bottom and out to the busy city. I love London. I love that no matter what the time, there's always something going on or someone who's awake.

The spring afternoon is still a little fresh, making me regret not grabbing my coat, or even a scarf, before I left. I pull my blazer tighter around myself and make the short journey to the shop.

The door's locked when I get there, and the bright neon sign that clearly showed it was open last night is currently saying closed.

Unsure of what to do, I lift my hand to knock. Only a second later, the shop front is illuminated, and the sound of movement inside filters down to me, but when the door opens it's not the guy from last night.

"Oh… uh… hi. Is… uh… D here?"

The guy folds his arms over his chest and looks me up and down. He chuckles, although I've no idea what he finds so amusing.

"D," he shouts over his shoulder, "there's some posh bird here to see you."

My teeth grind that he's stereotyped me quite so quickly, but I refuse to allow him to see that his assumptions about me affect me in any way.

"Ah, good. I was worried you might change your mind."

"Not at all," I say, stepping past the judgemental arsehole and into the studio reception-cum-waiting room.

"That's Spike. Feel free to ignore him. He's not got laid in about a million years, it makes him a little cranky." I fight to contain a laugh, especially when I turn toward Spike to find his lips pursed and his eyes narrowed in frustration. All it does is confirm that D's words are correct.

"Is that fucking necessary? Posh doesn't need to know how inactive my cock is, especially not when she's only just walked through the fucking door. Unless..." He stalks towards me and I automatically back up. I can't deny that he's a good looking guy, but there's no way I'm going there.

"I don't think so."

"You sure? You look like you could do with a bit of rough." He winks, and I want the ground to swallow me up.

"Down, Spike. This is Tabitha, or Biff. She's our new admin, so I suggest you be nice to her if you want to stop organising your own appointments and shit. I don't need a sexual harassment case on my hands before she's even fucking started."

I can't help but laugh at the look on Spike's face. "Don't worry. I'm sure you'll find some desperate old spinster soon."

He looks me up and down again, something in his eyes changed. "Appearances aside, I think you're going to get on well here."

I smile at him. "Mine's a coffee. Milk, no sugar. I'm already sweet enough." His chin drops.

"I thought you were our new assistant. Why am I still making the coffee?"

"Know your place, Spike. Now do as the lady says. You know my order."

"Yeah, it comes with a side of fuck off!" He flips D off before disappearing through a door that I can only assume goes to a kitchen.

"I probably should have warned you that you've agreed to work around a bunch of arseholes."

"I know how to handle myself around horny men, don't worry."

After finishing my A levels, before I grew any kind of backbone where my parents were concerned, I agreed to work for my dad. I was his little office bitch and spent an horrendous year of my life being bossed around by men who thought that just because they had a cock hanging between their legs it made them better than me. I might have fucking hated that year, but it taught me a few things, not just about business but also how to deal with men who think they're something fucking special just because they're a tiny bit successful and make more money than me. I've no doubt that my time at Anderson Development Group gave me all the skills I'm going to need to handle these artists.

"So I see. So, this is your desk. When you're on

shift you'll be the first person people see when they're inside, so it's important that you look good. But from what I've seen, I don't think we'll have an issue. I've sorted you out logins for the computer and the software we use. Most of it is pretty self-explanatory. I'm pretty IT illiterate and I've figured most of it out, put it that way."

D's showing me how they book clients in when someone else joins us. This time it's someone I recognise from my previous visit, although it's immediately obvious that he doesn't remember me like I do him. But then I guess he was the one delivering the pain, not receiving it.

"Biff, this is Titch. Titch, this is Biff, our new admin. Be nice."

"Nice? I'm always nice. Nice to meet you, Biff. You have any issues with this one, you come and see me. He might look tough, but I know all his secrets." Titch winks, a smile curling at his lips that shows he's a little more interested than he's making out, and quickly disappears towards his room.

It's not long until the first clients of the afternoon arrive, and I'm left alone to try to get to grips with everything.

Between clients, D pops his head out of his room to check I'm okay, and every hour I make a round of coffee for everyone. That sure seems to get me in their good books.

"I think I could get used to having you around,"

Spike says when I deliver probably his fourth coffee of the day. "Only thing that would make it better is if it were whisky."

"Not sure the person at the end of your needle would agree." He chuckles and turns back to the design he was working on when I interrupted.

My first day flies by. D tells me to head home not long after nine o'clock. They've all got hours of tattooing to go yet, seeing as Saturday night is their busiest night of the week, but he insists I get a decent night's sleep.

Continue reading Tabitha and Zach's story
HATE YOU!

ABOUT THE AUTHOR

Tracy Lorraine is a *USA Today* and *Wall Street Journal* bestselling new adult and contemporary romance author. Tracy has recently turned thirty and lives in a cute Cotswold village in England with her husband, baby girl and lovable but slightly crazy dog. Having always been a bookaholic with her head stuck in her Kindle, Tracy decided to try her hand at a story idea she dreamt up and hasn't looked back since.

Be the first to find out about new releases and offers. Sign up to my newsletter here.

If you want to know what I'm up to and see teasers and snippets of what I'm working on, then you need to be in my Facebook group. Join Tracy's Angels here.

Keep up to date with Tracy's books at

www.tracylorraine.com

ALSO BY TRACY LORRAINE

Falling Series

Falling for Ryan: Part One #1

Falling for Ryan: Part Two #2

Falling for Jax #3

Falling for Daniel (A Falling Series Novella)

Falling for Ruben #4

Falling for Fin #5

Falling for Lucas #6

Falling for Caleb #7

Falling for Declan #8

Falling For Liam #9

Forbidden Series

Falling for the Forbidden #1

Losing the Forbidden #2

Fighting for the Forbidden #3

Craving Redemption #4

Demanding Redemption #5

Avoiding Temptation #6

Chasing Temptation #7

Rebel Ink Series

Hate You #1

Trick You #2

Defy You #3

Play You #4

Inked (A Rebel Ink/Driven Crossover)

Rosewood High Series

Thorn #1

Paine #2

Savage #3

Fierce #4

Hunter #5

Faze (#6 Prequel)

Fury #6

Legend #7

Maddison Kings University Series

TMYM: Prequel

TRYS #1

TDYW #2

TBYS #3

TVYC #4

TDYD #5

TDYR #6

TRYD #7

Knight's Ridge Empire Series

Wicked Summer Knight: Prequel (Stella & Seb)

Wicked Knight #1 (Stella & Seb)

Wicked Princess #2 (Stella & Seb)

Wicked Empire #3 (Stella & Seb)

Deviant Knight #4 (Emmie & Theo)

Deviant Princess #5 (Emmie & Theo

Deviant Reign #6 (Emmie & Theo)

One Reckless Knight (Jodie & Toby)

Reckless Knight #7 (Jodie & Toby)

Reckless Princess #8 (Jodie & Toby)

Reckless Dynasty #9 (Jodie & Toby)

Ruined Series

Ruined Plans #1

Ruined by Lies #2

Ruined Promises #3

Never Forget Series

Never Forget Him #1

Never Forget Us #2

Everywhere & Nowhere #3

Chasing Series

Chasing Logan

The Cocktail Girls

His Manhattan

Her Kensington

Printed in Great Britain
by Amazon

80269187R00212